Judas

Books by Frederick Ramsay

The Ike Schwartz Mysteries
Artscape
Secrets
Buffalo Mountain
Stranger Room
Choker

Other Novels
Impulse
Judas
Predators

Judas

The Gospel of Betrayal

Frederick Ramsay

Perfect Niche Publishing

Perfect Niche Publishing
an imprint of Poisoned Pen Press
6962 E. First Ave., Ste. 103
Scottsdale, AZ 85251
www.poisonedpenpress.com
info@poisonedpenpress.com

Printed in the United States of America

To the late C. Stephen Mann, Ph.D.
Priest, scholar, mentor, and friend

Acknowledgments

A special thanks to Robert Rosenwald and Perfect Niche Publishing for taking a passion of mine and making it theirs as well.

My thanks, also, to Raymond Strait, who first declared that this book and, by indirection, this author, had some merit. Also, my gratitude to Jean Jenkins, editor and friend, for her thoughtful suggestions and encouragement, and to my old critique group, Nancy, Bette, and John, more thanks.

I am grateful to the staff of St. George's College, Jerusalem, for their instruction in the Palestine of Jesus' Time, and the people of Israel for their kindness and hospitality on my several journeys to their land.

Another special thanks to Connie Collins, without whose work the study guide appendix would never have seen the light of day.

Finally, and most importantly, my great thanks to my wife, Susan, who never stopped believing in this project.

ISRAEL
at the
Time of Christ
30 A.D.

Scale of Miles
0 5 10 15 20 25 30

Mediterranean Sea

Sidon
Tyre
PHOENICIA
MT. HERMON
ABILENE
Caesarea Philipi
PANEAS
ULATHA
ITURAEA
TRACHONITIS
Lake Semechonitis
GALILEE
Capernaum
Sea of Galilee
Bethsaida Julias
BATANAEA
GAULANITIS
Cana
Nazareth
MT. TABOR
AURANITIS
MT. CARMEL
DECAPOLIS
Caesarea
MT. GERZIM
SAMARIA
PEREA
Joppa
Jericho
JERUSALEM
Bethlehem
Bethany
JUDEA
Lake Asphaltitis (Dead Sea)
Gaza
N   A   B
Arabah Valley
Petra, Sela (Kadesh Barnea)
N

Foreword

First, a disclaimer: I am not a biblical scholar by any definition of the word. And, like most novelists, I rely heavily on the resonance between plausibility and circumstance to discern the truth of a matter. I would be remiss, then, if I didn't make clear that this is, in every sense, a work of fiction. As such, it qualifies as a midrash, a retelling of scripture in an allegorical or metaphorical form.

For centuries, biblical scholars of every stripe, divines, poets, and philosophers have attempted to unravel the Gordian knot that Judas Iscariot presents to understanding the Christian story. There are numerous theories, musings, speculations, and explanations about what he did and why he did it. Depending on an author's particular bias, they range from virulent anti-Semitism to painful political correctness. Judas is described as evil incarnate or the willing coconspirator with a politicized Jesus in his quest for martyrdom. All fail to address a fundamental aspect of the Gospel narrative: None of Jesus' followers knew, or could even guess, what the outcome of their time together would be, how the story would end. The Gospels, then, were all written teleologically. That is, their authors assembled the narrative specifically to lead the reader to Easter. Too often we read into the actions of one of the major players in the Gospel, interpretations contingent on our knowing that ending. But what if we were ignorant of it? What interpretation would we put on the same actions, then? In any event, this is not the traditional rendering of the character of Judas.

I have appended a few notes to the end of the book that expand on or explain the basis of some of the assumptions made in the course of assembling the story.

Also, thanks to Connie Collins, you will find a study guide intended for both individual and group use.

Finally, it is my hope that many who read this will be sufficiently intrigued by the fictional account to read the authentic one.

Frederick Ramsay

Chapter One

I learned the stories of my earliest childhood from my mother and, later, from Nahum the Surveyor. My mother would not speak of those events at first, but when she thought me old enough, she answered my questions, and over time I pieced together the whole of it.

Her family came from the Galilee. By all accounts they flourished in that most prosperous portion of the Palestine of Rome. Her father worked a plot of land on a hillside south of Sepphoris. He had a devoted wife, four sons, a beautiful daughter, servants, flocks, and, remarkably, his own well. On the Sabbath, the honor of reading from the Law or Prophets often fell to him. The community held him in high esteem—a Righteous Man, they said—the greatest compliment our culture offers. His name was Judas, the same as mine.

One day he looked upon his sons and daughter, his flocks and fields, and declared it was time to free the nation. He made no close inspection of holy writ, did not attempt to divine the will of God in omens and signs, indulged in no long speeches filled with holy rhetoric. He simply decided God had called him out as the successor to Zadok to free the land and restore His Kingdom. As things turned out, it might have been better if he had consulted the Lord. There are risks attached to presuming to know the mind of God.

My grandmother paled when she heard but knew better than to argue. She dispatched her two younger sons south to relatives in Nain. She wanted to send her daughter, Miriam, also, but grandfather would not hear of it.

"How will it look," he complained, "if I ask them to join me, but have sent my jewel away for fear of losing her? No, Miriam must stay with her older brothers." And so she stayed.

In a week or two he persuaded fifty men to follow him. They, in turn, gathered another hundred. Then, one sultry summer day, this band of foolish but brave men attacked the armory at Sepphoris. The contingent of Roman soldiers assigned to guard the building lacked both the numbers and determination to hold out for long against these Galilean zealots. The armory fell into the hands of the rebels within an hour.

Armed and flushed with success, they turned to face the relief column sent to retake the armory. They expected that once the news of their triumph spread, hundreds more would join them and that the fire they lighted would sweep across the land, driving the hated Romans into the Great Sea.

They were wrong.

The next day two hundred legionnaires arrived from Caesarea, lead by their Centurions and a tribune from the Syrian barracks—a man with a reputation for handling these annoying disturbances. The sight of those seasoned soldiers, beating time on their shields, marching inexorably toward them, struck terror in their souls. The fainthearted fled like Saul before the Philistines.

By nightfall of the third day, my grandfather, his sons, and all of the men and boys who joined him, as well as many who had not, were either captured or killed, and my grandfather's irrational defiance was replaced by calculated Roman terror.

Sepphoris exploded with the cries of its terrified citizens and fire put to the torch at the Tribune's order. Flames could be seen for miles, lighting the night sky a brilliant red-orange. Silhouetted against that, black and ominous, rows of crosses lined the road to Nazareth. Men and older boys, naked, bleeding, and nailed to the hard wood, hung near death. The younger men raised their voices in agony. Older men, those still alive,

222

remained grim and silent, refusing to give their persecutors the satisfaction of hearing them cry out.

In the darkness, beyond the crosses, screams and moans drifted across the land with the black smoke from burning houses—women and girls, paying the price for their husbands' and fathers' foolishness. Farther up the road, inside the bright well of firelight, soldiers, their tunics already soaked red with the blood of countless men, methodically slaughtered children while their mothers and grandmothers—those not being otherwise abused—watched. The author of this carnage, a man whose ambition for high office and innate sense of Roman superiority enabled him to accept, even enjoy these things, looked on impassive, his armor unspotted and gleaming.

People from the countryside as far south as Nazareth were rousted from their homes and herded to this place to bear witness to Roman power and the folly of standing against it. An example needed to be made of these rebels of the Galilee, this Judas, this self-proclaimed Messiah and his ragged band of dissidents and fanatics. They came, trembling, looking for friends and relatives, and a few even fearful of discovery—those who fled the armory earlier, before the end, before the horror began. They came to witness. Many swore silently that some day, somehow, they would avenge this indecency. God would raise up a Messiah, a new David, who would lead an army against this blasphemous abomination from across the sea and cast it out forever.

Women keened, men lowered their heads, jaws clenched, fighting their guilt and despair. Children, forced to see this terrible thing, clung to their mothers' robes and hid their faces. All except one boy, who stood quietly beside his mother, holding her hand and gazing clear-eyed at the crucified men in front of him. His gaze seemed far away, as though he were seeing his future.

Soldiers, eyes bright with the madness of the moment, dragged a young girl past them, her clothing in tatters, legs streaked with blood. Her eyes pleaded for help. None came.

Judas' daughter, his beautiful Miriam, who should have been safely away in Nain, was hauled before the Tribune, who had her stripped and raped in front of her father and then released her to a gang of soldiers who took their pleasure with her. Before the cohort finally marched away from the smoking ruins, one young man came back for her. He placed her with the camp followers to become his woman. In so doing, he probably saved her life. When the terrified residents returned to the ashes of their city, they finished punishing any rebels the Romans may have overlooked.

This chaos was my birthright.

Chapter Two

Caesarea Maritima

Our street stretched from the open market around the corner to the gate in the city's southern wall. I spent my childhood watching caravans assemble there. The animals would swing into line and then the caravan masters would shout "*Sah, Sah, Sah.*" Camels and asses, piled high with bundles and bales, trundled off, harness bells jingling, drivers yelping, traveling to places far away.

Those were the good days, the days before the madness. Not my madness—the empire's. I am not mad. I am a murderer and a thief. That is what they have made of me, my former friends and, of course, the mighty Roman Empire. Neither am I possessed or the willing tool of the Evil One. That is what they wish people to believe, what they require. "Give us someone not of our number, not from the Galilee to be the instrument of evil," they say. It was to be expected this betrayal of the Betrayer. It is in the Book. But I didn't know it at the time. He knew, of course.

How to explain the intense hatred we had for our Roman oppressors? Certainly, history will not record it. Conquerors write history, not the conquered, not their victims. History is about great men, not the terrible things they do. Battles cease but not the flow of suffering humanity. Oppressors need to put down their conquered people even after the war is finished and the blood has been washed away by a thousand rains. No one writes about the lives they grind beneath their heel—crushed with no more concern than for a lizard caught under a chariot's wheel. It's important to know the way it was then and how I, Jesus' most trusted disciple, became the man people revile.

"Judas," Mother bawled, "come in here right now." Awkward with Dinah on her hip, her eyes glanced up and down the street, searching for me. I had no desire to go back into a dark house. I spent too much of my life in darkness and shadows, but I am not unique in that. Roman society leaves most of its noncitizens clinging to its fringes like dust, an annoyance to be brushed away. My childhood in Caesarea and the three years in the Galilee with the Teacher were the only exceptions to a life of chronic darkness.

It seemed like the sun always shone in Caesarea. I did not know its name then. It was just the place where we lived. I remember our house and the beach, especially the beach. When we went there, we entered another world—windswept, clean, warm, and bright. I remember the blinding sun and how it hurt my eyes, so hot, so bright. The sea seemed to be on fire, glittering and flashing and alive.

Sometimes soldiers marched by, those men I would come to hate with such passion that even three years with the Master could not erase. The sun burnished their armor into molten copper. They tramped past our door nearly every day, rapping their shields with their spears, headed south to Jerusalem or Joppa or somewhere. And when the sun shone, I had to squeeze my eyelids together just to look at them.

I sat in the cold green water of the Great Sea and felt its depths in the wash and tug of the surf. The sea sucked at my legs, inviting me in to become a permanent resident of its murky depths, and blinded me as it mirrored the sun. The only way I could look at it was to hold my hands to my face and peer through sandy fingers. Sometimes I wonder if I wouldn't have been better served by accepting that invitation. A cool, clean end would be preferable to the living death forced on me now.

Ships from far away, from those places the men talked about, laden with the treasures of the empire, sailed toward me, around the jetty, and into the harbor. I went to the harbor only twice, once to visit the Greek surgeon who made me a Jew, and once to flee the police and certain death. But that would come later.

My mother entertained men. That is how she put it. She had visitors who came, and went, and left money—most of the time. My mother was not a woman of the streets, not then. She entertained men. For her it was an important distinction. Some would say that was a distinction without a difference.

"Judas," she said, the furrow between her eyebrows meant she was serious, "I entertain important men. It is how we live, Sweet. You will understand someday. Do not make Mummy's work harder. When my visitors are here, stay out of sight and for heaven's sake, don't let the Greeks see you." She lived in fear of *the Greeks,* by which she meant the eunuchs and the boy lovers, our neighbors in the south end of the city.

She served her visitors golden dates, dark figs, plump ripe pomegranates, olives, and honey cakes with wine. When they arrived and she was distracted, I would grab one of the cakes and stuff it into my mouth before she could turn and catch me. To this day, I believe those purloined honey cakes were the sweetest things I ever ate. I can still feel their stickiness on my fingers; savor their sweetness in my mouth. Only once did a honey cake betray me. I sat in our back court eating one left over from the previous nights entertaining. I laid it down next to me for a moment to lick my fingers and a wasp, a honey thief, settled on it. I foolishly reached to brush it away and it stung my finger. I howled so much I woke Mother. She explained the way of wasps to me. "They are evil," she said. Evil or not, I did not stop coveting honey cakes.

Men would sometimes tell stories about *The Mighty Heroes of Old,* which is how they would speak of them, *The Mighty Heroes*

of Old. They would amuse me while Mother prepared herself for the evening. I wondered about the stories. They filled the ears and mind of a child to overflowing. I had creatures lurking and skulking about in every corner of my head. Sometimes sleep would not come, so busy were these occupants, these tenants I had invited in but could not evict. Were they true? I needed to know.

"Yes, even I know because it is in the books of Moses that were read to me when I was little like you," Mother said, when I asked her after one of my particularly restless nights.

"You saw giants?"

"No. No, the giants were in the book. They are called Nifillim. There were other creatures, too, that came to earth and beautiful ladies entertained them. And David, our great king, killed Goliath, a giant, and saved the nation."

That was how she remembered the story. In her home, before she was taken away, education in the holy books was deemed a poor expenditure of time for girls and women, an education denied me as well. In Caesarea, the doors where people worshiped Mother's god remained firmly shut to us.

In the morning, her visitors would be gone and then we had money to spend. We walked to the market around the corner. It always excited me to see it, filled with hurrying people bargaining, buying, and selling. I remember the scents best. Meat cooking on spits, roasting lamb and goat, filled the air with smoke and the aroma of coriander. Spices exuded the mix of cinnamon, nutmeg, cardamom, curry, pepper, and ginger. There were things to eat, things to buy, copperware, fish, everything anyone could possibly want or need, or so I thought. If the entertaining went particularly well, we visited the cloth maker and the sandal maker and bought things to wear and the flashing, jangling ornaments Mother fancied. When there was no entertaining for a while, Mother took them back to market and sold them. That way we always had money to buy food.

I learned very early the power money wields over men. And that a man's life—any man's life—is worth more than a paltry thirty pieces of silver.

Chapter Three

"What have you done?" My mother stood in the road, hair flying, her face fractured with worry. "Where did you take her?"

"Who?"

"Your sister, where is she? You were supposed to watch her. She is your responsibility."

The road shimmered in the shadowless light of the sixth hour. The buildings, set side by side, were washed to whiteness by the sun. Mother had been sleeping and Dinah and I, unwilling to disturb her, walked down the road to see the stonemason's new lambs, born the day before.

"She is there." I pointed to the road where it turned and at that moment Dinah rounded the corner, swinging her arms and singing. Her steps made the dust puff up between her toes.

Mother had the disheveled look of someone brought suddenly from deep sleep to wakefulness. Her hair, unbound, spilled across her shoulders in a cascade of polished ebony. The heavy scent of nard clung to the air around her. She had thrown a loose azure robe over her shoulders which covered her, but not very well. The women from the shop next to ours shook their modestly covered heads, hair tucked out of sight, and clucked their disapproval.

"You should have told me," she said somewhat, but not wholly, mollified. "You should have told me." With that she wheeled and retreated into the house, into its cool gloom.

In truth, I had taken Dinah to see the lambs. I had other business with the stonemason. The day before, I had found a stone carving in the sand high up on the beach. It looked like a peculiarly plump woman with large breasts, short legs, the stomach of advanced pregnancy, and a painted face. It was crudely done, but I thought the stonemason would find it interesting. He turned it over in his hand. I watched his eyes.

"Astarte," he muttered under his breath, but I heard him. "Do you know what this is?" he said.

"Yes, it is Astarte." I said. I had no idea what that meant but I guessed he thought it important.

"Do you know what it is worth?" he asked, surprised at my presumed knowledge. He had me there.

He offered me a denarius and I asked for ten. His eyebrows shot up and he inhaled sharply. We settled for five. That is the way of the world. Men find profit from their neighbor's ignorance. If I were managing that transaction today, I would get the ten, perhaps more.

I arrived, my mother told me, wet and screaming in a small hut on the coast of the Great Sea along the *Via Maris* in one of the dusty outposts set every fifty *stadia* or so along the roadways to assure travelers safe passage throughout the empire. Legionnaires are assigned to them from time to time. I dropped into her life during one of my father's stints in such an outpost. She named me after my grandfather, Judas of the Galilee, an irony lost on my father. We lived there for about two years. Whether my mother was happy or sad I cannot say. She had no choice but to bear her lot as a soldier's wife. She never admitted that she was wife to no one and that her son was a *mamzer*, a bastard. My mother would have been twelve when she arrived at the outpost, thirteen when I was born.

One day he disappeared, his cohort called north to put down some minor insurrection. I suppose he believed whoever replaced him would also assume proprietorship of my mother.

She waited a week, and when she realized he was not coming back, decided to go to him. To a thirteen-year-old, that seemed the logical, sensible thing to do.

"Then," Mother said, "His detachment marched away. One morning at dawn, off they went, no good-byes, no notice, and no provision for those left behind—nothing."

Her eyes gazed past me, into the past, I suppose, inspecting it for some clue to explain what went wrong.

"What was I supposed to do? He did not even ask me to follow. I did not know about those things. I only knew he could not marry me. Because I was an Israelite and he a Roman soldier, it could not be. I knew that, but I thought we were like man and wife, and then there was you. Men do not desert their children, do they? So we joined a caravan going north."

Mother's eyes were wet from remembering.

A man in the caravan, an Egyptian, took a fancy to her. Zakis left his home in Alexandria and traveled north to Caesarea to work as a designer and maker of mosaics. He was very proud of his skill and, to amuse her and some of their fellow travelers, he took a handful of small tiles and, in a wink of an eye, created a picture of a camel or the face of one of his onlookers. His hands would fly about the stones like swallows in the evening. The people clapped and smiled when he finished.

They, Mother and Zakis, got along and one night, abandoning any lingering hopes she had of finding my father, we moved into his tent. It is from Zakis that Dinah received her golden curls. He moved us into the shop in Caesarea and worked there for a while, making floors for rich and important people. Then one day, he disappeared just like my father. I do not remember much about him, just that he seemed kind and smiled a lot.

Not long after he left, a rich merchant came by to commission a floor. Mother persuaded him to stay for a honey cake and some fruit. An hour later, a bargain struck, he took Zakis' place, though he did not live with us. She managed to meet his friends and when he, in turn, vanished, it was a simple matter for her to adopt a new way of life. That was when Mother began entertaining.

I did not understand the position it put us in at first. As a child, it was enough that we lived together and knew some measure of security. Later I grew to resent it and the burdens it placed on us.

"Judas, do not be angry with me. It is all that is left for me to do. I am unclean in the eyes of the Law. No one else will have me."

"It is a stupid law then. Only stupid people would make such a stupid law."

Mother gave me a look, not of anger, as I expected, but of fear. Not fear of some heavenly retribution, but rather for what might become of me. She had no family to turn to, and the thought that her son, born half pagan, might acquire the other half, made her tremble. I would not know that until later, of course. At the age of eight I had no real sense of it. To me there were the pagan gods and goddesses and then there was Mother's and the two never seemed to meet. It remained a mystery to me how all the other gods and goddesses seemed to get along very nicely and had not much to say about how people lived, and certainly not who or what was acceptable, but they were never able to join with Mother's, who did.

I have red hair, my only inheritance from my father. Not the gold-red they say King David had, but just red, like the "hen-naed whores of Babylon." One of Mother's friends said that. He meant me and assumed I would not know because he thought me too young to understand. People called my mother a whore but I thought, childishly, that it could not be true because her hair was as black as obsidian.

My father soon became the pebble in my sandal. I learned to hate the man who left us and drove my mother into the life she led. I chafed at the thought of being the illegitimate son of someone named Ceamon. There is no Ceamon in this part of the world so it became what it sounded like, Simon. Simon the Red, because of his hair. *Skyr* is the way we say it—red. No one called me Judas bar Simon. My status did not allow me the use

of my father's name. I had no father and, therefore, no patronymic. I became Judas Iscariot, Judas the Red, like my father,
no, like my grandfather. I would never be like my father, but I
ached to be like my grandfather, to be a hero.

Chapter Four

"We are going to the harbor," Mother announced, jaw set and determined. "We are going to put an end to this madness."

I had just dashed home from another encounter with some boys from the north end of town, my nose bleeding.

"Mother, they threw stones." I tried not to cry. I was, after all, the man in the house and it would not do to cry.

"Yes, I know," she said, and wiped my face with a cloth dampened with vinegar.

"They called you names and I said they shouldn't and that's when it started."

"I know."

"They shouldn't call you names."

"No, they shouldn't."

I spent much of my time at the close of my eighth year defending my mother's honor against the nastiness of boys from the other side of town. They would call her a whore and I would fight them, all the while knowing that they were right and fighting them, even winning, could not alter that fact.

This last time they pulled my clothes from me and, seeing I was not of the circumcision, threw rocks at me instead. I became the target of their contempt, not Mother. I should have been happy for that, but then one of their stones hit me in the face and I ran home. I could not understand what it was about that part of me that provoked the barrage. Mother tried to explain circumcision, but it made no sense. Most adult pagans do not understand it;

why should an eight-year-old boy? Bleeding stopped, Mother took me by the hand and led me to the docks.

Herod the Great built Caesarea, and, by anyone's account, it is a marvel. The harbor is huge. The docks front a broad street with shops and places for sailors to stay. Herod deemed it wiser to subsidize their lodgings and keep them in the harbor than risk them on the streets of Caesarea.

I craned my neck this way and that, looking at the ships and taking in the excitement. I did not notice where Mother led me. We stopped in front of a door marked with a Greek caduceus.

"Here," she said, "is where we will make you safe."

Safe? Safe from what? The place smelled faintly of olive oil and wine, sweat and vomit, and the sour residue of dirty clothes—a surgeon's place of business. She spoke briefly to the man. His eyes swept over me. They were red and still crusted with recent sleep. Coins were exchanged. Then I discovered what he had been engaged to do. Too late for me to run, and where would I have gone?

That day I became a Jew. No sacrifices were made in the temple on my behalf. No fatted calf slain in celebration, no chanting *mohel* wielded a quartz knife to mark my passage. Just my mother, the surgeon, and me. Later, I told my mother I would rather have my daily ration of rocks than go through that again.

"Tell me about my father." I must have asked her that a hundred times.

"Your father is a soldier."

"Does he march with the soldiers here?"

"No, not here, Sweet, he is far away. Your father came from one of those places where strange and wonderful creatures live and they speak in funny grunts like something is stuck in their throat and they paint themselves blue."

I laughed at that. I thought my mother was as good at telling stories as her friends. Blue, indeed.

"No," she said, "they really do, and instead of the Nifillim they have Little People." That is how she said it, like they were a race of men—Romans, Greeks, Little People.

"Little People? How little?"

"Some of the grown men are smaller than you."

My mother could be very funny. I thought it must be a wonderful place to live. Sometimes, when the sun lighted the sea to shimmering gold, I closed my eyes and thought about playing with little old men the same size as me. The only person my size I could play with was Dinah.

"You are in charge of Dinah," Mother said. "When I have my visitors, you watch her and keep her out of the front room."

She would be my responsibility for five more years. I took it seriously.

Someone had to.

Afternoons, if the weather was nice, we spent outside the walls at the beach. I played in the surf. Mother stayed under a screen with Dinah, because Mother needed to keep her skin white.

I preferred the sun.

When they both slept, I sat with my feet in the sea and tried to figure things out. Mother said the boys who lived near us were Greeks. I think she meant they are not Romans or Israelites, which is what she was. If my father was a soldier and my mother was a person of the land of the Israelites, what did that make me? It was a puzzle.

My name, she told me, is very important for the Israelites and I should be very proud of it. The Israelites lived on the north side of the city. We almost never saw them. When they did come by, they crossed the road to avoid us. Mother said they did it because of the entertaining.

Once we walked around the city to the north side. I do not remember why. We passed a deep depression in the ground. A stake with a leather thong attached stood at its center and stones were piled around the perimeter. I asked Mother what it was for. I guessed they put mean dogs in there or maybe they had cockfights. She got very pale and hurried me away. I did not see a pit like that again until years later at the gates of Magdala, when the good citizens of that smelly fishing village were about to destroy one of the Miriams—one of the Mary's.

◇◇◇

The desert man stood silhouetted in the doorway, bright sunlight at his back. His hand rested on the hilt of his belt knife.

"Where is it?"

His eyes flashed but his voice stayed even and controlled. I could not hear the anger even though I felt it. His ess sounds hissed, like someone tearing silk.

"What? Where is what?"

"My knife, boy, where is it?"

He came to our house the night before, dressed in the flowing layers of white robes desert men favor, and more knives than I have ever seen on one man. They were slung across his back, at his belt, and in the high leather coverings on his legs.

Sometime during the night one of them separated from the rest. He left later than usual in the morning. While Mother slept and Dinah played in the backcourt, I went about the business of cleaning up. I found the knife under a low table next to an empty wine flask. I turned it over in my hand, admired its red leather and silver sheath. Beautifully cut stones were set in its sheath and handle. The blade, hammered out from hard iron, curved like the new moon. I thought it the most beautiful knife I had ever seen. I coveted it. I tucked it away in my tunic. He had so many; he would not miss this one. Like a wasp, now I could sting.

"I don't know," I lied. Mother stirred and came into the room.

"Judas?" She glanced at me and at him.

"I am missing one of my knives," he lisped, tearing more silk. He spoke to Mother but his gaze never left me. I kept my eyes down. We searched everywhere. Mother suggested he might have lost it somewhere else.

"You were a little drunk when you arrived last night," she said. "Did you try the wine shop?"

He looked doubtful. Then he caught my eye. In that instant I think he knew. He opened his mouth to say something just as the great bronze horns sounded in the harbor. The tide had turned and the ships were putting out to sea. He cursed me and hurried away. I had my own knife. Now, I was armed…and a man…and a thief.

Chapter Five

I do not recall when I first felt the darkness approaching. It lurched toward me like a drunken sailor. I was ten years old and life, until then, had been bearable, all things taken into account. The three of us, Mother, Dinah, and I, had ample. We had the beach, a place to live, and money when we needed it. But that day I felt the way you do when you are about to be sick. You get sweaty and lightheaded and then, no matter how hard you try not to, your insides try to come out. Mother would have none of it.

"Gloomy Judas, what can happen? We have everything we need. We entertain important people…"

She stretched a point there. However much Mother wished it to be so, she had neither the breeding nor the background to be considered an *hetaera*. I let it pass as innocent fiction.

"Nothing will happen. Now go and help Dinah."

Mother hummed and sorted plates and saucers. Dinah had the task of filling them with dates and figs. She inspected each piece as if she were sorting pearls. Tongue between her teeth, she carefully arranged them on the plates making sure they made a symmetrical pile. The two of them were very cheerful. That night, Dinah would be part of the entertaining, at least for a while. It was to be a special night.

For the previous two months, Mother and Dinah posed for Leonides, the Greek sculptor. A wealthy sponsor had commissioned him to create a statue of a woman and a boy, fashioned, they said, after some Roman or Greek idol, Aphrodite and Eros, but I did not know it then. Pagan gods and goddesses were never something I cared much about.

"It is their goddess of love," Mother said, and scowled at some tarnish on a brass tray.

"I don't see why they need a goddess for that," I said. "There is not much in that department men have not already figured out for themselves." Pagans have a way of making sacred whatever behavior they wish to pursue. Pan, Bacchus, Aphrodite—the whole pantheon—offers sanctification for the mundane. It is the difference between us.

"It doesn't matter what they believe," Mother said. "It puts food in our mouths and if posing as their goddess makes that easier, then it's all right with me. Our God would not allow any of this, you know. It is a great sin." My mother never willingly faced the contradictions in her life. She could not afford to.

Leonides had finished the statue and intended to show it off to his patron at our house that night. He arrived late in the afternoon and set it up in one corner of the front room. That was the first time I saw it. The figures were naked and did, in fact, look like Mother and Dinah. Only he had made a little boy out of Dinah; and not a little Jewish boy either.

"There is only that 'little difference' between boys and girls," he laughed. "Men and women have 'big differences.' Look—a goddess and her boy."

The goddess stood, eyes downcast, and the boy leaned against her thigh, looking upward. Her hand covered one breast in an attempt at modesty, I suppose, and the boy's free hand covered his heart. It stood demure and even sweet in the corner, containing no hint at what it symbolized except, of course, its nakedness. For pagans, especially the Greeks, that is not the scandal it is for us.

"A nice line," Leonides said, eyeing his work with justifiable pride. He busied himself setting out lamps and arranging wall hangings to show the statue at its best. Then he left, I suppose, to spend some of his commission money.

He'd told my mother his family had wealth and influence, that they were members of the Athenian aristocracy. He said this, but no one believed him. What family in that position would allow their son to lower himself to the life of a stone cutter? It would be like finding Caesarean, Cleopatra's and Julius' son, working as a butcher.

Dinah said that posing was easy. "Judas, when I grow up I will be a poser for statues instead of entertaining like Mother."

"You want to spend your days standing naked in front of strangers?"

"It's not so bad," she said, brow furrowed like Mother's.

The idea of being undressed most of the time and in strange places with strange men apparently had not occurred to her. Dinah drifted through life an extremely shy child. People who knew us were often surprised to discover Mother had a daughter. It is a natural law, I think, that greatness in one thing will always be balanced by a weakness in another. Peacocks have breathtakingly beautiful iridescent plumage but screech like a woman in childbirth. Dinah was the most beautiful child I ever saw, but because she was so shy hardly anyone was aware of her existence.

I wondered how the evening would go. Leonides decided to have Mother and Dinah strike the same pose as the statue so his patron could experience the full measure of his genius. Dinah and Mother would stand naked before this man. Mother could manage certainly, but Dinah?

Mother told me to stay in the back, out of the way. It did not feel right. I knew something terrible would occur as surely as if chiseled into the plaster wall. At that moment, the sun went behind a cloud. I loosened my knife in its sheath and contemplated, with ten-year old instincts, the gathering darkness.

Chapter Six

The evening star had been shining for nearly three hours before Leonides reappeared. He reeled into the room, smelling of cheap wine and carrying a small brass bowl in which he'd placed glowing charcoal. He lighted some lamps, extinguished others, and sprinkled incense on the charcoal. The room turned a pale gold. The smoke from the incense drifted to the ceiling and layered slowly across the length of it. The transformation was remarkable. A moment later his patron arrived, accompanied by another man. The patron lumbered heavily into the room, squinting in the smoke and dim light. His face had the pasty look of someone who had not seen the sun for a long time, his skin like dough, and I thought if I poked him with my finger, the dent in his flesh would still be there in the morning. His toga hung loosely from him but did not hide the gross body beneath it. His companion, on the other hand, slipped into the room, shadow-like, lean, and dark. He wore dress armor and a short toga. He had golden eyes and the high aquiline nose common to Roman patricians. His look and manner were reptilian, like a snake.

There was no doubt what the first one did. Officialdom and bureaucrat were written all over him. The other man, however, could have been anybody or anything, a jailer or his prisoner, a general or a foot soldier. The patron addressed him as Tribune and that settled it. My instincts told me to be careful, he reeked of danger. I checked my knife again.

They settled down to eat and drink. Mother sang. Dinah sat behind her, only daring to peek out at the men from time to time. The statue sat on one side of the room cloaked in white sheeting.

"Well, sculptor, let's see it. You desire your money, I wish to see my statue," the patron said. His words wheezed out like the air from an empty wine skin.

The sculptor began to speak. He had a hard time keeping his feet under him. He laughed a lot and almost fell as he reached for the corner of the covering, missed twice, and finally, cloth in hand, yanked. The sheet snagged and nearly toppled the statue. When the cloth released, Leonides fell backwards to the floor. He staggered back to his feet and, without missing a beat, continued his speech, a very flowery speech filled with words of praise for himself and his art. The patron drummed his fingers and fidgeted. More wine was poured. His patron nodded and tossed him a purse that clinked heavily as it bounced on the floor.

"Enough of this," he barked. "Let's see the rest."

"Ah," Leonides said and bowed. "Now you will see the genius of Leonides."

Earlier, we'd strung a curtain across the other corner of the room. While the men's attention turned to the statue and Leonides' babbling, Mother and Dinah slipped behind it, undressed, oiled, and then powdered their hair and bodies with stone dust. The sculptor tugged at the curtain with almost the identical results he experienced with the statue. The curtain fell away and he sat down. Mother and Dinah held the exact pose as the statue. They were naked and I remember feeling proud and at the same time ashamed. They were beautiful. Leonides had taken great care in arranging the lamps and the effect brought a gasp from the patron. Mother and Dinah stood perfectly still. In the dim light, with their pale skins dusted white and eyes closed, they were the mirror image of the statue in the other corner. It was nearly impossible to tell living from stone. Leonides put his hand on Dinah—where she differed from the boy.

"You see," he giggled, "a genius."

The patron looked at Mother and then at Dinah. He licked his lips. "Get this fool out of here," he said. The other man, yellow snake eyes bright, grabbed the poor Greek by the throat, lifted him like a rag doll, and threw him out the door and into the street.

Then what I had feared, but could not define, happened.

The fat Roman beckoned to Mother. Always in the past, she set the terms of her services. No mention had been made of anything except posing. She hesitated. He snapped his fingers and Snake Eyes grabbed her by the hair and spun her around. Dinah screamed and tried to run but Snake Eyes, with his free hand, slapped her to the floor as easily as he would swat a fly. I watched, paralyzed. What happened next is not to be spoken of. The fat man grabbed Dinah by her wrist and pulled her to him. His friend, still holding Mother by her hair, bent her over his couch.

I launched myself into the room, knife drawn. Mother kicked her attacker. He only smiled. He struck her with a closed fist. I heard someone shouting and cursing…me. I looked at her and then at Dinah. The soft Roman had his hand over Dinah's mouth to stop her screaming. Her eyes were wide with terror and pleaded silently with me. She was my responsibility. I raised my knife over my head, ready to sink it to the hilt in that pudding-faced Roman. I think it may have been the only time in my life I was ever truly brave. As my arm swung down, I thought I heard noises at the door. Out of the corner of my eye I saw Snake Eyes swing at me. His arm looked as big as a galley oar. Everything went black.

Sunlight. That morning it hit my eyes like a hammer. My head pounded and I could remember nothing. When finally the previous evening came to me, my eyes popped open. All I could see was the mess on the floor in front of me. Tables overturned and plates scattered everywhere. Leonides' brass bowl lay upside down an arm's length away, its charcoal spilled out onto the carpet. Scorched wool and incense lingered in the air. I twisted around. Mother crouched in the corner, her face swollen. She had a piece of silk wall hanging around her to cover her nakedness. Dark bruises were beginning to form on her shoulders and under her eyes. Dinah sat in her lap, eyes that the day before had danced in anticipation now stared vacantly straight ahead, the dull eyes of the dead. Mother crooned and rocked her back and forth. Dinah was bleeding.

The room looked like an army had passed through it. Leonides' statue lay shattered on the floor, smeared with blood. The boy god, what was left of him, had been converted back to a girl. I tried to sit up. I hurt all over. I raised my head. There was blood on my hand, on the statue, everywhere. How had that happened? My knife stuck to my bloody hand. Mother rocked and crooned. Dinah turned her head and threw up on the floor. Something, someone, a man, looking like a pile of rags, lay behind the broken statue. I looked more closely—Leonides, covered with blood. I saw him thrown out; the Tribune did that before…

"He came back to help," Mother murmured.

I struggled to take it in. Leonides may have been silly, pompous, and vain, but he had honor, and he had been stabbed many times because of it. I looked at the knife in my hand. Who would believe I did not stab him? In the eyes of the Law I stood lower than a rich man's favorite dog. Who would believe me? I had no status, no father, nothing. They were Roman officials. Who would dare to question them? But why would I want this poor man dead? The Romans, certainly, I wanted to kill them, but not Leonides.

We cannot stay here.

My head pounded and I lifted my hand to my forehead and discovered it crusted with blood where Snake Eyes hit me. I staggered into the back room and found a pitcher of water. I washed my head, hand, and knife. Mother stirred and stood up. She had been severely beaten. There were bruises all over her body. I tried not to look. She drifted around the room retrieving her wraps, covering herself. Together we washed and dressed Dinah.

We cannot stay here.

Flies buzzed around the Greek. I shooed them away. I clenched my teeth and touched the body. I do not know what I expected. I thought it would be soft but instead it lay rigid, like the statue next to it. I opened his embroidered vest. The blood made it as stiff as tenting. I felt along his belt until I found his leather purse. It was heavy and clinked, filled with many coins, the commission paid for the statue. I wanted to run, just run, and never stop.

"We cannot stay here," I said.

Mother looked at me, brow furrowed. Horns sounded in the harbor. Boats were sailing. We scrambled about the house grabbing anything we could carry—the rest of our money, some clothing, Mother's paints and ointments and herbs. Dinah stood in the door watching without seeing. We dashed into the street and headed for the harbor. No words were spoken—none were needed.

Dinah could not keep up.

"Here," Mother said. "Take the bundles. I will carry Dinah." She hoisted her up on her hip and we raced on.

The street swarmed with people, a blessing. It gave us some cover. I saw the dark man, Snake Eyes, before he saw us. We ducked down behind a fruit vendor's stall until he and a cadre of soldiers trotted past us and out of sight. The horns sounded their last warning. We raced to the quay.

Only three boats remained when we arrived. We boarded the only one that would take us. I stood in the aft and watched Caesarea slip away. Dark clouds slowly swallowed the sun over the mountains to the east, a new day, a gray day. The ship tacked neatly through the gap in the northern jetty and turned westward.

"Where are we headed?" I asked.

"Corinth," the captain shouted, "The cloaca of the empire. That's where, Sonny."

The ship tossed in the chop as we cleared the harbor mouth. I turned my back on Caesarea and the land of my birth. I stood in the stern of that little coastal trader and contemplated the madness that now controlled our lives. I clenched my fists and swore to whatever gods there were, someday, some way, I would return and I would have my revenge. I would do whatever I must to bring those swaggering hypocrites, those arrogant purveyors of Roman justice who debauched women and children, into account.

Hatred is a hard thing to control. Like an alchemist's acid, which corrodes the hardest iron, hate eats at a person's soul. Though I struggled daily to contain it, in the end, it slowly and silently directed my feet into a path that would one day lead to tragedy.

Chapter Seven

"This is where you get off," the ship's captain growled. With that, our baggage was scooped up and thrown off, disappearing into the night high above our heads. The ship, which had carried us away from Caesarea, rocked and bumped against wooden bolsters beside a high, stone wall.

"Off, off," he said, waving his hands vaguely toward the wall.

"Is this Corinth?" Mother asked.

"It's as close as you will get, woman. Now get off."

Off? All we could see was the wall that rose two or three cubits over our head. Stone outcroppings were set into it, which served as steps. We climbed up and onto a rough paved street. The night enfolded us, moonless, and except for a few torches guttering every hundred paces or so, pitch black.

"Where are we?"

"Cenchrea." The captain had followed us up the steps and moved off to speak to a man I took to be the harbor master.

"You said Corinth. We paid for passage to Corinth."

"Corinth is that way, inland." He pointed into the night and added, "Woman, you are lucky I did not throw you and your brats overboard. I do not know what trouble you stirred up back there, but you brought it onto my ship. I am sure the authorities here would be more than happy to hold you until they found out why you left Caesarea in a hurry."

We gathered our bundles, shuffled a few steps into the darkness, and paused, hopeless and helpless, our few pitiful belongings at our feet. Dinah clung to Mother's leg. I drew my knife and huddled close to her as well. We had no idea where we were, where we should go, or what to do. The torches made uncertain pools of light along the length of the street. People drifted through them on their way to places we could not see. I made out thin lines of light seeping from under doorsills and around lintels. Mist drifted in from the harbor, blurring the light, intensifying the dark.

To our right, barely visible in the torchlight, a group of four women stood wraithlike, watching us, waiting. One of them studied us like she would a melon or a loaf of bread— should she buy or not? A door burst open and light and men poured out onto the street like water from an overturned pail. The men rolled about pummeling and cursing. As the door slapped shut, I thought I saw the glint of a knife blade. In the darkness that followed I heard a cry, then another, and then the sound of feet running away. There was a moan and then silence. I guessed one of the ships would be short a man in the morning.

Shadowy figures rose up near us, then drifted away. We wanted to run, but which way and where? We were lost and alone in a strange city on what seemed to be the darkest night of the year. Our ship poled away from the wall and disappeared into an inky harbor. I thought after all our efforts to escape certain death at the hands of Roman officials, we would end up murdered in the dark by some anonymous thief for our few meager possessions.

The woman said something to the others with her and they faded into the night. She waved at someone behind us and I heard the scurry of feet. She walked up to Mother and the two of them stepped away speaking in low voices. Mother seemed to think about whatever she said and then nodded. She came back to us, picked up Dinah, and said, "Come. We are going with this woman."

Her name was Darcas.

◇◇◇

Darcas exuded energy. A small, dark woman—not pretty like Mother—but her dress and carriage prompted men to look twice. Women in her profession sometimes acquire a wary, furtive look. Her long, thin face and her pointed nose reminded me of the wharf rats that scurried about near the harbor. She wore a lot of jangling bracelets and anklets. In fact, you could hear her coming long before you saw her. That turned out to be a blessing for Dinah and me. We decided, well actually, I decided—Dinah did not speak—that it would be wise to stay away from her, a good decision, as it turned out. Even though I knew, if it had not been for her, we might have been killed or sold into slavery the night we arrived, I also knew that Darcas could not be trusted.

Darcas put us into a cramped windowless room where Dinah and I slept at night, Mother during the day. The room was half the size of our back room in Caesarea. It lacked the sunny backcourt, the street filled with excitement, the scent of oils and spices, grunting camels, and the promise of adventure. It opened, instead, on a dim corridor ending in steps leading down to the atrium and the street. It did have a small hearth, which provided our only light and a place to warm our food. We paid for food and lodgings out of what Mother earned. Darcas took five tenths of that as her fee. The rest was spent on charges Darcas made for the food and rent. We struggled this way for a year.

Dinah remained mute and withdrawn. I had hoped the sea air, a change in the way we lived, anything, would bring back her sunny disposition. Nothing changed. As she grew, she showed signs of her womanhood. Not much, just the beginning of bumps under her tunic.

"I am worried about Dinah. She is not getting any better," I said early one afternoon while Mother fussed with her paints. She was due to go back to the atrium. She looked pale and drawn, and her hands shook as she struggled to paint her face.

"There is nothing wrong with Dinah. She will be fine once we are settled."

"It has been a year, Mother. This is as settled as we are likely to get."

"Judas, be a good boy and bring me my ointment, the one that smells of myrrh."

I handed her the pot. "She just sits and stares. She never talks, never smiles."

"Judas, please. I cannot do any more than I am already. I suffered worse things, and here I am. Dinah, pay attention to Mummy, you can't just mope about."

"Mother, she is only ten. They hurt her and...she didn't know..."

"Judas, this is about what women do. You have no idea. Dinah, speak up. Say something."

She never spoke.

Chapter Eight

There were other children like Dinah and me in the House of Darcas. Most of them were part of what the house offered in the atrium, competing with the women. Apparently, I was too ugly to be of much use, but Darcas wanted Dinah. She pestered Mother constantly for her to join the other children in the atrium.

"She would be very popular, because of her eastern looks and that golden hair. I could get a very good price for her," Darcas said and eyed Dinah with one of her shall-I-buy-or-not looks.

We needed the money. Darcas repeatedly increased her rents and what she charged for food. Some of the women could not pay, and were forced to leave or, if they wished to stay, indentured themselves. Most of them were simple country girls from the hills—girls whose parents or lovers left them to fend for themselves. They did not know enough to survive. Most of them did not even know their way home. Off and on, Darcas had a dozen slaves, which were very profitable for her. Some she worked to death, some she sold. I think Darcas had in mind to make slaves of us, too.

Our lot grew worse when the agents sent by the House of Leonides arrived. I saw the men speaking to Darcas, big men with eyes of ice, men who exuded power and confidence. I could see her talking and gesticulating the way she did when she was excited. They had followed our trail from Caesarea. Someone told them a woman and her children, a prostitute and her brood, was the way it was put, had sailed for Corinth. They scoured the waterfront and then the brothels. They planned to bring us their own form of justice. Leonides, it seemed, told us the truth about his family. I suppose Darcas found the reward too meager to give us up. But, from that day on, she owned us.

Once, Darcas brought a man to our room.

"You, boy," she said, "I need you to go to the herbalist and bring back a package for me." She handed me a coin and gave me a shove toward the door.

I did not go. I hid in the shadows in the corridor. When Dinah screamed, I ran back into the room. She was curled up in as small a ball as she could make, her arms wrapped around her head. The man was very angry and hitting and yelling in a tongue I did not understand. He yanked at her legs and arms. Darcas reached toward Dinah. The expression on her rat-face frightened me. She tried to pinion Dinah's arms. I drew my knife and stepped toward the man.

"Never mind," Darcas said, catching her breath and looking at me and then at my knife. Whether she thought I would use it or not, I do not know, but the thought of bloodshed in her house seemed enough to stop her.

"I have another girl who is a virgin and who will fight you, too," she said to the man, scowling at me.

They left, he complaining and she wheedling and apologizing.

I shook all over. So did Dinah. I held her in my arms until Mother came back to our room in the morning.

"Darcas will never do it again. She has promised," Mother said later.

"I don't believe her. We have to do something. We have to get away from here."

"And just how do you plan to do that?"

I did not have an answer for her.

◇◇◇

The city of Corinth is located on a thin peninsula that separates the Ionian Sea from the Saronic Gulf. It is really three cities, Cenchrea, its southern or eastern port, Lechaeum, its northwestern port, and the city that bears its name, which lies between the two, but closer to Lechaeum. Connecting all three and dividing the peninsula in half is a broad paved road, the Diolkos, a tramway that joins the two seas. The Diolkos is a miracle of engineering, as wonderful as anything in the empire, they say. Many years ago an attempt was made to dig a canal from one coast to the other but abandoned.

The bit of completed canal shallows out abruptly. Smaller boats maneuver right up to the Diolkos and onto rollers and marvelous machinery, and then onto land still completely laden. Enormous teams of oxen are brought, hitched up, and the ship and all of its trappings are transported the four and a half miles to the other coast. Ships too large for the rollers transfer their cargo onto pack animals and send it to Corinth or northward to the opposite coast where it is loaded onto another ship headed west. Of course, large ships, heavy merchantmen, and ships of war sail around the Pelopennisos, but small coastal trading ships can be carried overland. It is a dry land canal complete with walls, which keep the way clear for boat traffic. They say the Diolkos in Corinth determines the size and shape of all the trading boats in this part of the world, so profitable is this shortcut.

During the day, I wandered about the marketplace, the agora, looking for ways to get us free. One day while out exploring, I met Gaius. His mother worked in a house a short distance from ours.

"Why are you on the streets?" I asked. "You could work in the atrium." He was certainly handsome enough.

"Not me, not anymore. No more fat, sweaty men are going to have me that way ever again," he said, eyes flashing. "Besides, there is more money to be made on the streets than in the atrium." He showed me a fistful of coins.

"Where?" I wanted to see this gold mine of his. He motioned me to follow and we crossed the Diolkos and walked to the agora.

Cenchrea's agora is splashed across the width of the city beside the Diolkos. It is a grand sight with hundreds of gaily canvassed stalls and thousands of people moving about, bumping into one another, buying and selling. People bargain with their hands and voices, especially with their voices, yelling at each other at the top of their lungs. When the yelling reaches its shrillest, the sale is made.

"Watch," Gaius said, and slipped into the crowd.

I watched. He made his way toward a man shopping alone. Most people who regularly shopped in the agora knew it was best to come in twos and threes. But there were always a few who believed they could take care of themselves and a few who simply did not know any better and shopped alone.

Gaius, his knife tucked up his sleeve, sidled up to the man. In one quick motion, he cut the purse strings at the man's belt. As it fell, he grabbed it, and darted into the crowd. He was lucky. No one tried to stop him. A few moments later he was back at my side. He had more money in his hand than I had seen since the morning I lifted the sculptor's purse. He was right about one thing—more money could be made in the streets than in the House of Darcas.

"You should try it," he said. His face was flushed and I could see his heart racing.

"How many times have you done that?"

"Five or six."

"I will think about it," I said, tempted.

"Suit yourself, but thinking won't make you rich."

I stayed in the market to see if anyone else had discovered Gaius' secret. I saw dozens of boys like me, like Gaius, slipping through the crowd. All of them had indeed discovered his path to riches. I decided to study them. I would go to school, the school of the streets.

This is what I learned: All of those boys had dangerous cuts and bruises on their heads, arms, and legs from the near misses, the beatings they endured when they failed in their attempts at robbery, or when they slipped, trying to avoid their victim's staffs, cudgels, and kicks. The wounds were dangerous because the filth that collected in the city where we lived made it only a matter of time before the wounds festered and, perhaps, killed with the green poison.

Gaius had been lucky, either a genius at picking his victims, or his gods smiled on him. As for the rest, I watched as one boy edged up to a man bargaining for some sandals. Just as he stretched out his hand to cut loose a fat purse, its owner brought the hard knob of his staff across the boy's wrist. Unless I missed something, that boy had a broken wrist to go with his cuts and bruises. The people laughed at his shrieking. The man who struck him aimed a kick at his backside and sent him sprawling in the dirt. I would look elsewhere.

For children without families, position, or influence, work in the atria is safer. There you would grow old in a hurry, even succumb to one of the diseases that come with that life, but you would not die bleeding, shivering, and alone in an alley, to be thrown on a dung heap and hauled off like so much manure before your sixteenth year.

On the east end of the Diolkos, the empire was not so bright, not so grand.

Chapter Nine

Each day our situation grew worse. I helped out a little by running errands, polishing brassware, and scrubbing up after the cooks. But it was not enough. Mother got sick several days a month. Darcas kept up her insistence that Dinah be brought to the atrium. I sensed Mother weakening. She did not want to do it, but we were running out of ideas and time. Dark circles were beginning to appear under her eyes, circles that had to be covered with more and more paint. She looked worn out. One day when I saw her resolve beginning to crack, I said, "Let me go to the atrium. Don't send Dinah."

"Judas, Sweet, Darcas doesn't want you. She wants pretty boys and young girls like Dinah."

"If you send her there, she will die," I said, frustrated and angry.

"Judas, it is not your decision. I am her mother and I will decide. It shall be as the Lord directs."

"The Lord? Why is it always your god? What sort of god do you bow to, who allows these things to happen?"

"You hold your tongue."

"Mother, look at us. Look at what we have become. Think of what you are about to do."

Mother and I were becoming enemies. I did not wish it, but it was so. Dinah heard us arguing. I did not know if she understood, but the frown on her face made me think she did.

"Mother, wait a month. If we can't find something in a month…" I did not finish. Why make Dinah worry.

"One month? What can you do in a month? Judas, you are just a boy."

I spent a lot of time in the agora. With all the money that changes hands in that place I figured there must be something I could do besides cutting purses. Nearly all the merchants had boys working in their stalls with them. Twenty times I asked to be hired and always got the same reply, "Sorry." The boys working in the stalls were sons or nephews. But one man, a seller of copperware, had no son. He had a hired boy. At the time, I believed him to be the luckiest boy in the world.

"Do you need another boy?" I asked.

"No. The only time I hire boys is when one disappears."

"How often does that happen?"

"About every six months or so, but so far I have been lucky. This boy has been with me a year."

I followed the boy for over a week. I kept thinking, "If something were to happen to him, I could take his place with the seller of copperware. If something were to happen…"

I do not know how it came about. People flooded the streets to celebrate one of their gods' or goddesses' days. The street boys were busy plying their trade. When it got crowded like that, they could cut purses with relative ease. Escape became more difficult, but as the crowd shifted and moved, they did not have to go so far to be safe. So Gaius and his friends were at work, and I shadowed the boy.

We stood on the edge of the wall where the Diolkos shelved into the sea. There were no railings, only bollards and bronze rings set in the stone for the ships and barges to moor to while they waited their turn to be hauled out of the water and rolled north. If you were not careful, if you did not watch your step, you could easily trip and fall. I moved closer to the boy. He stood between me and the work I needed. He had no sister out of her senses, no mother who daily grew older and less able to function. That is what I told myself as I watched him out of the corner of my eye.

The priests from the temple of whatever god they celebrated that day paraded past. Trumpets blared. Banners snapped and swirled around and the sheer number of marchers forced the bystanders to move back out of the way and pressed us closer to the Diolkos. I heard a shout from the left. Someone nearly fell. People laughed and hauled a man back to safety, grinning and looking embarrassed. The shoving and pushing continued. Suddenly, the boy disappeared. He was there and then he was gone. I heard a thud and the sound of a wooden crate splintering, followed immediately by a scream. The parade passed on and the people surged forward again. I turned and looked down.

The boy lay moaning on the deck of a small coastal trader moored at the foot of the wall. He must have hit the crate first because straw, slats, and shards of pottery lay scattered around him. He stared at his leg, his face white as chalk. The leg stuck out at an impossible angle and the shaft bone protruded out of the thigh. The ship's master waved his arms furiously and bawled at the boy, but he did not listen. The master blustered on. The boy fainted.

I stared in disbelief and at the same time, relief. I wondered, did I do that? I could not remember. But I certainly wished it. I could have done it. I wanted to do it. Was wishing a thing the same as doing it? Would Mother's angry old god think that?

The life of a stall owner in the agora is not an easy one. I thought, naively, that all one had to do was buy goods cheap and sell for more. Trading is not so simple. The agora in Cenchrea, they say, is the best of the half dozen or so in and around Corinth. Many men wished to establish businesses there, and, therefore, vied for a space. That created a long waiting list. My new master, Amelabib, had to wait and then pay a big bribe to get in.

He also had to pay the market master a portion of his daily profits. The Roman officials did not know about this fee, but no one dared complain. The few that did were later found floating in the harbor. Also, he had to bribe the soldiers who patrolled the market, or they would look the other way when the gangs came, roving groups of thieves and cutthroats, the few street boys, like Gaius, who survived to become men. If the soldiers did not keep them in check, they could destroy a man and his stall in a wink of an eye. Then someone else would have to bribe the market master to take his place and so it went. Amelabib did not know from one day to the next if his bribes were sufficient to keep him in the market or even alive. By cutting his profits to the bone, he had managed to stay in the market for three years.

I quickly abandoned any ideas I might have had about owning my own stall. But I watched and I learned. Amelabib told his friends I was a quick student and he would have to be careful or he would end up working for me. They laughed when he said it. Money could be made in the agora. It just took a little imagination and a measure of cunning.

Chapter Ten

Amelabib, a short, stocky man, had the yellow hair you see often in Acacia, already streaked with gray, and his hands were permanently blackened from handling copper all day. Our booth displayed everything from cheap trinkets to elaborately worked salvers, pitchers, and bowls.

We had to be paid in denarii. It was the rule—no foreign currency was to be used to purchase goods in this area. Roman officials determined the taxes they charged based on the day's take, and they calculated their percentage in denarii. If someone tried to pay in coinage other than denarii, we had to send him to one of the official moneychangers. But often we changed the money for them and went to a moneychanger and converted it at the going rate. The officials understood this occasional necessity, and allowed it to go on in spite of the rules. Money changing without official permission, however, brought down a host of officials, including the local police and *judicato*. But a few people did, anyway. It seemed a better and safer way to make money than cutting purses.

One day Amelabib closed his stall early and took me to Corinth. He bought his copperware from an artisan on the other side of the city away from the Diolkos and inland, where all of the master craftsmen, the workers of metal and gems, the potters and shapers—all had their shops. It was nearly an hour before we reached the edge of the city. I could make out buildings up on the heights long before we reached the city. The Acrocorinth loomed above the city nearly touching the clouds, or so I thought. I had never seen anything quite like it.

If the south port of the tramway is the cloaca, Corinth is the head and heart. In Cenchrea, many buildings were made of wood and thatch, only a few of stone. They were brightly colored but small and mean compared to Corinth where all the buildings were of stone, white marble and pink granite, many painted in beautiful deep blues and reds, their column capitals gilded. When we turned into the straight street I saw it—Mother and Dinah posing again. I stopped and gaped. It looked so much like Leonides' work, for an instant I thought, how did they manage to get it repaired and shipped over here?

"You have not seen Greek statuary before?"

"Yes, I have seen statuary like this."

"It is Aphrodite and Eros, maybe you know them as Venus and Cupid?" Amelabib continued, "That is the way the goddess and the god always look. Artists look for models that have that look. You see the face and the way her body is proportioned…"

I did. Except for the nose, it could be Mother. My mother looked like Aphrodite, the goddess of love and fertility. No wonder Darcas wanted her so badly. If she were her slave, she could be sold for a very large sum.

"This is nothing," Amelabib lectured on. "In Athens, there are even more. Now there is the city for the world. Even Rome cannot match Athens for beauty."

I did not know about that. I had never been to either and had no plans to go. In fact, I had never ventured into the part of Caesarea where the statues and fine buildings were nor the part of the city which had brightly painted columns. I did not know about those things. We walked down the street but I could not take my mind off the figures.

We came upon one statue of a man in the middle of the street, bigger than life, and dressed in gilded armor. He had a helmet tucked under his arm and held an orb in his hand. The writing on the pedestal was in Latin and I could not read it. Amelabib squinted at it.

"It says, 'Now is a child born by heaven'...yes, born by heaven...'Smile...at the birth of this boy who will put an end to our wretched age...from whom golden people will spring... now does...Apollo...' My Latin is not so good."

"Who is this person?" I asked. He sounded wonderful to me.

Amelabib laughed very loudly. "It is Augustus, our late emperor, who says this of himself. He thought he was a god. All of these Roman emperors do that, even this new one, this Tiberius, probably. It is not enough for them to be the richest and most powerful men in the world, they must make themselves equal to the gods. What the gods think about this, I do not know."

We walked on. My mind wandered back to the statues and if, in fact, all the statues of Aphrodite looked like my mother. It was an unsettling discovery.

"Be still 'Little Hebrew,'" he said, his attention drawn to a disturbance up the street. He called me "Little Hebrew," and even though I tried to tell him I did not accept that status, he shook his head and said, "In this world we don't choose who we are, we just are. And you are Hebrew whether you like it or not."

I did not argue with him, but I confess, I had enough of the god who made me less than human, who punished people for the wrongs of others, and who let little girls be raped and made crazy. I wanted no part of him.

"Try to look Greek," he said under his breath, "the priestesses are coming."

I tried to look like what I thought a Greek must look like. But with my red hair, I doubted I fooled anyone. As it happened, the priestesses had more important things on their minds that day than one insignificant boy who did not care about his mother's or anyone else's god.

"There," he said, "you see there...all those beautiful girls?"

I saw them. They were very beautiful and dressed in stuff that let you see the outlines of their bodies.

"Who are they?" I asked.

"They are the women dedicated to Venus or Aphrodite, depending on whether you lust after women as a Greek or a Roman." He laughed again.

"People give their daughters to the temple in hopes of finding favor with the goddess and sometimes a rich reward, too."

"Give? They give their daughters to the goddess?"

"Yes. Most come from the poor farms and the families on the other side of the Diolkos. From families that cannot bring themselves to selling them into the 'profession of love,' if you know what I mean."

I knew what he meant.

"You see that temple up there?" He pointed toward the top of the Acrocorinth. I looked up at an enormous building. I guessed the men of Corinth must have their minds turned to love more than anything else. As if he read my thoughts, Amelabib said,

"This goddess has the biggest temple in every city. No surprise there, eh?"

"Where do they all come from? There must be hundreds of women and girls."

"There are two kinds of women in the temple. Some—those with much paint and red lips—are the temple prostitutes. They come and go depending on the needs of the priestess. The others are the Vestal Virgins. They must stay that way as a reminder they belong to the goddess. Those girls must be very special."

"How special?"

"They must be beautiful, of course, nothing less would be acceptable to the goddess, and they must be visited by the goddess herself. If they are accepted, they are taken into the temple and their parents may never see or speak to them again. Some say the parents are given the money collected in the offering salver that day."

"Visited? You mean the goddess appears to them?"

"It's like that…or something…a messenger from the goddess, I do not know. Those are the mysteries. All I know is the goddess marks some young girls in some special way and the priestesses in the temple know what that is, and take only those who have it."

I thought it must be like the wine stain the sandal maker in Caesarea had. He had a red blotch on his face he said the gods gave him. I scanned the Virgins. Their ages ranged from Dinah's to old women. None of them had a wine stain. One or two of them looked familiar, like someone I knew. But I did not know any girls outside of the House of Darcas and these would not be from any place like that.

We climbed upward. The city on its western edge backed up to the hills. Above us was the temple of Aphrodite.

We wandered around the heights toward the southern edge of the city. I could not take my eyes off the buildings and statuary and so I did not notice where we were going. I ran into Amelabib who had stopped abruptly at a small stall set in front of a low house, the coppersmith's home and shop. The coppersmith stood at his hearth, a big, rough-looking man, hands gnarled and black from years of working with copper, melting it, alloying it into bronze or brass, and hammering it out into pieces, some of such delicacy, I wondered how those cudgel-like hands could ever craft anything so beautiful. My master introduced me as his "Little Hebrew."

"Oh ho," the coppersmith boomed, "well, I am descended from the great Philistine metal workers. There is enmity between our people, so you'd better beware of me."

I did not know what he meant. The only Philistines I ever heard of were ancient people whose name had been twisted to Palestine, which was what Romans called the land of my birth.

I stood as tall as I could and tried to look brave. He laughed a big laugh. You cannot always tell when someone is joking with you, whether you are safe. That man could turn me over to the Romans on nearly any pretext, and because I had no entry pass, no citizenship, because Mother did what she did to survive, I would not have a chance of seeing freedom ever again. In that corrupt city, where nearly everything was for sale, he could and would do it if the circumstances were right.

On our way back, our bundles of jewelry and copperware carefully concealed beneath our cloaks, my master said, "You should have yourself fixed, you know. This is not a good place to be if you are a Hebrew."

"Fixed? What do you mean, 'fixed'?"

"You know, you should have yourself repaired…in that place!"

"That place?"

He waved his hands around, irritated with me. "I know of a Greek surgeon, a very good man, who can fix you back the way you were born. All of the Hebrews that come here to live go to him. You will be safer if you do that."

Ah, I thought—*that place*. I should undo with his Greek surgeon what the other one did, and for the same reason. It was unsafe in Corinth to be one of my mother's people and equally unsafe not to be one in Caesarea. I knew then that my mother's god must be mean and unmerciful. He punished me for being the illegitimate son of someone I never met. He made me an outcast wherever I went. He played cruel jokes on,me for not being circumcised and then for being circumcised and he made it very clear I could never have a part of this world except at its fringes. Not Greek, not Hebrew, nothing.

"I will think about it."

We did not talk much on the way back to Cenchrea. I was thinking about those girls and women. Why would anyone give a daughter to a goddess?

Chapter Eleven

I made my first illegal money. Not a lot, but some, and realized there could be a great deal more. It started simply enough. I changed some money in the street. Amelabib sent me to the moneychangers to convert the foreign coins we had taken in that day. On my way back, purse filled with dinarii, a man stopped me. Newly arrived to the city and not yet acquainted with the ways of the street and the market, he did not know better than to try to change his money in the street, did not know about the moneychangers or the fixed rate. I should have sent him to the official exchange but, without thinking of the consequences, I changed his money, at my rate, returned to the moneychangers and exchanged it again at theirs. I returned my master's money to him, but four denarii richer myself. No one saw me and even if they had, who would suspect a boy to have enough money to speculate in exchanges?

I decided then I would try my hand at the money changing business. There were risks, of course, and the need of ready cash to make the business work, but I guessed that if I were careful, started with this windfall of four denarii and held back a small measure of my wages in the future, I could make it work. Each day, I saved a few more coins. I was finally doing something about getting us away.

◇◇◇

One evening I returned late from the stall to our room. It was empty, no Dinah. She never ventured away from the safety of our cramped quarters. I picked up a lamp and went to find her. I checked the privy. I looked into the atrium. I could not find Mother or any sign of Dinah. I remembered the time Darcas brought the man to our room. Did she try it again with the same results? Did Dinah run? I searched the corridors and the buildings in the small courtyard at the back of the house. The privy stood at one end, open space beyond it, where animals were kept and deliveries made. Attached to the rear wall of the main building were a series of low sheds where Darcas stored her goods and things for which she had no immediate use.

I called Dinah's name, not loudly for fear of drawing attention from the atrium and Darcas. As I walked the length of the courtyard, I thought I heard a whimper. It sounded like a small animal and it came from one of the sheds at the far end of the court. All the sheds were sealed with chains and complicated devices that only opened when a specially fashioned strip of metal was inserted in it. I tried to force the device but failed. The shed leaned against the back wall of the main building. It looked solid. But what appeared to be an impenetrable wall turned out to be only thatch that had been plastered over and scored to look like stone blocks. Finally, I came to appreciate Darcas' tightfistedness.

I unsheathed my knife and slashed away at the shed where it joined the building. In a moment, I made a hole big enough to allow me to peer into the shed. Someone was in there. Another forty slashes with my knife and I had a hole big enough to squeeze through. I held up my lamp and peered into the darkness. Eyes stared back at me.

"Dinah, is that you? What are you doing in here?" Darcas must have decided to take the matter of Dinah's introduction to the atrium into her own hands.

She held her arm up and with her lost, faraway look, pointed her finger toward the door. I remembered something about that look. I had seen it recently and not on Dinah's face. No, I had seen it somewhere else, but where? Then I remembered.

"Dinah, it's me, Judas. I'm going to get you out of here."

She whimpered and pointed at the door again.

"Don't worry. Darcas won't know."

Of course, she would know. That was the problem.

I looked around me. The shed held copperware, pots and urns, vases, and salvers of various sizes and shapes, piles of it. Some had scenes worked into the rims and across the plate face. It was as good as, or better than, any of the pieces Amelabib and I purchased from the coppersmith in Corinth. There was a fortune here—a fortune for anyone who knew when and where to sell it.

I do not remember how long I sat there, alternately looking at the copper and Dinah. I could get her out, I knew, but if I took Dinah out, Darcas would know I had broken into her shed and she would turn me over to her guards or the police. If that happened, there would be no one to look after Dinah. Then there were all the goods, the copperware, not to mention the things in the other sheds. I guessed if she stinted building one shed, it was a good bet the others would be easy to break into.

I put my finger to my lips. "I'll be right back. You be as quiet as you can." Dinah stared at me. "And don't leave. Darcas might see you. Do you understand? Stay right here."

She nodded.

No one saw me. I needed a miracle.

Pagans believe gods involve themselves in their affairs, or at least they used to. Some bore children by women and goddesses sometimes bore men's children, and sometimes they were so mixed up you could not tell one from the other, which is why, I suppose, Caesar declared himself to be a god, as well. Why not? There is not much to choose between the lot of them and at least Caesar commanded an army, which gave him an edge over the people who ran temples and claimed power from gods. But my mother's god was another story. Ever since we arrived in Cenchrea, I had made a point of praying to her god. I never really expected any response, but I did it for her and in the secret hope I might be wrong about him.

"God of my mother," I prayed, "I need your help. Until this day you have caused me nothing but pain and sorrow and you probably will not even listen to me now because I have no father. Will you hear me, then, for the sake of my mother and this other fatherless child in the shed and deliver us from certain destruction?"

Nothing.

Then I saw Gaius. He looked terrible. His luck had run out and he had become a candidate for an early grave, as were the other six standing with him, as sorry a lot as you will ever see. Then I knew exactly what I must do.

"Thank you, god of my mother," I said under my breath.

Luckily, it was a pitch-black moonless night. I slipped back into the shed and removed the copperware and carefully put it into sacks I found lying on the clay floor of the shed. I thought how very convenient of Darcas to leave them lying about after she unpacked her loot. Dinah watched wide-eyed and wondering. It was a struggle, but I got the best pieces away and hidden. I piled some kindling against the shed to cover the mess I made of the wall. I greeted Gaius and his pitiful squad of cutpurses. I had a proposition for them.

Chapter Twelve

I went back for Dinah. Once out of the shed and safely on my way, I signaled to Gaius. His flock of spotted goats descended on the other sheds and within moments they were looting Darcas' life savings. I rushed into the atrium out of breath and sounded the alarm. Darcas and her bodyguards rushed out the door, headed toward the backcourt. Gaius and his band had managed, by then, to wreck half of it. How much they had stolen I did not know. They had time enough to make off with quite a lot but their greed was a match for Darcas' and so they had stayed, trying to grab everything. Others had joined in the looting and a riot began. I threw the lamp onto a pile of dry straw near the cookhouse doorway and it burst into flames, casting an eerie glow on the melee in the backcourt. In the midst of the noise and smoke, the cursing, and the sound of clubs striking skulls, Dinah and I slipped away. We were going to the city—to Corinth.

I found the temple of Aphrodite but only after stumbling about in the dark on a dozen streets. Finally I remembered I had to climb to the Acrocorinth. I let my feet find the grade upwards. I promised myself I would pay closer attention the next time I wandered through a city. I stopped in front of the temple. It loomed over us, even bigger than I remembered.

We stood in its shadows for a moment while I wrestled with what I should do next. I led Dinah up the marble steps and onto the portico. I hesitated, reluctant to enter, when the biggest Ethiopian I had ever seen stepped out in front of us. He asked what business I had in the temple. I stammered, momentarily tongue-tied, and wondered if the prudent thing might be to reverse and get as far away as fast as I could. I steeled myself, figuring I had not come all this way to turn and run.

"I bring a gift for the goddess," I said in my best Greek. My accent was that of Amelabib and sounded local and country. The Ethiopian glared at me and at Dinah. She moaned and scurried around behind me. The Ethiopian motioned us to follow him.

He led us along a path that circled the temple to a low build-ing at the rear. He knocked and had a conversation with someone inside. In a moment, an old woman came out carrying a torch. It burned as brightly as the absent moon. I pushed Dinah forward and whispered to her for the one-hundredth time, "You will be safe here. It is going to be all right."

Something about the old woman seemed to touch Dinah. She stood still and stared straight ahead. The old woman circled her and then gazed into Dinah's face for a long time. She murmured something to the Ethiopian. Their voices were so soft I could not hear what they said. The old woman looked up abruptly and said something to me in Latin.

"She says she has been visited," the Ethiopian translated. "The goddess knows this child." She said something else to the Ethiopian who turned back to me. "She wants to know her name."

I was very nervous. "Dinah," I mumbled.

"Di...?" the old woman said, "Dia...Diana?"

"Yes," I said, "her name is Diana."

The old woman led Dinah, now Diana, away. The Ethiopian signaled for me to wait. In a moment he returned and handed me some coins. I looked at them—silver and gold mixed in with a lot of bronze, a fortune, more than I could earn in a year. I thought, I will never see Dinah again. But she is safe at last. Not even Darcas will find Diana if she is looking for Dinah.

My next stop was the house of Amelabib. He gave me an angry look and complained about having his sleep disturbed before dawn but when he saw the copperware I had, his face brightened. I only showed him a small sample. We were close, but in the world I lived in, you could never really trust anyone. He saw the profit in my proposal. For a share we negotiated, Darcas' former cooper goods were to be sold from his stall. He asked no questions, I offered no explanations. It was a good arrangement. Soon I would have enough money to take Mother away.

The sun rose red and shimmering as I returned to the House of Darcas. The courtyard still reeked of burning thatch. Smoke hung low on the ground. Darcas raced back and forth cursing at her bodyguards and peering into the wreckage of her sheds. Gaius and his pack had been caught, but not before most of the goods they managed to take, were taken from them in turn, by others stronger and quicker than they. Life on the streets had not been good to Gaius. Too many beatings and too many days without food and sleep had dulled his wits. He could no longer function, even as a thief. He would be dead before the moon was full.

I slipped into the building and climbed wearily to our room. Mother was frantic.

"Where have you been? Have you seen Dinah? I can't find her anywhere and Darcas won't speak to me."

"She is safe. I took her away to a safe place."

"Oh. Good. You are a good son, Judas. Go fetch her back now."

"I can't bring her back."

"Can't? Why? What have you done with her? Where did you take her? Why can't?"

"She is safe. I took her to Corinth."

"To Corinth…Corinth?" she said, eyes round and frightened.

"I took her to the Temple of Venus—Aphrodite. She will live there now, and neither Darcas' men nor any others will be allowed near her. They will keep her safe. They gave me money."

Mother screamed. A sound of anguish so complete, it would make an angel weep. She leapt to her feet and pulled her hair. She tore her clothing. She ran to the hearth and heaped ashes on her head. She alternately moaned and bellowed like a cow dropping a calf.

"How could you? It is not permitted to sell children to Gentiles…you know that. You must go and bring her back."

"I cannot. It is done and I did not sell her. They gave me money. Here, take it."

She slapped the coins from my hand. They clattered and rang across the floor.

"Mother, it was the only way. Darcas had her locked up in a shed. She…You cannot stop her, I cannot stop her and Dinah… is special."

"I don't want to hear it. It would be better if Dinah were dead than sold to Gentiles. You have done a terrible thing…a terrible thing. We do not turn our own over to the Gentiles, and never for money, never. Dinah cannot go to the Gentiles."

She paced up and down flailing her arms, wailing, and looking at me wild-eyed and furious. "It is the same as death. You know the law. You cannot have done such a thing."

"Mother, for god's sake…"

"Do not talk about the Lord to me. If you had any sense you would know that—"

"Mother, stop it. That old god of yours has brought us nothing but pain. Dinah was going to die here, Mother. That is a fact. She is damaged and cannot help herself."

"Dinah is fine, only very quiet."

"Quiet? Mother, she is mad. What happened in Caesarea broke her."

She sat down heavily on the bench by the hearth and became very still. Her hands hung limply between her knees, her hair covered her eyes. I listened to her breathing. She stared down at her feet. I never noticed it before but she had very small, thin feet, the feet of a young girl. Somewhere in the midst of her pacing and yelling, she had lost one sandal. Tears streaked the paint on her face, which I realized with a shock, was no longer young. The kohl from her eyes now filled the lines around her mouth. In the three years since we left Caesarea, she had aged ten.

"Look at us," I said. "Look at what we have become. We live like this in a city, the name of which is the Greek word for what you do in the atrium."

She looked up sharply and then dropped her eyes again. We both stared at her feet.

"There is enough money here to go home. You could go back to Galilee and your people."

"Home? I have no home. I have no people. Judas, the moment you were born I lost any possibility of ever going home. This is what I am now."

"But…"

It was hopeless. What I had done, I had done. I did not regret it and if her people and her god could not see the sense in it, then I wanted nothing to do with it either. We sat in silence.

Finally, she stood and stalked to the door, one foot silent, one slapping, and said, in a voice so soft I had to strain to hear it, "Judas, you are dead to me."

"Mother?

Chapter Thirteen

After my mother declared me dead, I left the House of Darcas and made the streets my home. The sale of Darcas' copperware enabled me to expand my money changing enterprise. Within a year Amelabib was gone. He fell behind in his bribes and the gangs wrecked his stall and ruined him. Later, I switched from money changing to money lending, a less risky occupation. It did require some bribes, but what does not? And I required help to collect debts. Fortunately, the empire produces many slow men suited for that work and who ask little in return by way of wages. I practiced that trade, and one or two others I prefer not to recall, in several cities.

The empire exists through the delegation of decreasing power through its rigid class system. Senators, patricians, equestrians, on down to the meanest farmer are accorded respect by virtue of the wealth and position they have, acquire, or inherit. At the very bottom are the slaves, who have no rights of any kind, including the right to life. Slightly above them are people like me, the *humilores,* and so on, up the ladder. I came from the brothels and streets of Corinth. To climb from the ranks of the *humiliores* to *honestiores*—peons to honorable men, I needed to advance my education. So, I invested a modest portion of my earnings in Patros, a Greek scholar made superfluous by Rome's cultural pillage. I hired him to give me some polish. Brilliant when sober, which was not often, he instructed me in the finer points of life and culture so that I passed as a man of substance and breeding, that is, if you did not look too closely.

I would have stayed in Cenchrea except for the family of Leonides. From Patros, I learned about the goddess, Nemesis, who sees to the business of retribution. Leonides' family wished revenge, blood for blood. Nemesis never stops, never gives up. I would be pursued by these men for the rest of my life. I tried changing my name. I shaved my head, dyed my hair, everything I could think of, yet these merciless men kept finding me, driving me from one city to another. In my darker hours, I sometimes wished they would find me and put an end to it.

I traveled to Sepphoris armed with letters of credit, gold and silver coins safely sewn in my cloak and tunic, and determined to unravel my history. It seemed strange, walking into the land my mother once called home. In the years since she left, Sepphoris had been rebuilt. A few noticeably charred walls remained here and there, and the buildings lacked the style they once had, if I believed my mother's description, but the city lived on and the people prospered. Galilee has a way of healing its own. If things had been different, if Grandfather had not responded to an ancient yearning to be free, Sepphoris would have been my home. Now, I came as a stranger. No one had ever heard of Judas Iscariot, the grandson of Judas of the Galilee. And my mother was, at best, only a dim memory.

"You must talk to Nahum the Surveyor, he will know," the old woman said and pointed south and east.

"Where will I find him?"

She scowled and pointed again, back toward Nazareth. "He is working out there."

I looked down the road I'd just traveled on my way to the city. I saw nothing.

"There," she said again and shook her head, "on the hills."

Finally, shifting my gaze from the road, I saw three or four men on the parched hillside a mile or so away.

"Those men?"

"They are laying out the course for the aqueduct. It will be a good thing, the aqueduct," she said, "water." She peered at me with rheumy eyes. "Water," she repeated.

I thanked her and walked toward the workers. They were handling a series of poles. One man, Nahum, I guessed, seemed to be in charge.

As I drew nearer, I saw him sighting along a straight bar loosely fastened to one of the poles. It had another thin bar attached to it at right angles and that one pointed to the ground. He waved his arm up and then down and then held his hand out flat. A second man, two hundred paces away, stood next to a second pole set firmly in the hard clay. As the first gesticulated, the second slid a crosspiece up and down the pole. With the last signal, he placed a mark on the pole where the crosspiece had come to rest. I looked back and saw there were a series of those poles stretching across the hillsides, back toward Amatai, and each had a similar mark on it.

"Nahum?" I said. The man looked up from the bar.

"I am Nahum."

"They told me you would be the one to talk to."

"Yes? Talk about what?"

"The uprising here—eighteen years ago."

"I do not know any more than anyone else about that," he said and turned back to his work.

I pointed back toward the city. "They said, 'talk to Nahum, he will know.'"

He mopped his brow with the back of his hand and inspected me, one eyebrow cocked, whether being careful or suspicious, I could not tell. "And you are…?"

"Judas. I am named for my grandfather. Perhaps you knew him."

"Roman legionnaires crucified the Judas I knew—over there." He pointed toward the road I had just traveled. "Are we speaking of that Judas?"

"He died over there?"

He nodded.

"I would like you to tell me about that, if it is not too much trouble."

Sweat trickled down my back under my tunic. He squinted at the sun and at his men, then at me.

"It is nearly the sixth hour. We will stop then and eat a little something and rest in the shade of those olive trees. Wait for me there. I won't be long."

I thanked him and walked to the grove of trees. I sat with my back against the rough bark of an old olive tree and wondered if it had once been my grandfather's. The shade provided a welcome relief from the heat and the sun.

<><><>

Nahum limped toward me and collapsed in the shade. He unfolded a cloth containing his meager meal. He offered to share but I declined. He had barely enough for one.

"So, you are the grandson of Judas of the Galilee? Except for young Menahem, I did not know his sons had sons and surely none that could be as old as you." His eyebrows framed an unasked question.

"I am the son of his daughter, Miriam," I said. I stared at the dusty road in the valley where Nahum said my grandfather had been crucified.

"Miriam? But she is dead."

"Perhaps now, not then. Soldiers carried her off. I am the result."

"Ah…yes. Well…" He waited for more. I said nothing. What purpose would be served by telling him that Judas' daughter worked as a prostitute? He stared at my red hair and then nodded. "Yes, I see."

"I would like to know what happened here."

Nahum leaned back against the tree and gazed at the sky. Finally, his mind made up, he turned to me. "It is a long story and a brutal one. Are you sure you want to hear it?"

I nodded.

Chapter Fourteen

We sat in silence for a long time, he staring backward into time, and I forward, toward what I must do. He'd told me the whole of it, my grandfather's brave and foolish idea to free the country and the horror that followed. I realized, too late, I had greatly underestimated my mother's strength. No wonder she seemed so short with Dinah.

"You say you were part of the uprising. How can that be if the men were crucified?"

He showed me his wrists and the ragged scars where the nails had been driven through and his deformed ankles. I recalled his limp.

"It takes time to die on the cross. Our Roman conquerors were called away the next day. Not all died. Usually they will break the legs of those still living. Then death comes quickly. But they were in a hurry, so they ordered our people not to bring us down, to let us die. Who would follow such an order? It was Friday and Shabbat would begin. The dead must be in the ground, so we were taken down. I was one of the lucky ones."

What could I say? I closed my eyes and tried to see it, to take it in.

After a while he asked, "Are there others…brothers, sisters?" I hesitated, my gaze shifted westward, toward the sea, toward Corinth.

"No, none."

"Well, you have uncles in the area but—"

"But they would not welcome me under the circumstances."

"Unfortunately…it is our way."

"Yes."

"It would be best if you kept what you have told me to yourself, Judas. These are difficult times and some of the people here have not forgiven your grandfather, and with the circumstances of your birth…"

"I did not come here to find family. I do not want anything from them. If they had any interest in my mother or me, they would have saved us, they could have helped."

"Your uncles were only boys…children."

"And my mother's uncles?"

He dropped his gaze. "Why did you come here?"

"To find out what happened, and to measure the people's will. I am the grandson of Judas of the Galilee. I intend to pick up where he left off."

He looked at me, sadness etched his face. Finally he pointed to the hillside just to the south of where we were seated.

"This water system will connect springs and wells in these hills to provide good water for Sepphoris. The first well in the system once belonged to your grandfather. People here think it is the least he can do to atone for what he did nearly twenty years ago. Do you understand?"

"You are telling me that these people will not fight for me. Will they fight for anyone?"

"We live in expectation of a messiah."

"Messiah?"

"You do not know your scriptures? Surely you know about the messiah."

"You forget. No one ever invited me to share them."

"Yes, that is so. Some believe a new David will come and set us free. Some believe he is near."

"How near?"

He closed his eyes. Then, a decision made, he rose to his feet.

"I must finish this line today. I would be honored if the grandson of Judas of the Galilee would stay with me while he visits the land."

◇◇◇

The Galilee is the provisioner of all of Israel. The soil is dark and fertile. From it comes such abundance that those who work it can support their families and, in a good year, have sufficient surpluses to attain a small measure of wealth. Anything that can be grown will be found ripening on one of the terraced plots in the hills around the sea. Grapes, olives, pomegranates, figs, and dates of every size and variety hang heavy on branches. Flowering fruit trees bring the bees and their golden combs. Land that is not cultivated supports flocks of fat sheep and goats. Wines, oils, and dried fruit are shipped everywhere from this valley, through the port of Caesarea or on the backs of dusty camels and donkeys in caravans that crisscross the land.

In the center of this rich land lies the Sea of Tiberias—the Sea of Galilee, its greatest source of income. Fish is a staple food for the surrounding countryside and, more than that, one third of all the salt fish consumed by the legions of Rome comes from Galilee. This prosperous corner of the world is, indeed, "the land of milk and honey" promised to our ancestors. Perhaps it is this abundance that creates a yearning to be free, perhaps not. But more than its fish, fruit, oil, or flocks, the export, for which the Galilee is most famous, is rebellion.

Rebellion, I have discovered, does not always arise from political oppression or crushing poverty. It is just as likely to rise up in the hearts of prosperous and comfortable men who yearn to be free. The whole of our history is about such men, not conquest or overriding righteousness, but the endless pursuit of the Covenant, to live in the land God willed to us. In the Galilee the ideal burns like holy fire. Sometimes it seems no more than a flicker, sometimes a conflagration, but always there.

The only thing needed to kindle it anew? The long expected messiah, the new David. I wondered if I sought him, might I find him.

And where?

Chapter Fifteen

I lingered with Nahum. He told me he followed the practices of the Essenes. I did not know what that meant and his explanation did not help. If you have no knowledge of the books of Moses and God's prophets, variations in interpreting them mean little or nothing, not that ignorance has ever stopped anyone from trying. He began my education in the holy books my mother quoted but did not understand. If I proposed to ignite a fire, I needed to learn and learn all this, and quickly.

After weeks of searching, it became obvious to me the men I sought were not in the hills around Sepphoris, but east and south in the prosperous towns rimming the Sea. Nothing remained in my mother's hometown but bad memories. Nahum urged me to stay. "You have much to learn, Judas. Stay a while. This is your land and when you know it as I do, you will come to love it."

"Yes, I am sure you are right. But I must go. I thank you for your hospitality and your confidence. I wish you to have this." I handed him a letter of credit, a small one, but for him it must have seemed like a fortune. He inspected it carefully. His jaw dropped.

"It is too much. I cannot accept so much for so little. Even an innkeeper would not expect this."

"Take it for the future. Someday if I need you, you will have the means to respond."

I headed to Tiberias and, I hoped, one step nearer to my goal, one farther away from my nemesis.

I moved about the country for another month. Tiberias reminded me of Caesarea, a place for the wealthy and their hangers-on to be seen. Herod Antipas made it his capital and imported people to live there. More pagan than Jewish, he filled its streets and houses by offering freedom to slaves in exchange for their pledge to stay.

I made discreet inquiries, but no one would admit to knowing anybody. I spread some money around and learned I should seek out a certain Jesus Barabbas. But more money could not induce anyone to admit knowing him.

Then one afternoon a voice whispered in my ear, a voice from the shadows, "Go east toward Bethsaida and look for a man."

"What sort of man?"

"You will know him when you see him."

Not a very promising reply, but I had no alternative. I looked again but the shadows had no substance.

◇◇◇

I picked my way carefully among the smooth, black stones that line the sea shore. As I did so, I saw a lone fisherman hauling in his nets. At first, I guessed his awkwardness at the task resulted from his having to work alone. If I had been told the truth about how families dominate the occupation, this fisherman, struggling with his nets, represented a rarity, or he plied some other trade.

When I drew abreast he signaled for me to wait. He sculled shoreward.

"You are easy to spot," he said, eyeing me with disapproval. "Your hair. If you wish to fight Rome, you must do something about that hair."

"And you, old man, should do something about your fishing technique. I am from the other side of the world and even I can see you are no fisherman."

"That is as may be, but Romans know less about fishing than you. What they do know is watching and remembering. No one passes through a Roman checkpoint without being noted and reported. You have been noted and reported."

My face flushed with embarrassment. "But if I have been noted and reported, why am I still at liberty?"

"Probably because they decided you are not important or, and this is more likely, they expect you will eventually lead them to someone who is. You have been asking for Barabbas?"

"Yes."

"And if I know that, who else knows?"

It had not occurred to me that I had been indiscreet.

"You know, of course, you are not the only one looking for a notorious evil-doer."

"What do you mean?" I asked, but I knew the answer. The house of Leonides had picked up my trail again.

"There are men asking about you," he said. He pulled on his long oar and the boat pivoted. "Men are known by their enemies. You have powerful ones, it seems. That is what bought you this meeting. Go to Scythopolis, the Greek city, and wait at the turning of the road. Someone will meet you there. And for heaven's sake, do something about your hair."

Chapter Sixteen

I heard ringing of bronze wheels and the clatter of horses' hooves on cobblestones and warning cries from passersby just as a chariot bore down on me. I leapt aside and felt the rush of air as a lunatic boy nearly ran me down.

"Out of the way, Jew," the driver, who looked to be about twelve, bawled and cracked his whip in my general direction. I had not come all this way to be run over by some beardless Latin youth with too much money and too little sense. I shook my fist and sent a Corinthian curse at the charioteer's back. My introduction to Scythopolis.

Romans have no more regard for us than for animals. No, that is not correct. They hold their animals in higher esteem. Their horses and dogs are groomed and well fed. Their slaves and servants must compete with them for scraps of food. I once watched a Roman, a man of some standing, use one of his slaves to train his watchdog to attack. The slave was mauled and died. The Roman had the slave's body dragged away and ordered a reward for the dog.

Scythopolis or Nyssa-Scythopolis gets its name, I learned, from a Greek nymph who took care of the wine god. Why the Romans wanted a town named for that, I cannot imagine, but then, who can explain Rome? The locals call it Beth Shan, which means Secure House. Secure from what, I do not know. As long as Rome rules, there is only Roman security, and it seems those who claim lineage from Abraham must be content with that. Bands of raiders, those who preach rebellion, are turned in to the authorities by their own countrymen. Rome learned long ago that hunger provides spies and traitors. They maintain hunger by keeping the country taxed into poverty. That is our security.

As they did with nearly everything, the Romans made Scythopolis their own. They are not a people given to creativity. They take from others and bend it to their peculiar vision. Their genius lies in conquest and, in that, they are ruthless, predictable, and immensely successful. They will, if need be, destroy whole cities in a single day. That does not leave much in the way of choices for the rest of us.

Throughout my journey across Galilee, I heard rumors of men gathering in the wilderness, of bands collecting weapons and men, of raids on Roman camps. My grandfather's legacy, I thought. The men came primarily from the Galilee and south, down toward Gaza. Ragged bands that come together to attack legionnaires. They dart in and out of the wilderness, destroying a patrol here, stealing weapons or food there, and disappearing just as quickly. I planned to contribute to that effort. I had enough money to arm and supply such a band of men and lead it. I would be as merciless as any Roman.

I believed that eventually Rome would tire of the killing and lash out, not just at bands of raiders, but at everyone. Then those stiff-necked people would stop cowering in the dust and rise up like their ancestors before them and fight back. I dreamed of a day when all the dark dangerous men, soldiers, hangers-on, and tax farmers would finally be paid back for what they did to Dinah, Mother; did to all the women and children they left broken, homeless, and humiliated. And if the house of Leonides wished to take me, well, they must find me first.

Of course, many Jews would be slaughtered in the process, but I did not see that as my concern. What did I care about the Jews? People like me, the unaccepted and unclaimed, forced by their law to live as strangers among them, we are but a minor irritation, a flea in their tunic. I, on the other hand, cared only that hundreds of Roman soldiers would die in the process. Or so I told myself. It is easy to be brave in the abstract. Reality is another thing entirely, as I was about to discover.

Every Roman city I ever visited had a road running straight through it, the Straight Street. But Sycthopolis is different. Maybe the Greeks laid it out this way, or perhaps the Roman designer who came later to reset it had a sense of humor, or was too devoted to Bacchus to care. The street that ought to bisect this city had a right angle turn at its very center. It appeared so unexpectedly, the hubs of a thousand chariots turning the corner too sharply had chipped and scraped the curbstone into roundness.

Columned porticos and wide esplanades lined both sides of its *cardo*. The eastern portion of the road boasted a long reflecting pool lined by a colonnaded *stoa*. People could walk out of the way of the wheels of carts and the mad dashing of chariots. Colorful awnings fluttered between columns, and vendors hawked their wares. If I had not set my course as an agent of death, I might have settled there. But the stars were set in their courses, and so was I.

"Meet a man at the turning of the road," my counterfeit fisherman had said. Well, there was little doubt about where I needed to be. After my near fatal encounter with the chariot, I found a spot at the right angle turn and waited, watching people parade by, Romans in their long and short togas. Even the poorest of them had an air of prosperity. I don't think I ever saw a hungry Roman. The Greeks, on the other hand, looked a little seedy, I suppose because there had not been one of their race to amount to much since the great Alexander. Rome appropriated their culture, their gods, and their soul.

"You, Red Hair…yes, you."

The man appeared beside me, dressed like any of the hundreds of traders and travelers who crowded the street, unmistakably an Israelite. He motioned me to follow him. Surely, I thought, this must be the man. I followed him south along the main street, past the theater on my left and the baths on the right. Soon, we were walking south into the country away from the city's noise and confusion. We passed a great spring that gushed from the hillside. It appeared to be the city's only water source. It poured out from between two great boulders in the hillside and ran into the city in a shallow aqueduct. If I could find a way to shut off the water, I could defeat an entire city, a wonderful thought. I would share it with Barabbas when I met him, which I hoped would be soon.

"You," I called to the man who was leading me away from the city, "where are you taking me?"

He did not reply but flapped his arms about as if to say, be quiet and hurry. I increased my pace but I could not catch up. After an hour he was so far ahead of me I feared I would lose him. I started to call out again when he stopped suddenly and sat. As I approached he motioned for me to sit, too.

"Why are we sitting? I am certainly grateful for the rest, but..."

"Sit...eyes down," he growled between clenched teeth. I did as he ordered. No sooner had I tucked my sandals under me than I heard the noise of a large body of marching men. At first only the clank and jingle of metal against metal, then the glint of sunlight on short swords, shields, and helmets slung on straps over shoulders, the tramp of feet shod with the heavy leather and bronze fitted leggings, the sounds of burden bearers, camp followers, heavy breathing, grunts, and conversation as they approached.

They were just over the rise and as I lowered my head, they were on us. A centurion led a full Roman hundred north to Sycthopolis. I did not want to catch anyone's eye. I could be forced to carry their goods for the required mile and that would end any chance I had to meet Barabbas. We let them pass and then continued our breakneck pace southward, down the valley and along the King's Highway to the Jordan.

We traveled at that crazy pace all day and the next. My joints throbbed and my muscles felt like knotted cords, but as we walked, they loosened, the pain subsided, and I found it easier to keep up. I reckoned rebel bands in the wilderness must travel like that. To march at such a pace could put a person a great distance from his starting point in the course of only a few hours. A band of raiders moving across the wilderness at such a rate could strike several different points in a day and create the illusion there were two or three different bands instead of just one. I tucked that observation away for future consideration.

We arrived at Elijah's spring on the edge of Jericho about the sixth hour of our third day. Palm trees circled the well and offered shade to those waiting to fill their jars. The Judean wilderness rose steeply to our right, yellow-brown and arid, shimmering in the heat. Twenty or thirty people waited in line to draw water. My guide moved to the front with his dipper. No one objected. He quickly filled a small pail and brought it to me and we drank. It had been hours since I had any water. After he sipped his share and moved away, I finished the pail.

We rested for only a few moments, then he bounced up and we set off again. All I wanted to do was to stay there in the shade of the palms and rest. What difference would another day make? But when I got my feet under me and started to move I saw my guide already a hundred paces ahead. I hurried after him.

We left Jericho and walked west toward the setting sun and, if I remembered what I had been told, toward Jerusalem. The shadows in the valley soon deepened as the sun fell lower in the western sky.

As we climbed up the Wadi Qelt, my aches and pains returned. I longed to stop. At that instant he veered sharply from the path and motioned for me to sit. We were at a point along an aqueduct where a small leak created a lush green oasis, two palm trees and some soft grass. I collapsed. Never had anything felt so welcome. My guide left me but I did not care. I scooped water from the aqueduct and poured it over my head, washed my hands and feet, and drank.

I looked again for my silent guide. In the brief moment my eyes had wandered away, he'd vanished. I scanned the whole of the horizon, looked back down the valley. No one. Only shadows and silence. The sun dropped behind the western hills and the wilderness turned cold and dark, as though a curtain had been drawn across it.

Bandits and cutthroats of every sort inhabited those parts and while I did not fear them exactly, I was a stranger and alone and not sure what to expect. As I moved deeper into the darkness a rasping voice called, "Over here, Red Hair. Over here."

I jumped. The voice seemed to be right on top of me, but I saw no one. I peered into the gloom, looking for a clue, a flicker of firelight, anything.

"Now, Red Hair."

I had no choice. He could see me, but I could not see him, and that meant I had no hope of escape. I followed the sound into the dark and prayed to whatever gods ruled the land that when the sun rose again, I would still be alive. I stepped closer and saw he was waving me into a cave. Hand firm on the hilt of my knife, I stepped forward into either my last night on this earth, or the future I sought and had planned for since I left Caesarea years before.

Chapter Seventeen

To this day, I do not know what I expected when I set eyes on the famous Jesus Barabbas—something akin to one of the Greek demigods, I suppose, like Achilles, not quite human and yet, not beyond mortal contact. Maybe I thought this rebel would be a Jewish Alexander the Great or David himself. Whatever possibilities ran through my mind were quickly dashed by the man who crouched before me and who, he announced proudly, was indeed that very famous Jewish rebel and raider.

A small fire flickered in the deep recesses of the cave. I could make out baggage and bales deeper in. Close to its mouth, bundles had been arranged so that no light escaped to betray his presence. The result—a cave filled with smoke. Soon my eyes watered and I rubbed them with my sleeve. He laughed.

"Now you know why the soldiers call us 'red eyes.' They think it is because we are mad. It is good they think that, but it is only the smoke."

I nodded. My eyes adjusted to the light. "There are no others with you?" I asked. I peered into the depths of the cave as hard as I could, but saw nothing that resembled a man, much less a group of them.

"They are here…" he gestured vaguely, "and they are there… you understand how that must be."

He smiled. His teeth were broken and yellow and his grin looked like a wolf when it has chanced upon a flock of sheep.

My hand found the hilt of my knife. He saw the movement and his eyes hardened, but only briefly.

"Do not be afraid, Red Hair," he said. "There is no need for that. You have been searching for me and now you have found me. Now, you will tell me why you have been seeking Barabbas." He settled back on his haunches and peered expectantly at me through smoky firelight.

I studied the man. I saw strength in him. Anyone could see that. A sane person would not want to meet him in one of the dark alleys of Corinth. Even hunched over in the gloom he appeared larger than life, swarthy and broad across the chest, his beard long, cut in the fashion of the men of this land, but unkempt and scraggly. His hair had a reddish cast to it. Not red like mine, but rusty. He pulled his torn and dirty cloak around his shoulders and looked like a man on the run, which, of course, he was. I saw no weapons in his belt, no evidence of one on his person, but I had no doubt a short sword or a knife lay somewhere close by.

"I have come to make you an offer," I said.

"An offer? What sort of offer will this red-haired wanderer make me?" His eyes glazed over, and his expression became unreadable.

"First, I wish to join you in your fight against the Romans."

"First? There is more?"

"Well, yes, but I wanted to get that part said and agreed to."

"You wish to join my group of men and fight Romans. You did say Romans?"

"Yes, of course, the Roman legions. I have heard all about you in my travels, in places as far away as Ephesus and beyond."

"They speak of me, of Barabbas, in these places?" His eyebrows soared.

"Oh, yes, of Barabbas, the man who will drive the Romans out of this land."

Hearing of his fame so far away brought another frightening smile to his face.

"And you wish to join me in this?"

I felt more confident now. I believed he recognized me as someone who knew things and had been places. I nodded.

"I see. Tell me, have you ever actually killed anyone? A Roman soldier, perhaps, anyone? I ask this only because there are many young men roaming these hills who come to me, their heads filled with dreams of glory, but when the swords are drawn and the legionnaires approach, they disappear into the wilderness as quickly as they came. They go home to their mommas and tell their friends about their campaign in the wilderness with the great Barabbas. You will not be one of those? I only want the men who are ready to risk their lives and to kill. You are a killer, yes?"

I thought about Leonides and the blood on my hands. The authorities in Caesarea believed I killed that man. His family thought I did. I had come to understand that we are what others say we are, not what we believe about ourselves. Officials declared me a killer, so I am.

"Yes," I said.

"Ah, the Stone Carver. It is true then? You killed a favorite of the rich and powerful. Yes ? How?"

"How?"

"Yes, how did you do this killing?"

"With this knife." I jerked it free from its sheath. The blade caught the light and I thought I saw Barabbas stiffen.

"Ah, with that very knife? May I see it?"

I did not like this turn, but I could not refuse. I handed it to him.

"Very nice. May I ask where you got this? It is not from around here."

"I took it from a desert man."

"Took it? You took it from a desert man. And he let you? That does not sound like any desert man I ever met. You say you took it?"

"Yes."

He turned the knife over in his hand, scrutinizing it.

"Well, for the sake of progress, let us say you may join us. I will test this resolve of yours, you understand, but for a man who took this beautiful knife from a fierce desert man and has killed, how can I refuse?" He gave me another wolfish grin.

I relaxed a little, relieved and even happy. I had met the great Barabbas and had won him over. The rest would be easy, once he knew I came to help and could supply him with many of the things he needed.

"And the other thing you wished to ask of me?"

"Yes, the second part. I have access to certain sums of money." His eyes flickered for a moment. I could not read their meaning, but I plunged ahead anyway. "Enough to supply another band of fighters as large as your own, which I will lead."

"You will lead? What makes you think you can lead a band such as mine, Red Hair?"

"I have been saving and preparing for this moment from the day I realized it possible. Romans destroyed my family. Listen," I rushed on, "I am the grandson of Judas of the Galilee, and I swore many years ago to finish what he started and make them pay for what they did to me and mine. And now I have come to you prepared to do it."

"And that makes you special, Red Hair? Your grandfather, if indeed he was..." He looked at me and at my hair. "More than half the people in the Galilee and at least a third of those in all of Judea have suffered at the hands of the Romans. It comes from being a conquered people. Egyptians, Assyrians, Babylonians, Persians, Greeks, and now Romans, one after the other, have taken this land and done terrible things to its people. And when they are gone, someone else will take their place."

"Not if we raise men to fight," I said, and wondered at his lack of enthusiasm. This did not sound like the great Barabbas described to me.

"To do such a thing," he said slowly, "would require a great deal of money." He gave me an appraising look and I squirmed under his gaze. "You have such sums, no doubt, in that little pouch you carry? Or maybe they are in your belt. No, you've got them in your sandals."

He wished to provoke me, I knew. I stayed calm. I had the resources he needed and I decided to wait until he came to me. "Letters of credit," I said quietly, "guaranteed by Silvanus Quintas, a Roman banker, in fact."

His eyebrows lifted again, just a little this time. "No, you are not just one of the little boys who come to the wilderness to fight, only to run away, are you? You have thought this out." He said this slowly, thinking aloud. "Letters of credit could be hidden in many places, could they not? In one's cloak, for example, or tunic or even one's headdress. Isn't that so?"

I knew I had missed something important. I pressed on. The prospect of assembling a band of warriors from among Barabbas' best men blocked any second thoughts I should have had. My instincts told me to be careful but my heart urged me on. My mind was as cloudy as the smoke filled cave in which I sat. It never occurred to me that he might turn on me.

He scratched his head and then, having reached a decision clapped his hands. "Good. We will proceed. Red Hair and Barabbas will free the country from the invaders," he laughed. "We will drink some wine to seal the pact." He reached for a wineskin and started to hand it to me but stopped. He pulled back the skin and his smile disappeared. "You wish to kill Romans, yes?"

"Yes," I said, a little too loudly and wishing I had the wine.

"Who else are you willing to kill, to accomplish this end?"

"I don't understand."

"Red Hair, the Romans rule because they have power. Others, the people of this land, fear this power, and so they help them. Rome requires only a fraction of the men to occupy the country as it needed to conquer it in the first place. Do you understand?"

"Yes, I suppose that must be so."

"You suppose. No supposing. That is the way it is. Now, if we can create an opposite fear in the hearts of these sheep, a fear that will persuade them to stop helping the Romans, wouldn't that make it easier to attack our enemies?"

I heard his logic but was uneasy with the conclusion I expected to follow. I nodded my agreement.

"So, sometimes we must kill our own. We must take what we need from those who cannot stop us, so we can fight against those who can."

"You rob our people?"

"Rob, and if I have to, kill them. Who else? You have other candidates?"

What he said made sense, but surely, if there was to be a general uprising, people must be willing to follow a leader. If the leader turned out to be someone who had just stolen their goods or killed one of their family... My mind reeled.

"So, let us return to the Romans. I can see the idea of going against your own will take time for you to accept."

Not *my own*. Those people were no more my people than their god was my god. I was about to say so when he heaved himself to his feet and, crouching under the cave's low ceiling, moved back into its dark recesses.

"You wish to kill Romans, you said?" he asked from the darkness.

"Yes. As many as I can."

A moment later he reappeared, dragging what I thought was a very large bundle. The cave must have been deeper than I thought. There may have been many such bundles and who knew what else he had stored in its depths.

He tore the sacking away to reveal a man, a boy, hands and feet bound with a thick rope and another across his mouth to prevent his speaking. He wore only a soldier's soiled undergarments. His body armor had been stripped from him. How much of the conversation he had heard and understood, I did not know, but the look of terror in his eyes made me believe he had at least grasped the essentials.

"Very well, Red Hair," Barabbas said. "Kill this one." He picked up my knife, tested its edge, and handed it to me. "Cut his throat."

I held the knife in my left hand. I shifted it to my right. Sweat broke out on my forehead and my palms were so wet I thought the knife would slip away.

"Here…now?"

"Why not? You told me of your great hatred for the Romans, not just this Roman or that Roman, but all Romans. 'They destroyed my family,' you said. 'I am the grandson of Judas of the Galilee,' you said. So here is one. Kill him."

Time stood still. The soldier moaned, his eyes as big as bread rolls. He could not have been more than sixteen, I thought, probably just someone like me, who survived the streets and found his way into the service of Rome as an alternative to starvation. We stared at each other. We could be brothers. But he was a Roman soldier and my enemy.

"Kill him, man. Kill him, now."

I raised the knife. An eternity passed. I looked into the terrified eyes of that defenseless soldier and lowered the knife.

"Not such a killer as I was lead to believe," Barabbas said, voice flat.

He took the knife from my hand and with one quick motion drew it across the soldier's throat. The young man's eyes closed and then snapped open as his body jerked against his bonds as if it was trying to run after the life that drained out of him into a crimson pool at my feet. Then he went limp. Barabbas wiped the blood from the blade on the poor man's clothes and glowered at me.

"That is how you kill Romans, Red Hair. Not with words or letters of credit, but with knives and clubs and swords, with fists, and teeth, and nails, and anything that comes to hand."

"I know, but—"

"He was one of a squad of ten men who captured and then crucified one of my men. They nailed him to a cross, laughing at his screaming. They laughed and drew straws for the miserable clothes he had on his back. They sat, ate their midday meal, and watched him die as calmly as they would step on a beetle. No, this one was lucky. We were going to crucify him, too, on the Jericho road—one of theirs for one of ours. Now we must find another." As he said that, he looked steadily at me.

I thought I would be sick.

"You fool. Do you think killing Romans because they hurt your family will have an effect on anything? We kill one of them, they kill ten of us. I do not live out here in this godforsaken wilderness because I think I can save the world from Rome. No, Red Hair, I am here because this is what is left for me to do, to rob and plunder whatever comes my way. If they are Romans, so much the better, but for me, anyone, you understand, anyone is fair game."

Something had gone wrong. I had borne my hatred for years and believed if given the chance, I would gladly dispatch a Roman soldier. Yet something held me back. When presented with the choice to be the person I thought I was, I failed and, instead, made the choice Patros would have labeled as moral. I shook my head in frustration.

"Barabbas," I said, "I will not hesitate the next time. Listen, you need me. I can provide you with materials and resources—"

"Next time? With Barabbas there is no next time, boy."

I heard a sound behind me and, for the second time in my life, my world went black.

Chapter Eighteen

"Don't touch them. They are unclean."

"How can you tell, Ezra? That one looks like he might be breathing. We should be sure."

I heard the voices, men's voices, angry voices. My head buzzed like a beehive. I ached all over. Pain that failed to mask a sense of overwhelming foreboding.

"Alive or dead, Joseph, they are pagans. Look, the one in the ditch is not circumcised and this one, well, look at that hair. Did you ever see an Israelite with hair like that?"

"No, well not often but—"

"Even King David did not have hair like that. No, I think they are Romans or Samaritans. I think they have fallen into the hands of outlaws and if so, we do not want to be anywhere near them when the next patrol passes by."

Patrol? What patrol? Who would be patrolling? The sun beat down on my back and I could not move my arm.

I tried to open my eyes but they were plastered shut. Pain radiated along my side and down my leg. I remembered something about a journey and painful legs, but this pain came from somewhere else. I knew something had gone wrong but in my broken state, I could not think what. Where did my right arm go? I rubbed my eyes with my left hand. They felt gritty, sandy like the beach. I managed to get one opened, then the other. I saw a pair of sandals and the feet that occupied them.

"That one is alive. Look, he is moving."

"Cross over to the other side of the road. Do not get near them. We may not touch them."

"Yes, yes, I know. Who can they be?"

"Men foolish enough to travel this road at night, I suppose."

I turned my attention away from those carrion crows. An arm's length away someone lay in the ditch. I squinted through swollen eyelids at the feet, the legs, and finally the face of the murdered Roman. Barabbas had slit his throat the night before. I stared at his severed throat and the look of astonishment locked permanently on his face.

They left me naked except for the small loincloth around my waist. My Roman companion lacked even that.

Naked. No Clothes. No cloak, no tunic.

They'd stolen my clothes. A long time passed before that sank in. If they took my clothes, they also had my letters of credit and money. Everything, even my knife, the one I took from the desert man, all gone, taken by the one man I most wanted to help, the man I would have freely given them to, if asked.

I revised my opinion of Barabbas. His reputation as a liberator, a patriot, or even a nationalist needed amending. I had acquired another cause to avenge. He cared nothing about freedom. He roamed the wilderness a murderer and a thief, and the two of us lying on the road were merely his latest victims, nothing more. My eyes burned. Someone or several, I suppose, had beaten me and left me in the road to die next to this wretched soldier. Once again, just when I thought I managed to do the right thing, my resolve, like a leaf in the winter wind, blew away.

I lay on my stomach in the middle of a road somewhere, broken but alive. Barabbas did not leave me in the road, still breathing, out of any sense of mercy. Mercy could not last an hour with that man. And yet, I lived. Why? I really needed to know the answer to that question.

The sun came from a different angle. Not as hot as before, but I could still feel it on my back, which I knew must be badly burned. In the delirium of the moment, I turned philosophical. I knew I had been in this state before, not the first time I lost everything, and at least I was alive. With some luck and a little cunning, I could replace most of what had been taken from me. But then, the pain and urgency resurfaced. I knew that I had to get up, to stand, and leave this place.

My head ached. I lost my train of thought while I wrestled with why Barabbas did not kill me along with the Roman. Then everything went black again.

My mind, finally alert, brought me back and I knew why. Barabbas wanted me found with the dead soldier. He wanted the patrol or whoever monitored the road to think I had killed that miserable man. It would look like we had a fight, which ended in his death. The poor living in the wilderness often stripped corpses, which would explain why we were naked. Let stupid Judas the Red assume the blame for yet another murder. Barabbas and the Romans had more in common than either would admit.

Every bone in my body felt broken. Barabbas and his men must have beaten me for hours before they dragged us down to the road. Maybe they believed me dead after all. For a brief moment I wished it were so. I welcomed any end to the pain and humiliation I felt, even if it meant death. I staggered to my feet. I tried to run. I managed only a shuffle and careened down the road, I do not know in which direction I went. I just knew I needed to put some distance between me and that dead boy. I may have gone two hundred paces, maybe more, when everything went dark one last time.

I woke, staring at the ceiling of a building of some sort. I did not know what or where. A lamp burned nearby. Pain coursed through my body and I could barely lift my head or see anything except lamplight dancing on the wall. I heard men speaking quietly to one another and the clatter of crockery.

"Are you awake?" A woman's voice, a young woman by the sound of it. The last thing I remembered was heat, sun, and a dead soldier. I rolled my eyes toward the voice. Even that hurt. I could make out a girl's face, not a particularly pretty face, but a kind one with a lovely smile. I tried to speak but all I could manage was a croak.

"Shhh…" she whispered. "Do not try to say anything just yet. You have been injured. The healer said you were hit in the throat and it will take time to heal. Shhh…"

I tried again with the same results. I wanted to know how I came to this place. I tried gestures and finally she seemed to understand.

"Your friend, Nahum, brought you here."

Did I know someone named Nahum? I closed my eyes and tried to remember a Nahum.

"Your friend said he found you on the road. He said there were two of you. The other one seemed to be a dead Roman soldier. The patrol stood over him, stopping everybody and asking questions. He found you farther down the road and around a small bend. As they had not discovered you, he brought you here. We are only a short distance away."

With great difficulty and even more pain, I rolled my head around to see what sort of place I'd been brought to. With the girl's help, I managed to sit up, too quickly as it turned out, and the pain almost made me faint.

"It is the Inn of the Three Camels," she said.

I guessed the inn must be on the Jericho road, a small inn, no more than one large room with a few tables and benches. I lay on a pallet in an alcove at the rear, opposite the door. Did she say a patrol? I looked at her again. How to communicate with this woman? I waved my hands about…how to signal patrol? Finally after I acted out spears and shields—not without pain, she seemed to understand.

"The patrol? No, I don't think they will come. They did not then, and so it is not likely they will now." She said this with great confidence and smiled. I closed my eyes and tried to think. How long had I lain here?

"Oh, you have been here two days. Your friend, Nahum, paid for your stay and for your care and said to tell you he hoped you had nothing to do with what he saw on the road."

Nahum…Nahum…Nahum…I racked my brain. I could not remember anyone named Nahum and certainly not anyone generous enough to do such a thing for me. Ah, the Essene, it had to be him. What would he be doing here? So, I had been right when I said I might need his service in the future. How these things happen is, I think, a great mystery. My mother would have called it "an act of the Lord." Her god, she would insist, provided this good fortune. Well, I did not believe her god or any other had anything to do with it. Just a stroke of good luck, nothing more.

Chapter Nineteen

I must have dozed off. When next I raised my head the girl was gone. I tried to look around. I gritted my teeth and heaved myself up again.

A screen woven from river reeds separated me from the rest of the room. I was covered with a thin blanket. I discovered I had been dressed in a robe of some sort but my feet were bare. I had a bandage as big as a turban tied around my throbbing head.

As I took inventory of my situation and condition, I heard a commotion at the front of the inn. I craned my neck. Three soldiers pushed their way through the entrance and shouted at the innkeeper. He shook his head. They drew their short swords.

"We know someone was brought here two days ago, an injured man. Where is he?"

I blew out my lamp. The girl had been mistaken about the patrol. The innkeeper hesitated. Nahum had paid him to give me sanctuary. His honor was at stake. To turn me over brought disgrace on him and his family. At the same time everyone knew the soldiers could do a great deal of damage to his inn and to him personally if he refused to cooperate.

I waited. Only shadows and the reed screen kept me from discovery. When their eyes grew accustomed to the gloom, the soldiers would have me. One of them raised his sword. The innkeeper swallowed hard and pointed in my direction. I gulped and almost cried out in pain as my crushed throat contracted.

The soldiers wheeled in my direction and peered into the darkness. No escape. I resigned myself to my fate, first Barabbas and now this.

At that moment four other men shouldered their way in. They pushed past the Romans and walked straight toward me. The soldiers started to follow, then paused in confusion. Nemesis, I thought. Romans or the family of Leonides, which would be worse? Either way I would die.

"This is our brother who fell from the edge of the wadi. Isn't that right, Innkeeper?"

"Yes, that is so," he said, relieved. "The very one."

The soldiers looked at one another and then at the men. "Who are you? Why haven't we heard of an accident in the wadi?"

"We are friends of this man and have come to take him home."

The soldiers moved toward the back of the inn as well. "That is the man who killed our comrade."

"No, you are mistaken," one said. "Your comrade fell into the hands of Barabbas. Everyone knows that."

"We have information that on the very day our comrade was found in the road, this man arrived here covered with blood, our friend's blood."

"It is true he arrived here in that condition and on that day, but as the victim of a very bad fall into the wadi and in no way connected to your friend's murder. You should do us all a great service and be out seeking Barabbas. This man is a stranger to these parts and did not know the steep banks and foolishly left the road at dusk. He fell."

The two groups of men stared at each other as if they could, by sheer force of will, make the other step aside. I never saw anyone stand up to Roman soldiers like these men. I prepared myself for some bloodletting.

"Ask the innkeeper and these good people if we tell the truth," the first man said.

"It is so. Yes, yes. A very bad fall…" a nervous chorus of support from the small gathering.

The soldiers looked at each other and the people in the inn—unsure. The innkeeper pounded on the table where he kept his supply of wine.

"A drink for you, good soldiers. We are in your debt as you keep the roads clear of brigands and thieves." He poured out large cups of wine and offered it to them.

"The best," he declared, "from Cilicia." The soldiers took the wine, drank, and seemed to make a decision. Clearly, they would get no help from any of this group. Dragging a wounded prisoner any distance would be difficult. After a while the wine's mellowing effects set in, and they accepted the story about the fall. Life would be easier for them that way.

Once again I had been snatched from the terror of Roman justice, saved from being punished for murder I did not commit. I struggled to understand. I had no friends, yet it seemed whenever I needed help someone was there for me. The only boat leaving Caesarea that awful day fifteen years ago happened to have room for Mother, Dinah, and me. The boy who worked for Amelabib fell and broke his leg, Nahum, and now these men. I wondered if there was a plan, some divine current that kept me alive in spite of the difficulties that followed me.

My newfound friends approached my alcove. I tried to rise. My knotted muscles and the pain in my side from the blows allowed only a small hitch upward. They motioned for me to lie still. A fifth man entered the small space with a crude litter and they gently lifted me on it. One of the men chatted with the innkeeper, who then wrapped some bread and cheese in a cloth and handed it to him along with a full wineskin. They hoisted me up and carried me out into the afternoon sun. I did not know where they were taking me or why. We moved downhill and away, to where, I did not know.

Chapter Twenty

I spent the first weeks with my rescuers in an infirmary under the care of the resident healer, Eleazer. He hovered over me like a lioness watching her cub. Eleazer, it seemed, sailed through the days as one of life's cheerful and garrulous people. I could not speak, so he spoke for me, answering my unasked questions as he busied himself with his ointments and potions and tending my bruises. His infirmary smelled like a spice shop from the oils and balms he concocted. From his nonstop, one-sided conversation, I learned that I had been delivered to the Essene community at Kirbet-Qumran, the same group to which my friend Nahum belonged.

In my second week, three men visited me. By the seriousness of their expressions, bearing, and the deference Eleazer paid them, I assumed they must be very important. The oldest of the group did most of the talking. Later, I discovered he served the community as the high priest, not the high priest in Jerusalem whom I later learned they dismissed as a usurper, the corrupt end of the Hasmonian experience.

He stood in the doorway and studied me for a long time. His features mapped the whole history of the nation. He looked old enough to have crossed the Jordan with Joshua. I expected the quaver and rasp of the elderly, but this man's voice, deep and resonant, could belong to a young man. His expression resembled that of someone examining a piece of suspect fish.

"Nahum vouched for you. He says you are a generous man and worthy of delivery from the hands of Rome. He also said you came to Galilee seeking information on the whereabouts of certain men and you had plans to avenge yourself in some way. Is this true?"

I nodded.

"Since he found you near a Roman corpse, he supposed it possible you began that crusade. But, on second thought, he felt it unlikely you could have been beaten so badly and also have committed murder. In that, however, he could not be sure."

He paused and looked to his right and left, seeking confirmation from the two men with him. Reassured, he continued, "Because Nahum, whom we deem worthy and indisputably upright, spoke on your behalf, we brought you here, bound your wounds, and gave you sanctuary. We are no more concerned with the death of one Roman soldier than the affairs of any other pagan. However, before we can do more for you, we must have answers to some questions. Are you willing to answer truthfully the questions put to you?"

I pointed to my throat to indicate I could not speak and nodded again.

"Do not answer in haste, and be sure of what you do answer. We are skilled in divining the truth. Did you kill the Roman soldier?"

I shook my head.

They stood very still, stared at me, exchanged looks, and after what seemed like an eternity, and apparently satisfied I spoke the truth, they nodded and relaxed.

"Understand, if you were the killer of that man, the safety of all who live here would be jeopardized, and we would not permit you to stay."

He let me think about that for a moment. I wondered how good they really were at "divining the truth." Certainly all of the truth could not be forthcoming.

"You are of the circumcision."

A statement, not a question. I nodded. There could be no doubt about that. Why I, or anyone else for that matter, endured that peculiar anatomical revision remained a question for another day.

"Where are you from? Not here, we think."

I pointed at my throat again and gestured.

"Can you read and write?"

I was not sure how to answer. I could do both, thanks to Patros, my wine-soaked tutor, but I believe it is not always advisable to admit to everything. People sometimes think that if you are illiterate, you are also stupid, and will reveal things in their speech and manner they might not otherwise. That can be of great benefit in a situation involving negotiating rates or the price of things. Finally, I nodded.

We looked at one another and then, realizing my predicament, he told someone out of my line of sight to bring writing materials.

I was handed a wax tablet, the sort used to jot notes or do calculations. I took the stylus and wrote in Greek, *Some Greek, less Aramaic, no Hebrew.* I started to hand it over, then pulled it back and added, *I can do numbers, like the people from the East.*

They conferred among themselves.

"How can it be you read little Aramaic and no Hebrew, if you are of the circumcision?"

I did not know how to respond to that. Does God demand that if you are snipped short down there, you must also read and write Hebrew? I shrugged and then reached for the tablet.

I come from Corinth.

I thought Corinth a safer place to be from than Cenchrea, although there was a good possibility these men had never heard of either. I decided the rest of my travels could be discussed at some other time.

"Ah," he said, and nodded his head. The three men conferred.

I discovered later that men born in the Judea of Rome, or Israel, or Palestine—no matter which name I used, I offended someone—believed the Jews raised in foreign places lost all sight of their obligations under the Law. Therefore, these men viewed my selective ignorance as not only possible, but probable.

"Tell us of your family."

My mother and father are dead.

They looked at one another and murmured among themselves for a moment and then turned to me.

"You may stay here temporarily. If you wish to stay longer, after the third year, you must join the community. Everyone who lives here also works here, and so will you, if you stay. We have need of someone who can manage numbers like the men of Arabia. We will put you under the charge of our steward who has struggled with numbers for two years, since Jacob died. Jacob knew how to compute like the people of the east, but he could never teach Jeptha. Now, perhaps, you can help us."

I nodded.

"Then you will stay?"

Again I nodded. Where else could I go? Barabbas stole my clothes and my money. I would not last a day alone in the wilderness. Even if I could find a city in which to ply my trade, what would I use for capital? And then there was the family of Leonides. They would never think to look for me in this place. It had occurred to me as I convalesced that they may have been tracking me through my letters of credit. If they had, they would now be led to Barabbas. Perhaps they would be satisfied with taking that red-haired thief and leave this one in peace. Either way, I had no choice but to stay. In a year, with some careful manipulating of accounts, some creative ways of inventorying, I just might acquire the money I would need to start over.

Chapter Twenty-one

Masad Hasidim, home to the Essenes, is a collection of buildings set at the base of the foothills beside the Salt Sea. They are arranged in a cluster around a central great hall that doubles as a dining room and scriptorium. There is an elaborate series of cisterns and channels that keep the inhabitants supplied with water, which is a major concern as they are forever taking ritual baths.

I have never seen such compulsion. Romans are great ones for baths. They build them everywhere and use them often. But at Masad Hasidim, the Essenes climb in and out of their *mikvahs,* tubs before meals, after meals, instead of meals. They have taken to ritual bathing with the same fervor the followers of Bacchus have to wine.

More dwellings stand a short distance down the road. They house a separate part of the community. Wives and families of men who joined the community live there. Their rule requires celibacy, but it also prohibits abandoning families. The men visit their families from time to time, but do not stay.

Opposite the settlement, the hills rise steadily upward to the west, pockmarked with hundreds of caves and washes, providing hiding places for outlaws like Barabbas. They also hide the community's treasures. The caves store provisions, manuscripts, and documents no longer needed. The dry air in the valley of the Salt Sea means those scrolls and other writings, unless dug up by accident, will probably be preserved forever. Some of the caves are sealed, and some are not.

I assumed the sealed ones held secrets or wealth. In my first months, I determined to find out which. There might be an occasion in the future when I would need help in restoring my financial position. I never did. The community, I discovered, had a way of changing people. Except for the events of one fateful Passover, I might have been viewed as their greatest success.

When I recovered from my beating at the hands of Barabbas, I joined Jeptha, the rotund steward, and soon found myself occupied with the business affairs of the community. Jeptha, an honest and faithful man, had no sense of how things were done. Soon, he deferred to me as we arranged the community's accounts, stores, and transactions. He had no talent for numbers either, and so, inside a year, for all intent and purposes, I became the steward and he my assistant. I thought he might be annoyed by this turn of events, but he seemed relieved.

At the same time, to reduce the level of ignorance in things that mattered most to my hosts, I acquired a tutor, Reuel, who though only slightly older than I, had the benefit of a lifetime of study in the holy books and scrolls. Nahum had begun my instruction during my stay with him in Sepphoris. For that, and for saving my life, I owed him a huge debt of gratitude, but it was through Reuel I found the Lord. He had the look of one born to a life of asceticism, lean and angular, as if carved out of the tan stones from the hills.

He said we were born Jews. We could not escape that any more than we could escape the sun and the moon.

"We are born in pain and blood. We come into this world covered with the blood of our mothers and in her pains of childbirth. At birth we relive our history—the pain of captivity and deliverance, the blood of oppression and triumph. We are a people who endure. An obedient people, we are born to it. No matter how far we may stray from the Lord, we are still who we are and we must live it out. You were born in the blood of history, Judas. Neither you nor I can be anything but what we are."

If anyone told me I would someday worship the God of Abraham, I would have laughed and said they were drunk or worse. But after two years of Essene discipline and Reuel's tutelage, I did. I had lived so many years in the dark, and as long as I remained domiciled there, I could never know him. But on the sun-baked shores of the Salt Sea, I discovered the key to my survival.

My mother had not been schooled in the scrolls as she might, had she been a boy. Women, Reuel insisted, were not suitable vessels for the wine of the spirit. I did not know why, but it was their belief, and one shared with the populace in general. That being the case, all my mother knew of the Lord were scraps she gleaned from her occasional attendance at synagogue, seated on one of the side benches. A few things she may have learned from other women in their daily meetings at the well, the olive press, and monthly in the tents, during the times of impurity, but all before her twelfth year. After that, of course, she had no contact with her family or her people. She knew only small bits of the Law of Moses. She had been told what the Lord forbade his people, but never his desire for them. She knew what not to do, what not to eat, what not to say, and even what not to think. She dredged up what she knew or could remember from that limited fount to instruct me. None of it made any sense then, and after we parted, I had no interest in discovering what I might have missed, happy to put distance between myself and that angry, punishing god.

At Masad Hasidim, I discovered what holds our people together and what attracts Greeks and other nonbelievers to our way. I realized the rules and limits I chafed under as a child were part of a larger, practical, and functional whole. In a disordered and chaotic world, God offered order. To be a Jew is as much an exercise in discipline as spirituality. All that is required of us is to follow the Law. It needs none of the cerebration of Greek philosophy, none of the complex hierarchies of the Persians, and none of the beast and hero fables of the pagans, just submission to a way, to a truth, to a life.

Chapter Twenty-two

To my delight, I discovered the Essenes of Masad Hasidim knew my grandfather and his rebellion in Galilee, so I heard the story again, but not precisely as Nahum and my mother remembered it.

"A follower of Zadok, the last true priest of the temple," they said. "Everyone knows about Judas of the Galilee." And then they added, "But, he should have waited for the sign, for the righteous moment, when the forerunner appears and preaches the new Israel. That, you see, is our mission, that is what we are about—to preach the new mission."

"When will that happen?" I asked.

"In the Lord's time. And then," they said with a fierceness which matched that of Barabbas, "we will rise up and strike down those who oppose the Righteous Leader."

I accepted all of it, but in my heart, I yearned for the battle to begin immediately. I wanted to be there when the unrighteous met their doom, when the Romans, the men like Barabbas, and all those who prey on the poor and defenseless would be cast down into the pit. I did not want to wait. But Reuel said we had no choice in the matter.

"We will know neither the hour nor the day," he said. And I supposed it must be so, but it gave me small comfort.

Several young men came to Qumran to study under the watchful eye of the elders and the priests. Generally, they stayed a month or two, and then returned to their homes. Their tenure usually followed the seasons. These students provided a modest income to the community. In turn, the community provided tutors and a place to stay. One, named John, would dog my heels for the next several years. Born the son of a fisherman in Capernaum named Zebedee, he came and stayed. John's hands were soft like those of one who had never been asked to apply himself to the net or the plow. His clothes were not rich, but they were new and well made. John did not like me, then or now. I never knew why. He distrusted me from the outset. Perhaps he had a premonition, who can say? I avoided him, if I could; if not, I remained silent. Of course, that would change, but I could not conceive of even a possibility he or I would ever coexist peaceably.

About this time something happened that persuaded me I had become a different man and possibly worthy of some measure of esteem, after all. Jeptha, my putative overseer, set out for Jericho with coins to buy supplies. I calculated the amount he would need and watched as the treasurer counted out the coins from our meager store. He left with a substantial sum, more than I had laid eyes on in two years. I do not know if poor Jeptha had any sense of the relative fortune he carried or not. He stuffed them into his purse, laced that to his girdle and off he went.

Some hours later, I walked down to the Jericho road to stretch my legs and to be alone for a while. It had become a small indulgence I permitted myself after the rigors of Essene discipline during the day. I had to leap a gully where the lane leading from the settlement met the main road. As I did so, I saw where Jeptha had attempted the same maneuver but, because of his girth, must have slipped. I smiled at the image and would have walked on except a glint, a glitter, caught my eye. When I bent down to see what caused it, I discovered Jeptha's coins—all of them. His purse must have split in the fall.

I scooped up the coins. Mind you, I knew the sum and I knew it could be means to restore my previous status and independence. I could go to Beth Shan or Tiberius and start a new life. These thoughts coursed through my mind. My heart raced. Somewhere out there I could find my way again, search for my mother. I looked up and down an empty road. I could keep on walking and take this small fortune with me.

I turned back.

Once in the steward's closet, I put the coins, all of them, in a clay pot and waited. Moments later, Jeptha raced in, face stricken. I could smell his panic. Before he could speak, I handed him the pot and left him chanting prayers of thanksgiving.

I had changed.

◇◇◇

An outsider came into the community from time to time. He blew in like a great gust of desert wind. His name was also John, but no one ever confused him with the son of Zebedee. They said he'd come to the community as a boy after his parents died and left him orphaned. This John was unlike anyone I ever met. He'd spent years in Masad Hasidim but never joined the community, which, oddly, held him in great respect. They believed him a true prophet in the line of Samuel, Nathan, or Isaiah. When not at Masad Hasidim, he wandered alone in the wilderness, foraging for food in the honey hives and the locusts. He wore a tunic fashioned from coarse camel's hair, and the rest of his attire looked as if he had assembled it from the pickings off a trash pile. His disheveled appearance accentuated his habit of talking to himself, sometimes in the middle of the night, wild-eyed and agitated. Some declared him mad, while others believed a touch of madness marked a true prophet. I knew something about madness and madness was not in him.

He singled me out from the others. I do not know why. We would meet under the cyclamen tree that grew a few paces from the rear door of the dining room. We sat under that solitary tree and he spoke of times to come. His words evoked vivid images, as if he were revealing a vision from memory—images of beasts and a sacrificial lamb, but not one from temple, a lamb from the Lord.

"You mean like the one he gave Abraham to replace Isaac?" I said, and he looked startled and then nodded.

"Yes, yes...that is the very thing."

This John talked as if the Messiah could come within the year—a wonderful and awful thought. It held no interest to the rest of the community. They lived with the conviction the next chapter of the book would not be written in the High Places of Abraham, Isaac, and Jacob, nor acted out in the holy city of David, but in a new place, in a new temple with a new people, a people drawn from the old but made new. This group of steely-eyed men believed they were the remnant God would use to build his new people. I had my doubts. I was not one who willingly deferred that day. I wanted no, craved, John's imminent Messiah, our David in waiting.

As my final year wound to a close, I took stock of my life. I was as much a Jew as I would ever be. The time had come for me to commit or move on. Where I would go and what I would do, I did not know.

About that time, John left. His agitated state had increased in his last days with us, and finally he decided the Lord had called him out. He said he needed to go to the Jordan, somewhere near the spot it meets the road to Jerusalem, to prepare the way for the "Coming One."

"It is time," he'd said. "It will happen soon. Judas, you should come with me."

I ached for him to be right in that. I wanted to be with him to meet the Messiah, this new David. If it turned out not to be so, I could always find another way to settle old scores, only this time outfitted in the armor of God. Either way, I believed my days at Masad Hasidim were done.

And this shall be the Rule for the men of the Community who have freely pledged themselves, to be converted from all evil and cling to all of His Commandments…

The Fifth rule of the community, read to me until engraved in my memory—the next step if I remained.

I left to follow John.

Chapter Twenty-three

Masad Hasidim is a day's journey from the bend in the road where John set up camp. He'd selected a spot where the Jordan River sweeps away from the road a few hundred paces and then curves back, creating a large, shady semicircle, a place favored by travelers to stop and rest beneath sycamore trees, a place to spend the night in the safety of others. The river widens and shallows out so that you can practically wade across to the other side if you wish.

I heard him long before I saw him standing in the middle of the river, bellowing scraps of Isaiah and shaking his fist at a dozen travelers who stood wide-eyed, listening to this doomsday prophet of the Jordan.

"Do not remember former things or dwell on the past. For behold. I do a new thing. It springs forth, you see? I will make a straight way in the wilderness and rivers in the desert."

John's tone had become urgent. In Qumran he described the Messiah's arrival as something that might happen in the near future. At the Jordan, he spoke as if it could be at any moment. His gaze shifted from his audience to the road, looking north and south, as if he expected to see the Messiah marching toward him that very moment. He preached to anyone who would listen.

Preach is probably not the right word. He exhorted, he scolded, he pleaded, and he accused his listeners of every spiritual failure and breach of the Law imaginable, always at the top of his voice, strident, reckless, and intemperate. Once, someone shouted, "How can you say we will all be destroyed? Are we not the sons of Abraham? Are we not the chosen ones of the Covenant?"

"You believe your father's faith or that of your father's father will spare you from the final judgment? I tell you this, if God wanted, he could raise up a whole new generation from the stones you stand on."

People called him the Baptizer. He invited penitents, those who would put up with his sermonizing, to enter the river for baptism, the ritual bath common to these people and especially to the Essenes, who believe washing confirms a person's rejection of sin. Many came. They stripped, stepped into the Jordan, and performed the ritual. Others went directly to John, who lowered them into the water and held them under. They came up sputtering and thrashing and, usually, unhappy. But he said, "Baptism...to drown a little, to die to the old life and be reborn in the new." Some days there would be singing and the washing went on for hours. Other days, the crowds seemed indifferent, even hostile.

John preached on.

◇◇◇

Days became weeks and John continued to castigate the crowds to return to the Way. Only by being honest with their neighbors and with themselves, he declared, could they be saved. He even lectured the few soldiers sent by the prefect to see to it the "Hebrew holy man" caused no trouble. Some laughed, but one or two looked uncomfortable.

"And what shall we do?" one asked.

"Do not extort money, do not accuse falsely, and be content with your pay," John replied.

What a wonderful turn of events, I thought, if John were to convert Roman legionnaires to the God of Abraham. Perhaps they were the stones that the Lord could raise up as the newly covenanted people. But on reflection, I realized it would be easier to change real stones than change the flinty hearts of these implacably brutal men. But should it ever happen, I wanted to be the *mohel* handling the bris knife that day.

I assumed my nemesis still sought me. More than once, I felt the need to retire to the hills. Men who might have been Leonides' agents sometimes wandered into the area asking questions. I never knew.

I do not recall how long we had been at the river before I noticed a shift in John's rhetoric. The change was dramatic. He quoted almost continuously from the scroll of Isaiah with a note of desperation in his voice.

Pharisees listened to the man they all acknowledged, however reluctantly, to be a true prophet. Judging by the fear reflected in their faces, and their comments, they faced a dilemma. What if John spoke the truth about the Messiah's coming? Was this just another in a long string of dashed hopes, of Messianic claimants turned failed generals, or did he speak the truth? And if so, who was this new claimant?

"Are you the one?" they asked. I could not tell if they were hopeful or fearful of the answer he would give.

"No," he said, "not I. The one you seek is far greater than I can ever be. I am not even worthy to lace up his sandals."

"Who then?" they asked. John only shook his head.

Later, I asked if he knew the "Coming One." He stared off into the wilderness and waved his hand back and forth. I could not tell if that meant he did not know or he knew, but would not say.

"Judas, look after your soul. Inspect the things in your heart that do not please God. Purge them, get rid of them. Then you will be ready for the Messiah."

Purge my heart and soul? Of what, I wanted to know. I had become a believing and practicing Jew. I kept the Law. I prayed and purified myself often, as I had been taught. I studied the scrolls. What to purge? He looked at me, reading my thoughts.

"You will be with the Messiah and it will be important for you to be cleansed of your anger and your hatred."

"Is that possible? Every person in this land has been badly used by these Roman adventurers. How am I, how are they, how are any of us, to purge that?"

"If we want justice and peace, if we want God's blessing to fall on us, we must. Believe me when I tell you this: it is not Rome who destroys us. We destroy ourselves. We can only defeat them by changing our way of thinking, by returning to the way of the Lord. You and I, all the people of this land, must get straight with the Lord. He will deliver us where we cannot."

"But are we not seeking a new David who will raise a mighty army and drive the Romans from our land, or a Moses who will lead us out of this bondage and into another time of peace and harmony? Is that not what we have been promised?"

Without realizing it, I had raised my voice and the men nearby stared at me.

"You are the prophet. You said you are the one of which Isaiah spoke, to call the people to prepare the way. You must know."

I pleaded with him. I had to know. I sacrificed so much, been denied so much. There had to be an end. I could not let it go. The anger and need for revenge had kept me alive for nearly two decades. Repent of it? Purge it? Never.

"But you must," he said softly.

Chapter Twenty-four

At that time, I was closest to Andrew, a young fisherman from Capernaum. Sometimes his brother, Simon, joined us but he rarely stayed for more than a few days. As the eldest, running the family business fell to him, and he had a wife and responsibilities in Capernaum as well. The two of them were a study in contrasts. Where Andrew was short, lean, and cheerful, his brother was tall, broad, and brooding. I believed if he wanted to, he could lift one of his boats by himself. Andrew smiled; Simon scowled.

Also among our number were Nathaniel, the son of Tolomai; Philip; and the other John, the son of Zebedee. I thought I had seen his back when I left Masad Hasidim, but there he was, and as it turned out, we would be together for another three years. He behaved cordially enough, but I sensed his lingering doubts. Thomas drifted in later.

"Judas," they said to me, "what will you do when the Messiah comes?"

"Drive the Romans into the sea," I said and we all laughed.

All of us thought that then. We would change our thinking later, but then, the idea that the Messiah would be anything but a man at the head of a conquering army seemed inconceivable. Rome appeared invincible, yet we were persuaded that somehow this Messiah would be the instrument of its destruction. And so, we waited.

A month passed and another, still no sign. People started coming to the river specifically to see and hear John. His reputation had reached the cities and towns, and people flocked to the river.

"You brood of vipers," he roared and pointed at this person or that. "Who warned you to run from the wrath to come? Do you think you can escape it? Bear fruit that is in keeping with a repentant heart."

Once, a tax collector came to the river. He stood apart from the rest. No one would have anything to do with him. "And I," he shouted, "What must I do?"

The crowd grumbled and jeered at him. "Give us our money back," and "Go hang yourself, tax farmer."

"Collect only what you must and be merciful," said John.

Then turning to the crowd, he added, "And you, how is it you are so quick to condemn. Some of your brothers are being crushed by the taxes the temple and the empire impose on them. How many of you have offered them money so that they would not lose their land? Each time you look only to yourself instead of your brother, you are doubly disobedient and put more distance between yourself and the Lord."

About that time many who were with us from the beginning disappeared. I supposed they feared what might happen to them if John did not rein in his rhetoric. By the fourth month, the tension became unbearable. I do not know if John's tone put us on edge, or if something larger and less obvious caused it. The sort of people who came to the river changed. The cadre of curiosity seekers remained, but their numbers dwindled. Now we saw people committed to John's message. The Messiah would come they said, sometimes hopefully, sometimes with conviction, and they wanted to be ready.

The air, heavy and expectant, did not stir. Something was going to happen and soon.

◇◇◇

The day started out hot and sultry, nothing stirred. Birds did not sing, even the insects moved as if trapped in tree sap. The weather in the valley is usually hot and dry, so much so that it is unwise to stray too far from water. But that day the air steamed like a Roman bath. People shed cloaks and knotted or pulled the hems of their tunics up and tucked them into their belts. Some fashioned fans from palm fronds. The hills offered no breeze, no relief. The Baptizer sat in the shade beside the riverbank, his energy spent.

It reminded me of summer days by the Great Sea. Everything would be still and oppressive. Then, about the tenth hour, when the sun began its descent, clouds would pile into dark gray mountains in the south and, in what seemed like the time it takes to catch your breath, lightning cracked the sky and a storm raced in from the sea. The wind brought cooler, salty air to the shore in great gusts. Boats whose owners missed the warnings were tossed about like children's toys. Then, as quickly as it began, the storm blew by, leaving cool air and relief.

That's how it felt at the river that day. About the sixth hour, groups of pilgrims, like clouds, massed around the Baptizer. Things seemed fuzzy and confusing, out of focus, like looking through a bit of the glass Romans fancy.

Then, as if by magic, a tall man appeared in the crowd's midst. I had been watching the road. Somehow he slipped my notice. He stood at least a head taller than everyone, even the Baptizer, who was tall enough himself and as easy to spot as a tree in a field.

John went to him, said something, and the man replied. John shook his head and looked puzzled. Finally, he shrugged and they went to the deep spot in the river and John baptized him. He stayed under a long time. Unlike nearly everyone before him, when he emerged, he did not splash and sputter. He rose up out of the water like a fast growing tree. I cannot describe the look on his face. At once an expression of complete peace and at the same time, for a brief moment, his eyes flashed like lightning.

And then it happened. I heard it in my ear or perhaps only in my mind. I glanced at the others. Some seemed to hear it, too, some not. It sounded like rushing wind or the roar of the sea…

no, thunder. But all in my head. I heard: "This is the anointed one, the son I love, and he is the one that pleases me." At that same moment, a bird, a dove, I think, landed on his shoulder and then vanished.

A gentle breeze blew away the last of the heat and made the air fresher and cooler. I looked at John hoping to make some sense of what had happened. He stood unmoving in the water, expressionless.

◇◇◇

We ate our stew in silence. I could tell Andrew was about to burst, but we waited, each of us eager. John would tell us what we needed to know in his own time.

"Teacher—" Andrew began. He could not wait.

John held up his hand, palm out. He shook his head like an ox plagued by summer flies and said, "Perhaps we will talk tomorrow, but tonight I must listen to the Lord."

He left the circle of firelight and disappeared into the night. We would hear nothing more from him. Andrew looked at each of us in turn, eyes bright with excitement.

"What do you think? The man at the river this afternoon, was he the Messiah?"

"We don't know who he is, much less who he might be," Thomas said. "There must be more to it than that."

I wanted to tell them what I had heard. Perhaps I imagined it. I decided to wait. The next day would be soon enough. The fire collapsed into coals. Sleep. We needed sleep. It came immediately, like an order from God.

Chapter Twenty-five

The next morning our numbers were reduced. A small crowd gathered by the river but the Baptizer sat apart, silent. He gazed into the distance, waiting for some one or some thing.

When we were alone, I said, "Teacher, I thought I heard a voice yesterday."

He looked at me, startled. "You heard? What did you hear?"

"A voice that said, 'This is my son, the one I love, in him I am pleased'…something like that. And there was a dove."

"Well, that is all there is to know."

"But what does it mean?"

He half turned. "It means that you must go with him, that's all."

"Him? Who?"

"My kinsman, Jesus of Nazareth."

At that moment, the man, Jesus, walked toward us.

"Is it you, then?" John said. And turned to us, "Behold the Lamb of God. He is the one I meant when I said 'who comes after me is greater.' When he rose from the water, I thought I heard a voice and saw a dove come to him as well. You saw and you heard, Judas, you of all of them. You are to go with him and serve him now."

Andrew and I hurried after the man.

"Teacher," Andrew called, "where are you staying?"

"You shall see."

We walked north, away from the river, away from the Baptizer—Andrew, John, the son of Zebedee, Jesus of Nazareth, and me.

◇◇◇

I rose and rubbed the sleep from my eyes. Jesus stood away from the fire, praying. He held his hands out from his sides, palms up, and head bowed. He rocked gently back and forth, praying with his whole body in the singsong manner of the devout. I stood a few paces away and began my morning prayers, too, but I admit I watched him out of the corner of my eye. If the Lord were listening, I doubt anything I said that morning, made much sense.

In midsentence, he lifted his arms, his cloak fell from his head and face to the sky, seemed to be in direct dialog with the Lord himself. I would witness that movement many times over the next three years.

Finished, he turned to me. "Are you hungry, Judas?"

I smelled broiled fish. He handed me a piece of flat bread and a bit of fish and we ate. Andrew and John had wandered off to find some of the others, and we were alone. I finished and tried not to stare at him.

"It is not important." he said, "how you came to the Father, only that you did. There is no reason why anyone should know the nature of your circumcision. I tell you this now so that you can choose your path. You, of all who come to me, will be asked to sacrifice the most and receive the least in return. You were chosen because you understand these things."

I survived past my thirteenth year because I made a point of knowing things. But there, standing in the morning mist somewhere away from the Jordan, I knew nothing. At that instant, Andrew danced into our makeshift camp.

"I found the others. They are upstream a little way. I told them about you."

Jesus kicked some dirt on the fire, his eyes still on me. "Will you follow me?"

I gathered my things and began walking. I needed time to think. He must be the Messiah. John said so. I had no reason to doubt. Less clear to me were the implications of what that meant. Jesus did not quite measure up to what I imagined a new David would be.

In those days, the Messianic expectation burned in the hearts of all Israel. Those very expectations drove us to that moment and that place. But we could not agree as to exactly what the Messiah would do or who he might be. You know the expression: "Three Jews, four opinions." Some, like me, looked for a king, a new David, to lead an army and restore the Kingdom. More thoughtful and, I thought, timid people expected Elijah, the forerunner. Others waited for a second Moses to lead us out of this new bondage. As we walked among Galilee's lush hills, I tried to plumb Jesus' mind. I listened to him speak, I prayed for discernment, and still I could not be sure. David, Elijah, or Moses?

On one particular Sabbath, we entered a synagogue near Nazareth and took our places on the backbench. I anticipated a lively dispute because, by then, I had heard enough of his teaching to guess some sparks would fly. The president of the assembly recognized Jesus as local and, as a courtesy, asked him to read. Jesus took the scroll and opened it. I have no idea whether the scroll just happened to open to the passage it did, if he turned to the next lesson in the synagogue's lectionary, or if he picked it on purpose. However it happened, he read from Isaiah where it is written:

> *The spirit of the Lord is upon me because he has anointed me to preach the good news to the poor. It is I he has sent to declare freedom for prisoners, and sight to the blind, the release of the oppressed, and to proclaim the year of the Lord's favor.*

Then he carefully rolled the scroll and said, calm as you please, "Today this scripture is fulfilled in your presence."

His poise and the force of his words resonated with us and a few others, I think. But most of the listeners sat glued to their benches, murmuring among themselves—"Isn't this Joseph, the builder's son?…Who does he think he is?"

In the midst of all the muttering, he added, "You are probably wondering why I, of all people, am bold enough to say this. You have in mind I should do here in Nazareth what I have done elsewhere. All I can offer is the proverb about the physician healing himself. Well, the truth is, a prophet is never honored in his own home. If I were to do anything here, it would prove nothing. I will always just be your neighbor's son."

He went on to remind them the only person who offered to shelter and feed Elijah was a poor gentile widow. He would have expanded on that point but the congregation grew angry and shoved us all out onto the street. I guessed we would not be going back to that synagogue anytime soon.

Andrew, Philip, John, Nathaniel, and I left the Jordan together. Thomas rejoined us as we were entering the Galilee. I do not know where he had been. He had a habit of disappearing from time to time and returning some days later looking a little worse for wear. I wondered, sometimes, why he joined us in the first place. He was not particularly pious or versed in the scriptures. He would poke fun at John, whom he called "our Pharisee," a name John did not like, but which fit.

As we walked along the shores of the sea, Jesus beckoned to James, John's brother, and Simon, Andrew's brother. Jesus told them there were enough men catching fish; what he needed was fishers to catch men. They laughed. James, the son of Alphaeus and another of that company, also named Judas, came with us as well. That made ten of us, enough for a *minyan*.

I had no idea what I let myself in for when Jesus gave me the responsibility for the community purse. I had to be sure there was always enough to keep us fed and sheltered. I paid taxes nearly everywhere we went. When I first arrived in Galilee, I saw the crushing burden taxes imposed by the empire, by regional rulers, and the temple. But I passed them off as the usual oppression found throughout the empire. Paying these taxes and meeting the cost of feeding and housing ten to twenty men and women every day grew into a daunting task. And to make matters worse, Jesus insisted on giving our money away to every beggar and sorry case that wandered into camp. He assumed that no matter what strains were placed on the purse, whatever demands were made, I would find a way to make it come out right.

The others marveled at the way I could find food, shelter, and money. I even surprised myself. "Surely, you have become a thief, Judas." Simon said. He joked, of course, and I did not mind it, at least not at first, but I wished he understood how hard I worked to do those things. John took to calling me "the Thief" or just "Thief," but he intended no humor in his words.

Chapter Twenty-six

Before he joined us, Thomas used to scrape his face like the Gentiles. But in our company he let his beard grow out. While John remained standoffish and suspicious, Thomas grew open and friendly. We spoke often about the Messiah, about Jesus, and what he would do when he decided to declare himself. I told Thomas we should collect as much money as possible. The weapons and men we needed would cost a great deal, he said. He did not believe it could be done. I assured him it could. I had done it before and I could do it again. He wanted to know how and when. I almost told him, but felt unsure of my place in the company and decided not to risk it just then. As things turned out, it was just as well.

One evening when the others, the fishermen, busied themselves with their nets and boats, Thomas and I wandered off into the hills. I asked him what brought him to us.

"I do not mean to pry," I said, "but you are not like the others. You seem to stand back and watch us like we are a caravan passing by."

"And you—are you so much like these fisher folk?"

He had me there. I shrugged and smiled.

"This not the life I would have chosen. I came to this place against my will," he said. I waited and finally he grinned.

"It is a long story. Are you sure you wish to hear it?"

"Yes, if you wish to tell it."

"It starts with a well that was not really a well." He paused a moment, I suppose to gather his thoughts. "We dug almost twenty cubits straight down and hadn't even found damp earth, much less water. My father had this dream about water, and decided it meant we were to have our own well. 'It would be a fine thing,' he said, 'to have a well. It would bring honor to the family.' My father was very sensitive to the need for honor. He didn't get much respect in our village and wanted to reclaim some of what he had before, when we lived in Nazareth. The well seemed like a good idea. We argued about whether we should keep digging or not.

"I came home early one afternoon and Rebecca, my sister, stood by it, frightened and unable to move. A Roman soldier, his back to me, had dropped his belt, laid his helmet to one side, and plunged his short sword into the earth. It stood erect at his feet. I could not see his face except as reflected in the terror on Rebecca's. I picked up a rock. It's what we did then, all of us. We weren't allowed arms, not so close to the Roman garrison and so we, the young men that is, used to throw stones at soldiers, our act of rebellion against an occupying army, against our oppressors. What else could we do? We would toss stones and since the soldiers had no stomach for a two mile run in the hills, they never caught us. We fought Rome where our fathers could not.

"This stone was palm-sized, heavy, and of dark basalt. I threw it at the soldier as hard as I could and then braced for the dash I would make into the hills. Just as the stone left my hand, something, my grunting at the launch probably, made him turn. The stone caught him on the temple, just behind his right eye. He groaned and dropped to his knees like a stunned ox. His eyes snapped back and he pitched forward on his face. Dust billowed up around him, you know, like it will when a tree falls. Nobody moved. Finally, I said, 'Rebecca, run before he wakes up.' She ran down the hill to find my father. The soldier still lay on his face. I walked up to him and nudged him with my toe. Nothing happened so I kicked him. Still nothing. Dead! How could that be?

"I remember growing up and wondering how David killed Goliath. I loved the story but had my doubts. How could one smooth stone drop such a giant? Had they told me the truth, or did they improve the story to make a point—tiny Israel and mighty Philista, the hand of God on our side? Well, when I saw that soldier crumple in our yard, I knew it had to be true. I had only wanted to give Rebecca a chance to run. Instead I slew Goliath. The rush of pride I felt only lasted a moment. Then I realized what I had done and the consequences that would follow. I had killed one of Caesar's legionnaires. I, my family, and maybe the whole village were doomed.

"What happened next wasn't part of any conscious decision. I guessed nothing I would do could make things worse. I dragged the corpse over to the wellhead and dumped it in. He landed in a heap in the bottom, curled up like a baby. I picked up the helmet and sword and tossed them in, too. I didn't dare reward myself with my giant's sword and armor like David. Then, with the energy that comes from mortal fear, I began to fill in the well.

"My father joined me. Soon the soldier disappeared under rocks and dirt. Rebecca hissed at us. The rest of the Patrol had started up the hill. My father busied himself in the garden. I grabbed some clay pots and carried them to the back door. Rebecca disappeared into the house and hid under a pile of blankets. They came up the hill and stopped just beyond the court wall.

"Their leader wanted to know what happened to their comrade. The patrol had come to our village looking for weapons, it seemed.

"So he says, 'He was seen at your house,' looking at me hard, and then turned to my father, 'Old man, have you seen him?'

"My father looked at me and then at the soldier. I couldn't read his expression but I knew he was pondering which lie would work.

"He said, 'Yes, he came by here awhile ago. He told us we were to say he was not well and returned to your camp. He said

I should tell you that.' My father made a living negotiating the sale of caravan goods and other services. To do that he had a manner of speaking that was ingenuous and utterly sincere. It served him well in the past and I prayed with all my heart it would work this time as well.

"The soldier thought a moment...'He was unwell and wished to return to camp?' My father nodded. Then the soldier looked him in the face, 'He *said* you were to say that, but that is not what he really meant, am I right?' My father shuffled his feet. 'Where did he go?' The soldier demanded, as if to say we couldn't fool him.

"'That way,' my father said, and pointed over the hills toward the house of Isis, the prostitute. 'There are bandits and thieves in the hills over there.'

"'Dagon is a fool,' the soldier said. 'I'll deal with him when he comes back to camp. He peered down our well, now not as deep as before, 'What's this?' he demanded.

"We are digging a well," I said. 'A well?' he said. 'Were you given permission to dig a well?'

"My father said, 'we didn't know we needed it.'

"'You know it now.' He turned to the rest of the patrol. 'Fill in this hole.' And we watched, biting our tongues, while the soldiers finished burying their comrade.

"After the patrol marched away, Father turned to me. 'Thomas, you cannot stay here. That soldier may be a fool, but his commander is not, and there will be questions. Your brother Aaron and I must go to Damascus tomorrow. I have business there. Your mother and sister will return to Nazareth to her sister's. You must go south, somewhere where they will not look for you and where no one in the village will guess you might be.'"

"We argued about that. I said, 'Let me go to one of the cities of the Decapolis, Caesarea Phillipi or Gerasa.' And he said, 'No, not there.' So I suggested Tiberius. 'They won't look for me there.'

'That is precisely where they will look. But that is where we will tell people you are going...yes, that is what we will do. No, you are to go south to the Jordan. There is a holy man there, a prophet, after the way of Elijah. You will go to him.'

"Can you imagine that, Judas? A holy man and me?

"Judas, you are not from around here. Galileans believe things of the spirit are important, but to be attended to by others. The people of Judea, for example, place great stock in that, but not us. And that is why my father chose the Jordan and, as it turned out, the Baptizer. It would be the last place anyone would look for me. I protested. The thought of cooling my heels in the Jordan with a desert fanatic struck me as worse punishment than being hung for murder. But my father couldn't be dissuaded. His word was law in our house, however much I chafed under it.

"They packed my traveling bag for me and provided me with money, and here I am. Whether this is to be my calling or not, I cannot say. I await word from my father."

I decided then that I would like this skeptic.

Chapter Twenty-seven

We were beside the Sea of Galilee, and a large group, perhaps a hundred or more, gathered. Jesus said, "Peter, bring one of your boats around that I may put some distance between myself and the crowd."

Peter and Andrew launched one of their boats. Jesus stepped into it and allowed it to drift out a dozen cubits from the shore. The hills behind sloped gently upward, away from the shore, creating a natural amphitheater. The air was very still, and his voice carried over the water, so anyone on the shore could easily hear him.

He began a speech he'd made before and would again. Each time he added or left out bits, but it remained substantially the same.

"Blessed are you who are poor, for you shall be the inheritors of the kingdom. Blessed are those who are hungry and thirsty, for you shall be satisfied. Blessed are those who cry out and weep from suffering, for soon you shall laugh. Blessed are you when others hate you, or reject you or scorn you or call you evil because of me.

"But woe to the rich and pompous, for they have already received all they will ever get. And woe to the well fed and fat among you, for soon they will know hunger. And woe to the men who laugh at my words and at those not as fortunate, for they will soon receive their share of weeping and mourning. And woe to you also, who think you are wise and whom others speak so highly of, for that was how they spoke of those who destroyed the prophets."

I loved hearing words that convicted the people who acted so terribly to me and Dinah and Mother. Oh, yes, it would be a fine day when the self-righteous were brought down to our level.

Then he said, "Love your enemies. Bless those who curse you. Pray for them. If someone strikes you on the side of your face, let him hit you on the other side. If someone takes your cloak, let him have your tunic as well."

I thought, nobody but a fool would behave that way, and I glanced at the faces around me and realized I was not alone in that.

"If someone takes something that belongs to you, do not demand they give it back. Treat them in the same manner you would have them treat you. Do not judge or condemn others and you will not be judged. If you expect to be forgiven, you must first forgive. Give and it will be returned to you, a full measure and more."

While all of this sank in, one of the men in the crowd shouted at him, "Rabbi Jesus, Moses gave us the Law and he received it from the Lord. Are you saying you can make Law, as well? Just who do you think you are, God?"

That question would haunt me for the next three years.

Jesus made a habit of calling one or the other of us to him at night, before he prayed. I do not know what he said to the others, but that night as we sat under the stars, he looked at me for a long time like a physician studies his patient.

"Judas," he said, "what is it you seek?"

"Rabbi?" I said, unsure what he wanted of me. "I seek many things. I wish to see the oppressors removed from our land. Then, you have trusted me with the purse. I wish to serve you faithfully, as you are the one to lead us…I wish to know more of the Father of whom you speak—"

"That is too much, Judas, and not enough. I ask you to tell me the single thing that brings you to me?"

I could not answer. I thought I had spoken truly. I did want to do those things and more. It could not be of any import to him that I ached to see my mother, half of me believing her dead and the other afraid she might still be alive. Old women practicing her profession do not fare so well.

"I do not know how to answer," I said.

"Judas, a worker went into a field one day and discovered treasure buried in the middle of it. He immediately went out and sought money to buy the field. He had to borrow from relatives and friends and to each he told a different story about the field. To one he said it would yield in abundance, and to another he said sheep could safely graze there, and so on. By the end of the day he had enough to buy the field. You see how it is?"

I did not. Parables were a part of our daily fare, and I should have been able to untangle this one, but I could not. I suppose knowing it pointed to me made it difficult. We do not usually want to be fed the truth about ourselves, and I was certain I would soon have it in a large portion.

"You have told me many things about who you are and how you came to this place. It is to do the Lord's work, to avenge your family, to serve...you beg for a loan so you can buy the field. I will gladly *give* you the purchase price, but you must be honest with me and tell me about the treasure."

As I said, I would hear the truth. But in fairness, I had not thought about why I came along. I thought I followed John and he sent me to Jesus. But I had not sought John. Anger and hatred brought me to him. I wracked my brains for an answer, and I resented this man for making me feel guilty for having to do so.

"We are not so unalike, Judas," he said. I frowned at this comparison. There was precious little between us that could be thought of as sameness. "No, it is true. People questioned my birth. My mother always sounded vague on the matter and so there was doubt. Those men in Nazareth, the ones who evicted us from their synagogue, they doubted that part of me, you see? So, what is the treasure you are willing to risk so much for?"

I sorted through all my reasons. What did I value so much that I would risk the family of Leonides, Barabbas' band of cutthroats, Rome, and now walk the path this man would have me follow, a path that common sense said could only lead to trouble?

"I think," I said finally, uncertainly, "that I wish to find my family." I didn't know what I meant by that. It just came to me. The chances of finding my mother were slim, if they existed at all. Perhaps, I thought, she would hear of this outlaw rabbi, what he did and said to women trapped in her condition, and seek us out. I didn't know. And then there was Dinah in Corinth.

As I thought on these things, Jesus stood and indicated I should walk with him.

"You see," he said, "we are alike in this respect. We yearn to be accepted, to have a family that is settled, comfortable, and normal. But that cannot be, Judas. We are who we are. Or futures are woven on the Father's loom and into the fabric of our life. We are born to play out our parts. You and I, we come from different places and see the world through different eyes, yet it is the things we share that bring us together and hold us. You have survived in spite of what the world sent your way, and you shall in the future. I will not."

I started to protest but he waved me off. He stared off into the night sky for a while and then turned to me.

"You will see," he said.

I did, but not in time.

Chapter Twenty-eight

When we traveled in or around Nazareth, Jesus' mother would sometimes join us, but as she was no longer young, she only traveled short distances. I often dropped back and walked with her. Even at forty-five, she carried herself like a woman half her age. She asked about my family. I repeated my orphan story. I saw no purpose in burdening her with the truth. The Romans have a saying for it, *veritas odium parit,* truth begets hatred. Some things are best left unsaid.

She told me amazing stories about his birth and childhood. Once, she said, he played with some children in a stream. It was the Sabbath. Jesus had formed clay into the likeness of small birds. His skill was remarkable and the images he created could be taken for the quail that frequented the area.

While they were about this, a boy from the outlying area slipped in among them. He was a child of uncertain parentage and who was often taunted by the others. When they saw him, they ridiculed him and, turning to Jesus, demanded he be sent away. "Our fathers told us this person is outside the Law," they said.

Jesus replied, "The Law says we must love our neighbors as ourselves," and added they should also love this boy.

Well, one of the boys, jealous of Jesus' popularity, reported what Jesus had said to his father, a Pharisee. This man called on the elders. As they drew near, Jesus held out his hand and perhaps four score quail descended to the place where the little clay birds were.

When the Pharisees and the elders arrived, the father said to Jesus, "Where are these images you have made in defiance of the Sabbath?"

Jesus swept his arm in an arc and pointed at the quail milling about on the bank.

"I see no images," the Pharisee said.

His son, in distress, ran to the flock, "They are here among these birds." With that, the flock took flight. When they had flown away, no clay birds were left. Had they been transformed into living birds? Or had the quail trampled them into formlessness? Who knows?

And then there were her stories of messengers, worshiping shepherds, and visitors from the east with wonderful gifts. A wonderful birth, she said, for the man born to save the nation. I tried to remember the words Amelabib had recited to me years before in the street in Corinth.

Now is a child born by heaven...Smile...at the birth of this boy who will put an end to our wretched age...from whom golden people will spring...

Had I remembered it correctly? I could not be sure. But what Augustus thought of himself seemed strangely prophetic for what must have seemed to be an insignificant boy born in a forgotten corner of his empire toward the end of his reign.

I did not know whether to believe her or not.

Once, while he spoke, a man pushed forward to say Jesus' mother and brothers wished to see him, and would he stop and go to them.

Jesus said, "My mother and my brothers are all of you who hear and respond to the word of God," and continued his teaching. The answer puzzled and annoyed me. I never knew even the semblance of a family. My mother, father, and such relatives I could claim had deserted me. I ached for family, and he rejected everything I most coveted.

Later, when the crowd left, he started to walk away with his family, but then hesitated, turned, and came back to me. I still chewed on my resentment.

"Don't you see, Judas," he said, "my words give you that which you most desire—you are my brother, my family. That is how the Kingdom of God is to be built. And it begins here, with you."

◇◇◇

We arrived at the gates of Magdala toward evening. A crowd milled around, shouting and shoving. Some held stones. Jesus' eyes narrowed, and he quickened his pace. A wild-eyed woman thrashed about in the center of the throng, cursing and whooping. Two strong men pinioned her arms but could not hold her fast. She kicked and twisted this way and that, revealing the flesh of her legs. Her headdress had fallen off—or perhaps she never had one, and her hair tumbled like tarnished brass around her shoulders. The words coming from her lips would make the roughest seaman blush. Her clothes were, or had been, of some quality at one time, but hung in dirty tatters. Her face was streaked with grime that came only partly from her struggling. That face had not seen water for a long time.

"Don't go near her," John muttered. "Look at her. She is filthy. Her hair is unbound, and she displays her body like a prostitute. Do not touch her. She is unclean, Master."

Jesus' practice of touching the ritually unclean alarmed John more than any of us. I do not know if John feared the consequences or, because he had been trained by some of the brightest pharisaic minds in the country, worried how his former colleagues might interpret it. In any event, he refused to speak about it, then or ever, as if by not doing so, he could deny it happened.

Jesus smiled, raised his arm, and said, "Release her."

"But Rabbi, she is dangerous," one man said. "She was betrothed to one of the elders in the city, and for the last three months, she has been ranting and raving. I will not tell you all she has said and done, but it is enough to justify stoning."

"Let her go," Jesus repeated.

The woman fell to her hands and knees. She growled. She spun in small circles and bared her teeth, spittle at the corners of her mouth. Jesus raised his hand and she cringed as if he were about to strike her. She snarled and wailed.

"Be still," he said, and then, "come out of her." I had seen this before, of course, but this time, there seemed to be more than one demon tormenting her. She howled and writhed on the ground. Her eyes rolled back. Suddenly, she stopped kicking, her legs shot straight out, and she lay stiff as a board.

We waited, wondering if she were dead. Then she gave out a sound as sorrowful as a winter wind, a low moan…then another and another, seven times…and went limp. No one stirred. Finally, she sat up and looked around in wonderment, first at the people, then at Jesus, and then at the mess she had made of her clothes. She rearranged her rags as best she could and gathered her hair in an attempt to assemble something of a headdress. But now her eyes were clear, her gaze steady. The onlookers were amazed.

"Get up, woman." Jesus said. "You are needed."

Her name was Miriam, Mary, the same as the mother of Jesus, the same as my mother.

Most of the time, I spent with Jesus and the others who formed the center of his followers. Our custom was no different than any of the itinerant rabbis whom we encountered from time to time. Jesus would walk several paces in front. We followed. If he wished to say something, he would call one or the other of us to him or he would turn and address us all. Close behind us were other followers and, of course, the women. In time, they would become a scandal in the eyes of those who opposed us. His mother and the Magdalan offered to leave us, but Jesus insisted they stay. "If the meek are to inherit the earth," he said with a smile, "surely the women will qualify as major inheritors."

Since I left my mother in the ashes at the House of Darcas, I had not known or allowed myself to be close to any woman. Well, except as a young man I did visit the women who plied my mother's trade from time to time. Since I came to this land, I kept myself apart. I felt safer that way. It is a dangerous thing to be too close to anyone when you pursue a vision like the one I harbored. At least that is what I told myself.

The women who walked with us were very different than the women I knew in my youth. Those women had a hard side to them. They trusted no one, would confide in no one—at least not in men. I am sure they talked among themselves. But men were outside the circle. The Magdalan, on the other hand, spoke in the soft tones of the privileged. I gathered she had known that life. She told me she intended to marry and then things "went bad." That is how she put it. I am sure the appeal she held for me arose from the contrasts between us. I came from the gutter, she from a society that barely knew or acknowledged someone like me.

◇◇◇

One day, as we approached our base in Capernaum, we were met by its elders. "Rabbi Jesus," one of them said, "We have been sent by the centurion, Cornelius. His servant is very sick. He bids you to come and heal him, if you would."

"No, it is a trick," I warned. "Don't be fooled. They wish to take you, Teacher."

"No, no," the elders replied, hands in the air, "this man is not like the others. He deserves your help."

"We will go to him," Jesus said. I was furious. I did not come to this land to see Romans receive the mercy they refused others. We traveled no more than a mile when the friends of the centurion approached us again.

"Rabbi, our master greets you and says you are not to trouble yourself. He said you need only to say the word and his servant will be healed. He is used to giving orders. If he tells someone to 'go,' they go and if he says to 'come,' they come. He believes you can do the same. You need only to say so and his servant will be healed."

Jesus stared at them for a long time and then turned to us.

"I have not seen this kind of faith anywhere in this land. Listen and learn."

I thought about the centurion's servant, Mary from Magdala, and myself, and worried about this strange man who led us to only the Lord knew where.

Chapter Twenty-nine

A Pharisee named Simon invited us to his home. To this day, I do not know why Jesus accommodated those smug Pharisees. They were only interested in what he had to say so they could build a case against him. But Jesus brushed off our warnings.

"Master," Peter said through clenched teeth, "they wish to shame you."

"We shall see," Jesus said and reclined on his couch.

When we entered, our host already occupied the place of honor. Sycophants from the town scrambled to fill the remaining couches near him and created a serious breach of courtesy. Jesus had been invited to the meal as the guest of honor. The Pharisee made it clear he wished to hear what Jesus had to say, yet he appropriated the place of honor for himself. His friends, who came to see the rabbi from Nazareth put in his place, flanked Simon right and left. Smug and arrogant, faces alight with anticipation, they dipped crusts of bread in the dishes of olive oil and spices, oblivious to the amenities of hospitality that require the guest of honor eat first. Other people were let into the room, not to eat, but following custom, to be in the presence of their betters and, in this case, to hear what this strange rabbi had to say.

As we settled on our couches and the town folk lined up along the walls, a woman entered. There could be little doubt about her profession. Her hair cascaded over her shoulders and down to her waist. Her eyes were lined with kohl, her cheeks red with the powder I remember seeing in my mother's kit. She worked her way around the couches and settled at Jesus' feet. Peter and James gestured for her to go away but Jesus stopped them. All conversation ceased. She reached into her robe and removed a small vial. She wrestled with its stopper but in her haste to open it, the neck broke away and perfumed ointment spilled out. The vial alone would have brought forty denarii. The perfume in it was probably worth twice that. The aroma permeated the room.

Without hesitation, she started to anoint Jesus' feet. Her tears also fell on his feet and she tried to wipe them away with her hair. Everyone started talking at once. The Pharisees clucked like chickens. The other spectators were either shocked or amused, assuming someone was playing a bad joke on our host. But I knew this woman's story. I had lived it.

"What a waste," I said to John. "Imagine how much food that perfume would have bought for the poor." It was all I could think to say. The look of contempt on our host's face seemed to say, 'What kind of prophet is this that allows this low person to touch him in this manner?'

Jesus raised his hand. The company quieted down.

"Simon, I wish to tell you a story," he said.

The Pharisee smirked and grimaced at his friends. Jesus waited until the snickering died down and then began.

"There were two men who owed money to a well known moneylender. One owed him five hundred denarii, and the other fifty. Neither of them could pay him back, so he canceled their debts. Which one of them, do you think, loved him more?"

"Obviously the one who had the greater debt canceled."

Jesus paused and studied his host for a moment. "When I entered your house, you did not give me water to wash my feet or a towel to dry them, but this woman wet my feet with her tears and dried them with her hair. You did not give me a kiss of welcome, but this woman has not stopped kissing me from the time she settled at my feet. You did not put oil on my head as is the custom, but look, she anoints me. I tell you, her many sins will be forgiven, for she has shown much love. Those who forgive little—love little. Do you understand?" Then he twisted around on his couch and said to the woman, "Your sins are forgiven."

The woman ceased weeping and with enormous dignity, rose and left the room. As she did so, I glanced at our host and his friends. Their faces had lost their smug, self-satisfied look. Their expressions ranged from shock to fury. I had no doubt we had not heard the last of this encounter.

The woman followed us from Simon's house, at a distance, of course, and that night when we settled into our camp, Jesus gestured for her to join us. The others, uncomfortable with this display of intimacy with an unclean person, moved away from her. She told us her name was Rehab. I do not think she told the truth. Many women forced into the life she led assume that name. I suppose they believe identifying with the prostitute who helped Joshua conquer Jericho somehow lessened the stigma attached to their profession. I cannot judge these women, certainly. My mother practiced that profession because it was the only life left to her.

To this day I do not know if we have a ritual that will cleanse such women to allow them back into society. I think not. But even if we do, I do not believe anyone would accept its results. There is something about that particular sin that challenges our ability to forgive. She sensed our discomfort, or perhaps she knew her place. In either case she accepted the food and moved some distance away to eat.

Mary, the Magdalan, seemed less concerned with Rehab's presence than the men, but she kept her distance as well. I took her to task for that. It was a cowardly thing for me to do, as I reflect on it. The truly bad-mannered responses came from the men, and I should have gone after them, not her. But I suppose I thought she should have been softer in her response; given what we all assumed had been her lot before.

"You do not know what you are talking about," she said with some heat. "There are differences in these things."

I suppose she meant that women like Rehab who stepped over the Torah's moral boundaries were to be held to a different standard than women who maintained occasional lapses, those not marked by the exchange of denarii. Mary accepted her restoration at the hands of Jesus and her role of renewed righteousness. But neither she nor any of the others granted the same to Rehab. It remains a great mystery to me how we come to believe these things. If I understand anything about the mind of God, it is this: There is no hierarchy of sins. You either miss the mark or you do not. Matthew, our tax gatherer, exploited his countrymen for years—a great sin. Yet Jesus forgave him and except for some minor annoyance on the part of the disciples who had been injured by him, his forgiveness was accepted.

Chapter Thirty

Sukkoth arrived, and we were to go to Jerusalem. Jesus sent for me. I found him sitting in the deepening evening shadows. He asked me to walk with him so that he could give me some instructions. "Your marching orders," he said with a smile. I was to go to Jerusalem and make arrangements for our stay. Jesus gave me names of people to visit on the way south—women, mostly, who would provide us with funds. Jesus and the others would follow in a few days.

We were quiet for a while, and I waited. It is the way with student and teacher. He seemed to have something on his mind that troubled him. Finally he turned to me and said, "The Baptizer is dead."

We all knew he would be martyred. It was only a matter of time, a prophet's destiny. Still I felt the loss.

"It is the way with our people." He sounded bitter and resigned.

"Teacher, may I speak plainly?"

"Of course, you may."

I nodded, took a breath, and began, "The Baptizer is dead. That leaves only you. When will you declare yourself and strike out at Rome?"

"Strike out?"

"Yes. Strike out. Raise an army, whatever it takes to free us from them. You have the power and the people will rise up—"

He raised his hand to silence me, but I could not stop.

"No, you must listen. I have seen your power. We all have. You can do whatever you wish. If we were more careful with the resources we have, with our money…you allowed that woman to squander over a hundred denarii on your feet…you feed the poor and we have to forage for food…we needn't do that. There is no reason for anyone to go hungry or wanting. Rabbi, if you wanted to, you could turn stones to bread. You could feed the world."

"Stones? I should turn stones to bread? That is not the bread they need, Judas. We do not live on bread only. They need to feast on the Word. When they do that, the bread will be there, as much as they require."

"But, people look for, no, need signs. You could give them one."

"It's signs now, is it? What have I done these last months? Must I go through this again?"

"Of course, they should believe. You raised that boy from the dead and—"

"And in the face of all that, have the people, as you say, risen up? You know they haven't."

"It does not seem to be enough. Listen, if we stood on the top of that mountain over there to the west, we could see the world. You could rule all those kingdoms and empires if you wanted to. You could just step in and do it."

"To do what, impose an Israelite king in the place of a Roman Caesar? We have done that many times before and look at what it brought us. Judas, to rule over a worldly kingdom, I would have to be a worldly ruler, manipulating circumstances, collecting taxes, marshalling an army, worrying about plots and schemes from other ambitious men. To hold it together, I would one day fall at the feet of the Prince of Darkness. It is the inherent nature of temporal power and there is no escaping it. I cannot do it. I can only serve the Lord."

"Then give the people one great sign. Something they cannot pass off as just the act of one more miracle worker."

"And what do you suggest? Should I jump off the pinnacle of the temple and float to the ground? The psalmist says, 'The angels will bear me up so I may not dash my feet against the stones.' Is that what you had in mind, my friend?"

"Why not? Then there would be no doubt. Everyone, even those self-righteous, officious donkeys that dog our heels day and night, even they would have to admit you are the One. Imagine what that could mean."

"Judas, you are the most resilient of all who walk with me. You were not raised in the faith and what faith you do have, you acquired through study, prayer, and struggle. It will serve you well when things are dark and you are a long way from this place. But you know it is also written 'we are not to put God to the test.'"

"But the Lord is deaf to the cries of his people. Look around you. If the Romans are not rolling over us, the 'keepers of the Law' are. The Lord cannot want us to suffer so. Children are left fatherless and that is the least of the ills they have to face. Widows are left to die and these priests, these presumed, strutting, heirs of Aaron, grow fat on the sacrifices of the very people they are charged with helping. Why would God want that?"

"Do you remember from your studies, the story of Gideon?"

"Yes, I think so. He had a wine press or something, and the Midianites were in the land."

"He was on the way to his little store of grain which he was threshing out in an old wine press when the messenger of the Lord met him. Remember? The angel greeted him as a 'man of valor' and said the Lord God was with him. Gideon was a man much like you. He wanted to know why, if God stood with him, people had to suffer."

"Master, I don't see how—"

"Listen. Do you remember what the angel said to Gideon?"

"Yes. No. I'm not sure."

"Well, he did not say, 'Be patient, the Lord has a plan,' and he did not say, 'It's all a great mystery.' He did not say, 'Wait for a sign,' either. The angel said, 'Go and free your people.' Do you see?"

I did not.

"The Lord expects his people to do it. He put his creation in their hands and he expects them to use the gifts he gives to do what needs to be done. We are to believe, to obey, and to act in his name. And we are not to wait for him to come and do the work for us, as the Greek gods and goddess do in their stories."

"But, if we are to do it ourselves, shouldn't we be raising an army?"

"The Kingdom of God will come when the hearts of men are changed. It is not of the world. Our history tells us anything else is doomed to fail. You will see in time, Judas. Trust me. What I say will come to pass, and you will play a role in it."

"I don't think that likely, Lord. One of the others, perhaps, but not I. I carry the purse. I am your 'thief' and I am happy in that. I expect no more."

I meant those words. I was content to do the one thing I did well and walk with the rest. I left it to quicker minds than mine to discern the complexities of the kingdom. But I still could not see how it would ever come about without force.

"I will see you in Bethany," he said and walked away.

I felt like a bean pod that had been shelled. What did it mean? No army, no assault on the Roman beast, nothing? Why did I stay in this man's service? He had a power about him that drew you in the way the sea's strong currents pull you into their depths. He gripped me in exactly that way.

Rehab sat away from the rest of us, alone, as was her custom. She seemed very sad. The other women did not welcome her, even though Jesus said, on more than one occasion, words to the effect, "Don't be hasty in judging others, unless you would likewise be judged." I went to her and sat with my bowl of stew and bread. We sat in silence. I could feel the others' eyes, men and women, boring holes in my tunic, but I stayed. I knew this Rehab, as they did not, could not.

"I must leave you," she said finally.

"Leave us? Why?"

"It looks bad to others, to those whom your Master wishes to teach."

"He said this?"

"No, of course not. He would not. But I think he worries."

I thought she was probably right in that, but it was not my place to say so.

"He has forgiven you. He said your sins were forgiven. What else is there?"

"Only The Lord on High can forgive sins. Is your Jesus able to do this, too?"

People like Rehab and me, who struggled at the dirty edges of society, needed to believe it. No one else would have us.

"I believe he can," I said, with more certainty than I felt. "You can change your life. Reclaim it and return to the world new."

She gave me a long sideways look that stirred something in me that I would not describe as holy.

"All that remains for me is the life I have now or to take up gleaning in the corn fields like Ruth in the hopes of finding my Boaz. Shall I do that, Judas? Shall I risk starvation and worse at the hands of the men in the fields? Or shall I stay with the only life I know? You tell me how, Judas, keeper of the purse? How does a woman like me 'return to the world new?' Can I go back to my family? Will they kill a fatted calf for me? You know I cannot and they will not. What advice can I have from the clever man from Corinth?"

Her outburst caught me off guard. I should have known better, of course. People assume that women in brothels and in the profession of pleasure are slow. But it is not so. Many of the women I knew in the House of Darcas spoke with the accents of the refined and educated. They all had their reasons for being where they were and most had stories like my mother's. Though a few willingly chose the life.

"There is the other thing as well," she said.

"The other thing?" I said, uncomfortable.

"It is the way some of you look at me."

I said nothing but I knew what she meant. I had not lived as long as I had in the presence of men seeking the pleasures of the flesh not to recognize the glances sent her way, not just by those we met on our journeys, but from some of our number as well.

"You see how it is?"

"I will miss you," I said.

Chapter Thirty-one

Pilgrims flocked to the temple from all over the world, bringing their sacrifices to the altar. Bellowing bulls, bleating sheep, smoke, and the smell of burning flesh filled the air. Crowds pushed and shoved their way in and out of the courts. The din was unbelievable.

Around the periphery of the largest court, Herod had built low-hanging roofs supported by pillars, much like a narrow *cardo*. Rabbis and teachers from all over the countryside and, indeed, from all over the world, took places in the shade of these arches and called out to the crowds. Passersby stopped to listen. Some lingered, caught up in the particular topic or harangue, but most moved on, listening first to one, then another. Jesus took his place a distance from the more popular rabbis and began his teaching. Soon a large crowd gathered around him. It was usual for one to dispute with the teachers, and that day was no exception. Jesus had just finished speaking about the Kingdom and urging his listeners to live beyond the burdens of this world when a lawyer interrupted him.

"Teacher, that is all well and good, but what must I do to inherit eternal life?"

"What is the Law? How do you read it?"

The lawyer recited: "Love the Lord with all your heart and with all your soul and with all your strength and with your entire mind, and also, love your neighbor as yourself."

"Yes, that is so. Do it and you will live."

"And who, exactly, is my neighbor?" he asked, his eyebrows arched.

Jesus gazed patiently at this upstart and then, giving me a fleeting smile, said, "There was a certain man who was traveling on the Jericho road. On the way, bandits attacked him. They beat him, stripped him of his clothes and money, and left him for dead. A short time later, a priest from the temple, traveling down to Jericho, saw the man. When he did, he crossed the road so as to pass by on the other side.

"A little later a Levite came along. He saw him and passed by on the other side as well. Then, a third man, a Samaritan, came by. When he got to the man, he took pity on him. He attended to him and bandaged his wounds. He put him on his own donkey and took him to an inn. The next day he gave the innkeeper money and said, 'Look after him. If there are any other charges, I will repay you when I return.' You tell me, which of the three do you think was a neighbor to the man who was left in the road for dead?"

The lawyer said, "I guess the Samaritan who gave him aid."

Jesus said to him, "If the misguided Samaritan can do something like that, then surely you can do the same."

The young lawyer's face reddened, and he seemed about to say something when a group elbowed their way into our midst and shoved a woman to the ground. She looked terrified. The men appeared to be officials, or Pharisees, or both, and they were on a mission. They hoisted the woman to her feet, spun her around, and turned to Jesus.

"Teacher, we caught this woman in the very act of adultery. Moses commanded us to stone such women. Now what do you say we should do?"

They stood close to Jesus, hands on hips. The moment moved like honey in winter. The woman could have been my mother. My heart ached for her. I felt rage begin to well up in me. I was back in Caesarea. I opened my mouth to say something when

I felt Jesus' hand on my arm, a brief touch, but it brought me back to the present.

Jesus stared at the ground, then leaned forward and seemed to write in the dust with his finger.

Impatient, they asked him. "Well? Have you no answer?"

Jesus straightened up and gazed wearily at their leader.

"If one of you can claim to be without sin, throw the first stone. Be very sure that you understand…anyone without *any* sin…cast a stone."

Then he leaned forward and scribbled on the ground again. The woman's accusers shuffled their feet and muttered and then, one by one, drifted away. Jesus straightened up and looked at the woman.

"Woman, where were your accusers?" He looked at the rest of the crowd. "Will no one condemn her?" They lowered their eyes. He looked back at the woman. "Has no one condemned you?"

"No, Teacher," she said nervously.

"Nor shall I. Go and leave your life of sin."

There was a stirring among the crowd. Many seemed pleased with Jesus' response. Others looked worried or offended. And again the words, "Who does he think he is?"

I had to leave to pay our temple taxes. As I made my way toward an exit, I sensed someone close on my heels. When I turned to look, I saw several men moving toward me. Had Leonides' people found me again? I ducked through the temple's passageways and burst into the street. If they wanted me, they would have to catch me.

Chapter Thirty-two

The men worked their way through the crowd toward me. I quickened my steps, dodged down a side street, cut though a shop, and dashed out its back door and into an adjoining street. I pressed against a wall in the shadow of some hanging carpets and waited—no one. I eased back onto the street and retraced my steps. They burst through a doorway ten paces in front of me. I dashed off again. They closed in. I increased my efforts to lose them, wiggling through the mass of humanity crowding the street. Either they knew these streets very well or they were experts at tracking. I picked up the pace, but these were determined men and I did not dare run. That would have been the surest way to lose them, but running in the streets of Jerusalem on a High Holy Day would attract the notice of every Roman soldier in my path. If any one of my pursuers were to yell "murderer," I would be done for. Of course, any inappropriate move on their part and they might feel the heavy hand of a legionnaire as well. Realizing then, that what works against me also works for me, I turned to face them.

Three men pulled up in front of me. One stepped forward, a fat man, heavy from too much good living and not enough sweating. He stretched out his arm, palm toward me. They did not look like the stony men who pursued me before, my nemeses. So who were these men? The fat one removed a perfumed linen cloth from his sleeve and wiped his brow. Only soft Pharisees seemed to have them, or something else, up their sleeve, not hard men, not men from Athens.

"We would have a word with you." the fat one said, panting.

We stepped out of the crowd and into a small space between two shops.

"We have listened with great attentiveness to your master's teaching, and we are impressed. Some even say he is the Messiah, do they not?"

I did not trust these men. They seemed too well turned out to be genuinely interested in Jesus. But I could see no harm in agreeing with such an open remark. I shrugged and waited.

"You are Judas, sometimes known as Iscariot. You have been a follower of Jesus of Nazareth, his trusted disciple. We know this and that is why we sought you out." He paused, letting that sink in.

"He trusts all his friends."

"Perhaps, but only you are trusted with the purse. Only you may be found far away from the others when there are important negotiations to be made and tasks to be done. We could easily have approached any of the others, but because of your special position, we thought it best to come to you."

I said nothing.

"Let me speak plainly," he continued, with a quick, worried glance over his shoulder. "We represent a small but growing number of men in Jerusalem and elsewhere who also seek the Messiah. We have studied the prophets and are certain that the time is near for the Lord to act. We have position and influence. We want to believe, as you do, that this man is the 'Coming One,' but we have reservations. Our colleagues are not willing to commit to him or his cause. For us to do so and then discover we were in error would do irreparable damage to us personally and to any future hopes we may have. You see our predicament?"

I shook my head.

"For example, that scene at the temple just now with…that woman…Jesus seems to have no sense of propriety when it comes to people like that. And more importantly, one might be led to believe he sees himself as a judge equal to the Lord. He said he forgave her sins. Only the Lord can forgive sins."

"He didn't say, 'Your sins are forgiven.' He said, 'Leave that sinful life behind,' and he would not condemn her. It's not the same thing."

"Perhaps not, but to the ordinary listener, one not skilled in the niceties of disputation, it amounts to the same thing. And in the past he has forgiven sins. There was a woman in the house of Simon, whose sins he forgave. There have been other instances…"

I said nothing and waited for his next words.

"We are sincere in our desire to find the Messiah. Of all the men wandering about this land in the last generation, and the testimony of the Baptizer…your Jesus seems likeliest. Our problem is what people say about him and what he says about himself do not always appear congruent. We must know all there is to know about him, and it must be from someone like you, someone who walks with him daily and he trusts completely. Do you see our point?"

Certainly, it could not hurt Jesus if they heard the truth. The stories circulating about Jesus were often hugely exaggerated. One claimed Jesus changed the colors in a vat of dye so the dyer would not be found to have made a mistake and be punished by his master. Where that story began, I do not know; probably from a dyer seeking attention. People are not satisfied with just the truth. They need to make it bigger and, sometimes, to put themselves in its middle. If this natural inclination to exaggerate, to overlook reality, were not stemmed, we would soon face a serious credibility problem.

"What is it you wish from me?" I asked, my suspicions still intact.

"Only the truth," he said, and spread his arms wide. "We want you to write the things that happen, the things he says. Write only what you are comfortable in sharing with us. And do not worry whether we understand. We will study what you write and decide for ourselves. If we can support Jesus, we will send for you. If not, we will dispose of your letters and remain silent. In any case, what can be the harm in that?"

What indeed? If the truth were known and reported, what harm could come of that? But if those other wild stories continued to circulate, there could be trouble. A record of the important points kept by someone who had witnessed them could only strengthen our case. The men were right: I was the one person trusted by Jesus and levelheaded enough not to get carried away with flights of fancy, like Andrew, or misunderstand the essence of the thing, like Peter, or dress it up in John's theological abstractions. I could do it. Still, I hesitated. What would Jesus say?

"This is a delicate position," he added, sensing, I suppose, my concerns. "Perhaps it would be best if only we knew of these writings. Your associates may think you are over-reaching. Why not just deal with us? When the time comes and we announce our support for Jesus, we will acknowledge your contribution. I think that would work best."

As I listened, it dawned on me that I must have been placed in this position precisely for this task. When we met, did not Jesus tell me that I had been chosen? And now I knew why. I set aside my intuitive dislike for this sweaty official and his perfumed handkerchief. We needed something more—something from the established leadership, from the center of power. He asked only for the truth.

"Very well," I said. "I will do as you ask, if I can. I write passable Greek and some Aramaic…"

"Greek will be fine. It is for our eyes only."

"Where would you like me to start?"

"Ah, that is most important. Begin as far back as you can. There are things reported about the circumstances of Jesus' birth that raise serious doubts, questions, you understand, about his ability to be considered a whole Jew, much less the Messiah of Israel. It is the problem with his father, Joseph, you understand?"

Did I? People could be very hard on those with uncertain or mixed parentage, *mamzers* like me. Even though the scriptures are filled with one example after another of instances where great men arose from a mixed lineage, the descendants of Ruth and Boaz, for example, they worry too much about marriage with the historical inhabitants of the land and others who moved in with us. Pity the poor Samaritans.

"What else?" I write slowly. It would read well enough but I did not want to spend time on things that did not interest them or would not help in their decision.

"We would like to know what he says about the special relationship he has with the Lord. Every prophet has such a relationship. It is important we know his. The events of this morning need to be put in context. Tell us things he has done, healings, miracles, that sort of thing. And, oh yes, this is very important, any time he may have spent in the company of the Zealots, the Essenes, or any other dissident group. We must know if he could unite these people to our cause."

"I will write what I know to be true. I cannot capture all of the events, because I will not have time. But those things you ask, and those things I believe to be important, I will write."

"That will be enough. We will contact you in a week or ten days, if that is agreeable."

"I will try to be ready."

I doubted the other disciples would grasp the significance of what I had been asked to do. They were content in their belief that Jesus would magically unveil the new kingdom, or his army, or perform some mighty miracle and it would be done. They did not understand the world as I did. Common sense told me if any progress were to be made, it would have to involve many people including the entrenched ruling class.

"Love your enemy," he preached. Well, now I understood.

Chapter Thirty-three

Jesus wished to return to the Sea of Galilee, but this time he decided to press farther north, toward Caesarea Philippi and visit the towns in Bashan and the Decapolis. Why he picked that particular day to travel by boat across the sea escaped me. It would have been easier to walk along the shoreline than bob around in a damp, smelly fishing boat. He said he wanted to let our fishermen exercise their skills and they were hard at it, hauling in lines, setting and resetting sails. As long as we had a northerly breeze, we were fine. These men, Peter, James, and the rest, were in their element and having a grand time. I tried very hard not to notice the boat's rocking. Jesus, on the other hand, fell asleep in the stern. He had been teaching steadily for days and needed rest.

The first several hours were pleasant enough. Then, quite suddenly, the sky darkened. I saw worried looks exchanged between Peter and Andrew. They consulted with the others and looked shoreward. The wind had taken us far from land.

The wind increased and the sea became more violent. The boat pitched. Spray blew over the sides. We were soaked. Thunder crashed and lightning flickered menacingly on the roiling water. The men shortened sail and tied down baggage. Water accumulated in the boat's bottom. Peter took an oar and attempted to bring the bow into the wind. John and Thaddeus scrambled over the thwarts to Jesus. It did not look good. I figured if these fishermen, knowing storms as they did, were frightened, I should be, too. Jesus opened one eye and then the other as they screamed at him.

"Master, Master, wake up. We are all going to die."

He stared at us, cowering in the bilge, stood, faced the storm, and slowly raised his hands. The wind lessened. We were still tossing about but somehow we did not seem to be in as much peril. Then the storm left as quickly as it came.

"Where is your faith? What are you afraid of?" he said, shaking his head, and he resumed his place in the stern of the boat and closed his eyes. The sun came out and we sailed on. I looked at the others. They all assumed an expression as if to say they knew all along we were not in any danger. But the telltale red in their eyes told me something else.

We sailed to the area of the Decapolis where there were no Jews, the land of the Gerasenes, near Khersa. The coast rose steeply from the shore, forming a low bluff that hung out over the sea. We beached the boat and climbed toward the top.

When we reached the crest, we were met—perhaps overwhelmed would be a better way to put it—by the strangest sight I ever saw. A man crouched beside a pile of rocks near what appeared to be tombs. Behind him and reaching all the way up the bluff, a huge herd of swine rooted in what must have been the town's dump. The man hunkered down on his heels and stretched his arms in front, hands planted on the ground like one of the pigs. When he saw us, he howled. He bared his teeth and growled, like Mary had at Magdala. I glanced her way to watch her reaction. Her eyes were wide.

"Master..." she began.

"I see."

He walked toward the man, who was completely naked, his body covered with so much filth we had not noticed it before. We drew back. The howling stopped, replaced by low mutterings and words so blasphemous and vile that even I, who'd spent more years than I care to enumerate in the streets and brothels of the empire, blushed. I looked at Jesus, but he seemed as calm as if he were listening to King David play his harp.

The pigs stopped rooting, turned their heads, and watched us like an over-fed audience at a theater. We began to retreat, unsure which would be worse, pigs or this unclean and danger-ous man. When he saw Jesus walking calmly toward him, the man screamed obscenities at us. Mary covered her ears. Then, the man wheeled and focused on Jesus. He growled, "What do you want with me, Jesus, son of the God of Israel?"

Jesus raised his hand and said, "Come out of him." The man jerked about but continued to rave.

"You are torturing me," he screamed.

Jesus said, "Tell me your name."

"*Legion*," he barked. "*Legion*."

"Well, Legion, leave him…this moment. Infest those pigs if you must, but come out."

With that, the man leapt to his feet and ran at the pigs. They, in turn, panicked, raced to the top of the bluff, and before anyone could stop them—not that we would have, they were pigs after all—they tumbled off. Some were dashed on the rocks below; others fell into the sea.

At that moment, the man came to his senses. He stood in the field looking around as if he was not sure where he was or how he came to be there. Nathaniel, who had a better sense of propriety than the rest of us, took him down to the sea, washed him off as best he could, and put a cloak around him. When we took our leave, he asked to come with us, but Jesus said he should stay with his people and tell them what a mighty work the God of Israel had done.

I mention all these cleansings, these exorcisms, because they became symbolic of my journey. The first I witnessed involved a single spirit. Later with Mary, there were more. And now this man whose demons were legion. If he could manage this demonic legion, surely he need not fear the power of Rome and its legions. That was the thought that formed in my mind. I would change that view later, of course.

Chapter Thirty-four

Herod Philip built Caesarea Philippi in the north, almost to Dan. We made our way there moving from town to town. Sometimes there were large crowds, and sometimes only a few gathered. Caesarea Philippi is quite beautiful but, like his half-brother Antipas, Philip built a pagan capital. It had no synagogue and we gave it a wide berth. We used a nearby field to meet with the folk who lived and worked there and where we pitched camp. Andrew built a small fire, and we ate our evening meal. It had been a long and busy journey. We were tired and ready to relax, to speak of other things. In the quiet that followed, Jesus swallowed the last of his meal and refilled his cup from the wineskin, being careful to add some water to it. It had not traveled well.

In the quiet that followed, I asked the question that had bothered me since that painful day on the docks in Caesarea Maritima. I guessed it would cause some trouble but I needed to know. "Master, is circumcision really necessary?"

The others looked at me, mouths agape.

"It was given to us through our father Abraham," John said. "How can you ask such a foolish question?"

"No, no, it is a good question. I would like to hear the answer to that myself," Thomas said and winked.

Jesus frowned. "If it were necessary, in the sense you mean, children would be born circumcised. What is important is the circumcision of the spirit."

There was a shocked silence. I looked at John out of the corner of my eye. His face was a thundercloud. Peter's mouth dropped open. Everyone except the Magdalan looked uncomfortable. She hid a smile. I thought, born circumcised? We were, in a way. *In this world we don't choose who we are; we just are. And you are a Hebrew whether you like it or not.* Amelabib said that to me in Corinth, a lifetime ago. Circumcision of the spirit.

Then, he asked of no one in particular, "When you hear people speak of me, who do they say I am?"

Well, people said many things about him and not all of them were complimentary. "Some think you are a prophet like the Baptizer...or Elijah or one of the ones we read about in synagogue."

"Some say you are the Messiah promised by Isaiah."

"Well, then, who do *you* think I am?" he asked.

We were silent. The question hung in the air like an over-ripe pomegranate. I knew when it fell there could be a mess to clean up. I realized at that moment he had asked the single question that I, and I suspect the others, had avoided for over a year. He was the "Coming One." We did not have to know in what way or how. We needed only to accept it and believe whatever we wanted.

Suddenly, Peter blurted out in a voice as loud as if he'd been stung, "You are the Christ. You are the Son of the living God... you are..."

Words failed him and he crumpled to his knees. Then, like lightning, the realization of what Peter said, struck us all. Each of us, as the truth sank in, followed Peter and dropped to our knees. It was like a hammer had pounded us into the ground.

It took me a while to identify the soft sobbing and then locate it. Mary sat apart from the rest, crying quietly into her sleeve. We had recovered from our argument about Rehab and were again on friendly terms. This strange, tarnished woman intrigued me. I sat next to her and waited. After a while, her sobbing subsided.

"Judas?"

"Yes? Is there anything I can do?"

"No, nothing. Is that why you are here?"

"I heard you weeping."

"You were right about Rehab. We were wrong to judge her so harshly."

What could I say? It seemed unlikely that regret over poor Rehab would cause such a volume of tears.

"She felt unworthy to be in the presence of the rabbi. She thought her sins too great." Mary spoke as much to herself as to me. "Were her sins any greater than mine? I did with men what she does. That I was not in my right mind is no excuse. The truth..." She paused, deliberating whether I could be trusted with her story.

"I am not in a position to judge either you or Rehab," I said. She stared at me for a long time. Finally she lowered her eyes and told me her story.

"I never thought of myself as different. As a young child, I had episodes when I became a different person, but my parents put that down to an overactive imagination. I would be playing with the other children and then I would assume the role of an entirely different person. They thought I invented this new person and delighted in the novelty of it. But I really did become that person. I stopped being Miriam and became Salome. Well, when you are young, you don't know, do you? I mean, without some experience, you don't know what is normal. I did wonder, sometimes, why the other girls couldn't do it, too."

Madness, I heard madness. Not like Dinah, whose madness took her within herself, but the madness you see sometimes in the streets by people whose personae shift from lamb-like to leonine in the wink of an eye. A street entertainer I once knew had such a man on a leash, and he would goad him into becoming as many as a dozen different people. The force with which the man played each part made it amazing, frightening, actually, and the leash necessary. No actor in the theater could have done what that man did. And now this woman told me she suffered the same way.

"It amused my friends, but later, as I grew older, one or two of the women inside me turned me to doing things that no decent woman should do. The demons—"

"But it is over now. That life is behind you. Your past has been forgiven."

"Forgiven perhaps, but not forgotten. Where will I go, Judas? Who would have me?"

"I would," I said. She gave no sign she heard. I took her hand and, this time loud enough to be heard, said "I would."

"You? But you would be consorting with a woman who could never be accepted by any community."

"There are some things you should know about me," I said. And for the first time since I left my mother, I spoke of my past.

"Now, I am going to ask you to do as I have done." Jesus paused and seemed to weigh his next words.

"You have listened to me for all these months. You know my words. You know what I am likely to do or say in almost any circumstance. It is time for you to go and do the same."

We all looked at each other, unsure what he asked. Did he mean we should wander about performing miracles, preaching, and exhorting? What did he mean by *do the same*?

"I want you to go out in pairs. You will be given power. Your tongues will be loosened and your minds made clear. Seek those who need to hear the Word. If they are deaf, restore their hearing. If they are blind, restore their sight. Tell them of the good news God brings to the poor, the oppressed, and the hungry."

While we still grappled with the significance of our new understanding about him, he declared we must share in this ministry. He caught us by surprise. We thought of ourselves only as followers. The idea that we had to do something beyond that had never occurred to us.

◇◇◇

Thomas and I paired off and wandered about the countryside for nearly a week with little success. We were an unlikely pair—two doubters. We would have been better off yoked to one of the simple fishermen who did not struggle as I did with what we were about. We could preach the lessons, mind you. In fact, Thomas was quite good at it. He remembered the words and parables almost verbatim and even added some of his own from time to time. My teaching lacked fire and depth and clarity. Passable, but uninspired.

Thomas walked behind me, ranting on about the burden Jesus had laid on us and how he should have taught us how to do this or that, and on and on. I listened with half an ear. I knew from experience that no good comes from railing at the wind. Better to walk with your back to it.

The sun baked the land and dust covered our legs. As we traveled a back road toward a village I did not know existed, I saw a young girl of ten or eleven years, sitting off to one side. She reminded me of Dinah when I last saw her. However, where Dinah was fair, this girl was dark, and where Dinah was plump, she was thin. She looked like she had not eaten for weeks. I drew closer and I saw one other similarity. She had Dinah's vacant stare. Startled by the look, I drew up so sharply that Thomas, in full stride and absorbed in his running commentary on the unfairness of our situation, almost knocked me down.

"Thomas, stop. We must do for this child." I exclaimed, excited.

"Do? Do what for this child?"

"We must heal her…restore her to her senses."

"What? How?"

"I have no idea, but he said we have the power. We just say the words and call it down."

"What words? See, this is exactly what I was just talking about."

Thomas remained reluctant to put his faith on the line, but the sight of that girl, and the memories she evoked, drove me into uncharted territory. She stared unseeing and apparently unaware of our presence. I put my hand on her shoulder and she began to tremble. I knew the sequence. I had experienced it dozens of times. Dinah would start shaking and then the screaming would begin. I took a deep breath and muttered, "Do not be afraid, it will be all right."

Her eyes darted back and forth and locked on to mine. She calmed. Now what? I looked at Thomas but he only shrugged.

"God is with you…young woman…He wishes you to be made whole. In the name of Jesus, be restored." I said this with as much conviction as I could muster. Not much of a speech. Jesus would have said something wonderful, or nothing at all.

We waited. Had I done something wrong? Why didn't he give us the right words? Then the girl smiled and kissed my hand. Her eyes were clear. I had done it, well not I, exactly, but it worked. I looked at Thomas. He beamed and shuffled his feet in a little victory dance.

Chapter Thirty-five

Mary and I formed a conspiracy. The others wondered about us, but our relationship never progressed beyond the innocent keeping of secrets. I regretted it, but at the same time, rejoiced in the acquisition of something I had never truly had before—a friend.

I could not keep the writing from her.

"Can you trust those men?" she asked.

"It is not a matter of trust," I said. "They may or may not be what they seem, but if they aren't, why ask for the truth? That is all I write. What can they possibly do if they are only in possession of the truth?"

She looked doubtful. It was her nature. Women are far less trusting than men in matters of the world. In matters of faith, the reverse is true. Women are naturally spiritual and men must be drubbed into belief.

"*Cui bono*?" I asked, in about the only Latin I knew, "Who benefits? They gain nothing from associating with us. Incur risks, in fact. Besides, they could get everything I write from dozens of sources. The Master's reputation is common knowledge. I only provide an eyewitness and, I suppose, an authentic source."

"But," she said, and I knew I was about to receive a woman's logic. "If that is so, why are they asking you to write at all? It seems very strange to me they would go to all that trouble…"

Women, I thought, worry about the wrong things. She should be thinking about the benefit to us, not having dark doubts about a few Pharisees who could help, and certainly not hurt us.

"*Cui bono?*" I repeated. "We do."

I don't think she believed me, she but conceded that when it came to knowing how the world worked, I was the acknowledged expert.

◇◇◇

Once, when we neared Bethsaida, Jesus stopped and turned to the masses following us. There would be no relief until he spoke to them. We were in an area where the ground rose up from the sea. Throngs of people—men, women, and children—covered the hillsides. The wind blew in from the sea so his words carried back to the farthest listeners. He taught them about the kingdom. He told them of the blessings and the warnings. He preached as I never heard him preach before and they listened, eyes bright, mouths open as if to swallow his words.

The sun was low on the horizon when he finished. We waited, expecting the crowds to disperse, but they lingered, reluctant, it seemed, to miss anything that might yet come. Philip clutched at the rough fabric of his cloak and asked, "What are we to do with these people?"

"Send them away. It is late and we must move on," John said, alternately squinting at the setting sun and frowning at the milling throng.

Jesus said, "Feed them. It is time."

Philip looked this way and that as if unsure what to do next. I could count and estimate numbers better than anyone else, and yet even I could not guess how many were camped on that hillside. Thousands? It could easily be five thousand, more if the women and children were counted. Philip hurried over to me.

"How much money do we have?"

"What do you need money for?"

"To buy food. He wants to feed all these people and we must buy food."

"Where, exactly, do you plan to make such a purchase?"

We were at least an hour's journey from the closest place where food in sufficient quantities could be purchased. Philip looked around helplessly and threw up his hands.

He and Andrew scoured the area and found a few fish and some loaves of bread, which they presented to Jesus, half expecting him to rebuke them for their foolishness. But he did not. Instead, he held one of the loaves above his head and the crowd quieted. He said a blessing and broke the bread. There was an audible stirring in the crowd. Jesus repeated the blessing with the remaining loaves and fish. The crowd buzzed with excitement. Some cheered. He placed some of the fish and bread into each of twelve baskets and directed us to pass them around. Every person in turn dipped into the basket and took a small morsel and passed it along. People began to sing. A few danced on the hillside.

Later, as the crowd drifted away, Jesus asked Peter and James to gather up whatever had been left behind. We stared at him in wonder. How many crumbs could possibly be left over from two or three fish and some loaves? They returned from the hillside with all twelve baskets filled. I stood and gaped at them. Jesus walked past me and as he did so, he clapped me on the back, grinning as broadly as I had ever seen him.

"Where…how?" I stammered.

"Stones, Judas, don't you remember? They are from your stones."

Chapter Thirty-six

Jesus began speaking of his death, not an idea we either grasped or accepted. We had barely begun our journey and were not willing to hear about its premature end. The countryside and this disorganized accretion of farmers and fishermen were barely aroused in sufficient numbers to expect any of them to band together and face the might of Rome. It was too soon to speak of endings.

Acrid smoke from a guttering campfire added an extra irritant to these conversations. Peter protested vociferously. Occasionally, Jesus would snap at him. "You don't know what you ask of me, Peter. You do not understand."

"But Master, you cannot be put to the test." Peter preferred to put it that way. "Death" did not fit comfortably in his mouth.

"Peter, either I do the will of the Father or all will be lost."

"For the sake of all of us, for your mother and the many who have come to rely on you, do not say these things."

"If you acted any more like Satan, I would have to cast you out." Jesus said, his voice uncharacteristically curt. "Get behind me."

We sat in embarrassed silence. We all believed as Peter did and were upset he had to take the brunt of Jesus' anger.

"Master," I said, hoping to shift the talk along a different path, "how do we answer the critics who grumble about the women."

Jesus' head snapped around and his eyes glittered. "Women? What do they say about women?"

"Well..."

I caught sight of Mary out of the corner of my eye, saw her anger. I had stepped on a wasp's nest but I couldn't turn back.

"Some question the time you devote to women. They think women should stay at home, fetch water, and not traipse around with us." Peter nodded his head. Now that the conversation had shifted away from him and into the area he, too, worried about, he seemed much relieved.

"Do they?" Jesus asked, his face darkening.

"Yes, they do. These are good men but raised a certain way. It is hard for them to see how women can be an important part of the kingdom. They call you 'the Women's Rabbi.' Many left us because of this."

There are moments in life when you know you have over-stepped, drawn in where you did not want to go. This was one of those times. At that moment, I felt supremely stupid.

"Well, they should return to their studies," Jesus said between clenched jaws. "They should remember Ruth, and Rachel, and Jael, and Deborah. They should meditate on Rebecca and Sarah, especially Sarah. They should think about their own mothers and ask themselves where they would be if their mothers had never been born. Some day they will hear that heaven lies at the feet of mothers. For as it is necessary for each individual to have been born of a woman, so the covenanted people of God had to be born, as a nation and as individuals. Each must have a mother. Without one, without our women, none of us would be here today. The land would belong to the tribes of Canaan. Tell them that."

Once, outside a town, I cannot recall which or where it was now. In the Galilee, certainly, the subject of law came up. You understand that is a topic which fascinates Jews beyond reason, it seems. Jesus said, "You remember the man at the lakeside asking me, 'Who do you think you are, God?'" Some of us remembered—I did.

"God gave the Law to Moses and he gave it to us. We are people of the Law. Scribes, lawyers, and rabbis study it day and night, and write about it. You know it from the Torah. You were raised in it, correct?"

Everyone mumbled and nodded except me. I did not have advantage of a lifetime of study in the holy books and scrolls. Only John knew the books well, I think.

"In this," Jesus continued, "we are unlike any other race or nation. Our law comes only from God. Rome has many laws, is famous for them. But those laws are the work of men, and however grand or just they may be, they are still only the work of men. Therefore, they can be changed as circumstances dictate. Our Law does not change. It is not subject to time or place. It does not vary from king to king because it is the immutable Word.

"We live it day in and day out. Thus, it defines the core of our existence, the path we follow, our *Way*.

"As it is from God and unvarying, it also defines truth. Again, we are unique in this. The Greeks have given us philosophers. There are cynics, stoics, the disciples of Zeno, and many others. They search for truth through philosophy and intellectual exercise. Their truth, like Roman law, may shift over time, a moral precept may decline in their culture. They seek universal truth but live in a world where truth is transitory. For us, the Torah is *Truth*; we need look no further.

"And, therefore, it is our *Life*. We live within the Law, we believe it to be true, we obey it, and we accept that it is, for us, all we need to know to structure our lives. It is our Way; it is our Truth; it is our Life, you see. It and it alone, is our pathway to God."

He paused. It was a long speech. Not so long as some, but for the fifteen or twenty of us there, it seemed long. I could barely make out the faces of the others, but from what I could see, they were puzzled. John cleared his throat, uncertain if he should speak. Jesus nodded to him.

"The man hearing you describe the terms of the inheritance believed you were pronouncing Law, or at least adding to it. Is that why he said what he said?"

Jesus nodded again. John furrowed his brow in deep concentration.

"So then, if this man understood you correctly, Master, as you acted as Lawgiver, you may be thought of as the Way, and the Truth, and the Life and, therefore, the pathway to God."

Jesus smiled on his favorite pupil and nodded.

Chapter Thirty-seven

Thomas had grown out his beard, and by then he bore a striking resemblance to Jesus, so much so, we took to calling him *Didymus*, the twin. Jesus was, of course, taller and broader than Thomas, but their proportions were such that unless the two stood next to each other, strangers could easily confuse them.

"My twin," Jesus would say and clap Thomas on the back. Thomas would spread his arms wide and look heavenward like Jesus at prayer. We did not know if we should laugh with or be embarrassed for Thomas, but Jesus laughed and we relaxed and joined him.

"You have been doing some writing, Judas?" The question startled me. I thought Jesus was away in the hills praying, as he always did in the morning. I felt a pang of guilt for having gone behind his back and a little foolish for thinking I could.

"Yes, Master." What else could I say? I had nothing to hide. I had taken on this task to help our cause, to strengthen our position, not to compromise him.

"Why?"

I could not read his expression. I decided to tell him the whole story. If I had done something wrong, then I could make up for it somehow. If not, then he should know about this potential source of support.

"These are men, Master, with position and influence who can help us. But they cannot be seen with you except in large gatherings. You remember how Nicodemas came to you under cover of night. They wish to support us, to support you, and they asked only that I write what I remembered of your teaching, nothing more. They wish to be sure of you."

When I spoke these words, doubt crept into my heart. Said that way, I think I must have sensed their shallowness. But I had committed to that course and unless he called me off, I would stay with it.

"And you think they may help us?"

I shrugged. "Can it hurt? Master, the people are behind us. Every day, the crowds grow larger and the willingness to make a stand more obvious. These men can hasten that day."

"Judas, I have told you again and again, my kingdom is not of this world. Why do you persist on believing otherwise, you, of all people? You have seen the face of our oppressors. You have felt their wrath and you have measured their power. Do you truly believe our people will push them into the sea?"

"I do not know any other way to think about it. All I can conceive is marching against them. I don't have your vision. I only see what I know. Something will happen soon. I do not know how I know this, but I do. And I know it will concern you. I can only assume these men will be a part of that, somehow."

I do not know if the urgency of my voice or something else moved him, but he turned toward the hills and closed his eyes for a moment. The air seemed filled with the oily aroma from the olives hanging heavy on a nearby tree.

"Someday you will see as I do." He paused, letting his words hang in the air. He plucked an olive and crushed it, rubbing its oil into his hands.

"Then you feel it, too? Something in the air, something is about to happen?"

"Yes, something important, perhaps even terrible." I said, and in that brief moment, sensed my words, like the olive tree, bore more fruit than I imagined.

"It is the way the air tingles before a great storm or when the earth moves and brings down the mountains. It's like that, isn't it?" he said.

"I had not thought about it quite that way, but yes…something like that."

He shook his head like a man who has been clubbed, trying to clear it, to regain his balance, to collect his thoughts. He put his fingertips to his temples and squeezed his eyes shut. It was a gesture I had seen many times. He looked for a moment like a man afflicted with the headaches that flash fire. He would hold his head like that for a short time or even an hour and then it would be over. At first it frightened me and the others, but after a while, we grew used to it.

"Is something wrong, Rabbi?"

In a moment whatever possessed him passed and he turned his gaze back on me. He looked at me and with the saddest expression ever I remember seeing. I felt as if I had been stripped naked and every thought, every deed, every wrong I had ever done was laid out for him to see. He shook his head again and breathed a sigh.

"It is enough, Judas. God is directing both of us now. We must be in Jerusalem for Passover. You will make the arrangements as usual and…" He paused and stared at me with sad eyes for a long moment. "And you will know what you must do."

What would I know? He left me then, I suppose, to continue his prayers. I never knew what he did when he left our company. None of us did.

I turned away and walked along a shallow wadi toward an ancient sycamore. I smelled the honey before I saw the bees. A split in the trunk of the tree held the hive. Hundreds swarmed into its depths. I sat and contemplated bees. I knew little about them. I grew up in cities and beekeeping belonged to the country. I did know they would sting if aroused, and attempting to take their honey was the surest way to do that. Bees had short lives characterized by hard work, no recompense, and an anonymous death. Somewhere in the depths of the hive, the ruler, removed from all this activity, dictated their fate.

It would be easy to wax philosophical about that—bees are the conquered people, the ruler is Caesar, and so on, but that is not where my thoughts took me. Bees work for others. They contribute beyond their needs and combs fill to overflowing. My colleagues were like bees. They worked the nets together, each contributing a share.

I remembered the solitary wasp that stung me when I tried to retrieve my honey cake. Wasps do not make honey. Wasps do not gather in communities like bees. They fly alone, caring for no one but themselves. I worked alone and always, only for myself. I did not qualify as a bee. Did I ever belong with this man? Could I be transformed from solitary wasp to communal bee?

I wanted so much to share the vision. I understood how to make things happen in ways the others could barely comprehend. But I did it alone. I left the company and worked my own kind of miracles, *Judas the Thief.* A solitary wasp, a honey thief, allowed in the hive and lingering only because the ruler wishes it. Should I leave before they discover I am not one of them, or stay and pretend to be something I am not? Could a wasp destroy a hive?

"They are evil," Mother had said.

Chapter Thirty-eight

Smoke from a thousand campfires and the din of an equal number of voices filled the Kidron Valley. The bleating of at least as many calves and sheep added to the cacophony. The aroma of animals, people, and cookfires assaulted my senses. Why, I asked myself, must I cross this noisy, crowded valley and climb to the top of the Mount of Olives? To secure a donkey, and not just any donkey—a white one. Of all the things Jesus asked me to do, this ranked as the most incomprehensible and time-consuming. I approached twenty men before I found one willing to provide such an animal. He wanted two denarii for the day. I agreed, but insisted on seeing the beast first. It turned out to be a colt. That took me to my wit's end. I had wasted hours searching and then, to end with this undersized and ridiculous animal. I could not afford to squander any more time. It would have to do, but I told the donkey's owner that such a poor animal was not worth two denarii. I gave him one. He protested until I told him whom it was for, and then he shrugged and agreed.

Bethesda lies across the Kidron Valley and to the south. Mary and Martha and their brother Lazarus live there. Jesus would travel up from Jericho and turn south to Bethesda just outside the city wall. Then, on the day after the Sabbath, he would enter the city. He'd made it clear to me what I must do, and I knew better than to argue with him. He had his reasons.

My first task had been to find a family known to Jesus who, he said, would provide us rooms. I had been directed to go to the Essene quarter, the home to families who like Nahum the Surveyor, follow the way of the Essenes but prefer not to commit to its rigors. They adhere to the rules as best they can, including the calendar for feasts and holidays but remain scattered around the country, partly Essene, partly of the world. They are good people caught between two worlds. They found Jesus speaking to them.

"Look for a man carrying a jar of water," he had said. What kind of man, I wondered, would carry water? That is woman's work. Just then, a boy, a young man, approached me with an empty jar on his shoulder. "Are you looking for me?" he asked.

I nodded. "What is your name?"

"Mark," he said.

"Well, Mark, my master sends his greetings to you and your family, and desires a place for himself and his friends for the Passover feast. Can your father supply these things?"

"Yes, he has been expecting you. A room has been set aside for you over our lodgings."

Of course, the room was available. Somehow it no longer surprised me.

"My father says you will bring the food and wine."

Ah, to be sure, another expected response. Of course, Judas will provide the wine, the food, bread…everything.

He led me to his father who showed me the room above their lodgings large enough to serve a meal for the number of people who were with us and to sleep. The room would serve us well. We also planned to celebrate the Passover in the city. Satisfied, I thanked the man and his son. I had one more task to perform but, first, the purse needed replenishing.

I had only a few coins left and most were shekels. To function in this city I would need a great deal more. I recrossed the Kidron Valley and climbed the temple steps to the Hulda gates and watched as thousands of pilgrims streamed in and out, making their way up and back down again. This smelly, noisy mass of humanity filled the temple and all its passages. I joined them, pushing and shoving my way up the inner stairs to the moneychangers. They were out in force, changing money for travelers, to pay their temple tax, or buy doves, or rams, or other sacrifices with shekels.

No image, whether king, pretender, living, or dead may adorn a coin dedicated to the Lord's service. It would be reckoned a graven image and not permitted on the Mount. So the moneychangers were there as a service to the faithful and a source of significant income for the temple. They had been installed years ago to aid pilgrims. They charged no fees and only asked for a small donation to compensate them for their time and effort. But over the years they had become a pestilence. I made a good living in my days as a money changer and I drove some hard bargains, but compared to these vultures, I practically gave money away. They were charging twenty over a hundred that day. Twenty! Those wretches were gouging travelers from Egypt to Gaul. And John called *me* a thief.

However, it did provide me with a great opportunity. I positioned myself at the foot of the stairs leading up to the temple and offered to change money, making sure they knew my rate. Soon people were streaming back down to me. I began changing at fifteen. When I had nothing but Roman coins, I walked around the temple to the Praetorium in the Antonia Fortress, and offered to trade them to the Roman legionnaires for their shekels. They thought they were as shrewd as rats.

"What rate will you give us today, Jew?"

"Twenty," I said.

"Five."

"Fifteen."

"Twelve."

"Done."

At twelve on the hundred from these gutter rats and fifteen from the pilgrims I was netting twenty-seven, better than the thieves at the temple.

It was a good thing I did.

Chapter Thirty-nine

The next day dawned crisp and clear. Cool morning air carried the fragrance of anemones and the promise of better things to come. The city stirred even though it lacked an hour before shops opened. I had a few things to purchase and some followers to visit in the city. When I finished, I went to find Joseph of Arimathea, a member of the Sanhedrin and one of our supporters. Jesus did not tell me the depth of his commitment. I do not think he even asked. Jesus trusted him and, therefore, so must I. I did wonder if he had read my letters, if he were one of the anonymous insiders.

I located him standing among a small group in the shadows of Solomon's Porch. A group of lawyers and Pharisees were disputing about divorce and adultery, a conversation I did not wish to hear. They had no idea what life was like for those of us who were the consequence of such a union. For them, it made no difference whether a person fell or was pushed, there must be punishment, and because of the sin of Eve, it must be meted out to the woman first and only sometimes to the man. I do not know which caused me the greatest anguish in my childhood, these self-righteous upholders of the Law or Rome. These men thought like donkeys.

I made my presence known to Joseph and stood to one side and waited. If men were assigned to animal families, Joseph would be an eagle. With his hawk-like nose and piercing eyes, he could pose for the crest on a legion standard. He wore robes that marked him as a man of stature and substance. With his straight back, white beard, and angular features, he seemed taller than he really was.

When he'd heard enough, he walked away and, with a tilt of his head, motioned to me to follow. He did not want to be seen with me, at least not on the Temple Mount, not in public. When we cleared the temple, he slowed so that I could catch up and then we walked together, speaking in low voices as we elbowed through the crowd.

"Does Rabbi Jesus have a message for me?"

"He said to tell you he would arrive later today and there would be a task you would not like, but you must do."

"Task? What sort of task?"

"He said only that it would not be easy for you and you might be called on to defend him and you should not be afraid."

"Defend him from what? Against whom…when? Afraid of what? Was that all?"

I shrugged. We passed a stall selling fruit, some of it overripe. The aroma of rotting fruit had attracted flies and wasps. The flies did not discriminate between the fruit and passersby. The wasps concentrated on the sweet pulp. We hurried by swatting at flies while avoiding stirring up the wasps.

"Tell your master to be careful. There will trouble this Passover."

"What sort of trouble?"

"Pilate made it clear any disturbance this year, no matter how slight, would be dealt with severely. He is angrier than usual. He is capable of butchering anyone for even the slightest infraction. He has done it in the past and will again. And if that weren't enough, Barabbas has been taken into custody."

Barabbas in custody? That thief, that fraud, I wished I had brought him in. Good for the Romans. Today, I would hate them a little less.

"What has that to do with us?"

He spun around and looked at me, angry, then continued down the street. "His followers are in the city. They will stir up trouble. When the soldiers respond, they will take everyone and anyone they think could be a problem. They will not discriminate between Barabbas' people, the Siccori, Zealots, or you Galileans."

"Galileans?"

"Your people. His disciples. Don't you know?"

"I have never heard us called that."

"Yes, yes," he said, less angry now. "It is because so many of you are from that part of the country. Those who oppose you, the Sanhedrin and the High Priests, Caiaphas, and even old Annas, many powerful Pharisees, and most of the temple establishment—all of them constantly remind the prefect of the uprising in Sepphoris twenty years ago, the one he helped put down, as it happens. You won't remember. It happened before you were born, but Rabbi Jesus will."

I did not know why that failed rebellion surfaced so often in conversations and reminiscences. Jews are never far from their history. Rebellion rose up in the Galilee; Jesus came from the Galilee; therefore, there would be more uprisings in the Galilee, and Jesus must be part of a great Galilean plot. The movement against him would use anything, even that bit of specious reasoning, to bring him down. I wished such a conspiracy did exist. Before I could stop myself, I blurted out, "Good."

The old man spun on his heel and looked at me, puzzled.

"Good?" he said. "What could be good about that?"

"Sorry. Good that Barabbas has been put in prison," I said, covering my foolish outburst. "He is a danger to everything we are trying to accomplish."

"Yes, well, tell Rabbi Jesus to be very careful, to be discreet."

After a moment I asked, "Is there any talk in the Sanhedrin of support for Jesus, a small group, possibly?"

"Support for Jesus? Except for me and Nicodemas, there is no support for him at all. Quite the opposite, he is a major thorn in Caiaphas' side and the sycophants who surround him. That is why your master must be doubly careful. If they thought they could get away with it, they would happily turn him over to the prefect. They are offering large sums to anyone willing to testify against him. It is a very dangerous time. No, tell him not to look to the Sanhedrin for anything but trouble."

Somehow his words, though I heard them clearly, failed to register.

As our conversation unfolded, we moved steadily through the city streets. He barely acknowledged the salutes accorded him from those who recognized him. He stopped suddenly, turned, and stared at me as though he had never really seen me and wanted a good look.

"I must prepare myself to do a service for Rabbi Jesus that I will find difficult and distasteful. Is that the gist?"

"Yes, in so many words."

He nodded absently and melted into the crowd. I had my answer, but it troubled me. Why was he, of all people, not included in the group that contacted me? Surely they would know his sympathies. On the other hand, if they were unwilling to align themselves openly with Jesus, they would be reluctant to affiliate openly with Joseph. Satisfied, I returned to trying to figure out who the others might be, unwilling to consider any possibilities except those I most wished for.

Chapter Forty

Our steps had taken us to the Gannath Gate. The street teemed with people and soldiers pushing them back from the center of the street. Others handed out flowers, boughs, and coins. I turned to the man next to me.

"What is this?"

"Pilate is coming."

Soldiers made me nervous, our Roman overlord and his entourage, more so. I began to sidle away.

"Stay, stay," the man said and tugged at my sleeve. "They will give you money to cheer for the prefect and throw flowers in his path. It is easy money. See, he comes up from Joppa with all his baggage, through the gate over there, and marches to the Praetorium." He gave me a toothless grin. "Easy money."

I stepped back to the wall. I wished to see but not be seen. Preparation for Passover meant streets cleared of trash and detritus. Unlike many of the empire's cities, Jerusalem has no great sewer to manage the waste of its thousands of citizens. Instead, it is channeled along the streets through drains and into one of the wadis leading eastward. When the rains come, the accumulated filth washes down to the Salt Sea. Until that relief arrives, the wadi and, eventually, the city suffers from its stench. If it gets too bad, water from Pilate's aqueduct can be diverted into the morass and the worst of it sent streaming away.

Into this malodorous city, the prefect, the mighty Pilate, had to pass on his way to the Antonia Fortress. His presence remained a constant and important reminder of Roman authority and a warning to any who would challenge it. It was one of the few times during the year he visited Jerusalem, preferring the sun, the sea, and the familiar pagan culture of Caesarea Maritima.

A wagon filled with boughs of aromatic balsam and juniper appeared at the top of the street. Soldiers passed out the boughs. Another wagon appeared and then another, flowers, palms, and fir to be distributed to the crowd. People were told to lay them in the road when the prefect and his party arrived, each given a coin to assure they did as they were told. I took some boughs and the shekel. After all, money is money.

Soon I heard the blare of brass trumpets from the gate, drowning out the ram's horns from the temple. Then I heard the thunder of drums. I looked to my left. Legionnaires, in lockstep, marched to their beat.

Two hundreds from the Italian cohort stationed in the city—my clients from the shekel exchange—commanded by their centurions, led the way. More drums thundered. Standards of each unit passed by, streaming with ribbons designating battles fought, battles won. As they approached, we threw our boughs in their path. Three additional hundreds—soldiers from Caesarea—followed. More standards flashed, more banners fluttered, and more boughs and flowers were thrown. The sun hovered low in the east, but bright enough to light this spectacle. Greaves and the legionnaires' heavy soled sandals shone from grease and polishing. Their burnished shields glittered, and I was momentarily transported back to my childhood.

Two dozen chariots clattered down the street, each drawn by three of the tall horses from Scythia and manned by spear throwers and drivers. Horses snorted and pranced. People, at the prompting of the soldiers in our midst, began shouting.

"Hail to Pilate. Hail to the one who comes in the name of Caesar."

The soldiers' sandals, the horses' hooves, and the bronze-covered wheels of the chariots crushed the boughs. Soon the stench of the city was cloaked by the fragrance of fir, balsam, and flowers. Next, a train of enclosed wagons lumbered down the street. I guessed they contained dignitaries and their wives. More soldiers and chariots followed. Finally the prefect himself appeared, the famous Pilate, astride a white horse with saddlery and harness of polished black leather and gold studding.

"Hosanna, hosanna, blessings to the one who comes in the name of the Lord Caesar."

I knew him. I had seen him somewhere, but where? Memory failed me.

What a spectacle. I never saw anything like it—flowers, palm branches and sweet balsam, drums, soldiers, trumpets, all the panoply of Roman power and hubris, the Roman Empire on display. Even in this backwater province, this display of might, however meager by the standards of the capitol, made clear to anyone with a glimmer of intelligence that you engaged Rome at your peril.

I suppose these simple people found it exciting. Certainly it was impressive, but it depressed me. How could we ever defeat these people? Who could stand against all of that? Not Judas. Not the Galilee's fishermen, not even with Zealots and Assassins combined. In the face of that display, I knew then that all I dreamed, all I hoped for, had no more substance than smoke.

Chapter Forty-one

The eye-watering smoke from cooking fires drifted lazily across the Kidron Valley, forming a blue haze in the heavy afternoon air was as irritating as Barabbas' cave. Experienced pilgrims learned early to arrive in the city, days in advance of holidays, to stake out a claim on the heights. Latecomers had to endure the smoke and the waste that inevitably drifted downhill. The hills already bustled with people. In another three days, you would not be able to discern a hint of green where a bush might have been. Shelters would be packed together like pebbles on a beach.

Legionnaires worsened the tensions created by this flood of people. Groups of two or three moved through the throngs, which ebbed and flowed like a huge tidal basin, into the city and out. Nerves eventually frayed and hard words followed. Words led to fists, fists to clubs, and clubs to soldiers. Men were led away, and whether they would ever see their families again was, at best, uncertain. In the midst of it all, a thousand voices, speaking in dozens of tongues, babbled on, punctuated by the sharp bleating of calves, sheep, and the bright laughter of children.

Zealots and the followers of people like Barabbas drifted through the encampments preaching rebellion. Here and there, a would-be prophet chanted bits from the Isaiah scroll and called for the Messiah to deliver us. The air crackled like it does just before thunder and lightning strikes. It made my skin feel tight.

I found a narrow path that zigzagged up the slope. Apparently, even in their push to secure a good space, people had enough sense to leave a pathway to and from the city and the temple. But even so, I had to pick my way carefully to the top of the hill. Children tumbled past me, their shrill voices filling the air. Mothers called after them to stay close, and for pity's sake, keep away from the soldiers. Good advice, that.

Nearly out of breath and late, I arrived at the top of the hill overlooking the Kidron and found Jesus and the others. I told him about our arrangements, including the animal he requested. I repeated Joseph's warning. I put particular emphasis on the obvious, that there might be trouble stemming from any of several quarters and he should be very discreet while in the city.

"Discreet?" he laughed. "Have you ever known me to be discreet, Judas? We do not constrain the Father's will. The High Priest and his party do that. We are here to renew the Covenant. It cannot be twisted about to please just those who are frightened or too comfortable. Look around you. People are hungry, and the rich, who could do something about it, turn away. People are thrown off their land by their neighbors and are left to stand idly in the marketplaces while their families starve. They are crushed by taxes to build the temple. People are trampled by the selfishness of their neighbors. The Romans are not the enemy—we are killing our own. And for this Joseph says, 'Be discreet?'" I had no answer to the obvious. Still, I worried.

Jesus summoned Philip and Simon and directed them to fetch the donkey tethered to a ring in the wall a few paces from the path which led down from the Mount of Olives toward the temple. In a few minutes they returned, leading the pitiful animal. Jesus mounted. His legs were so long, he had to bend his knees like a man riding a camel so his feet did not drag on the ground. We all smiled at the sight.

Then he clucked and rode down the hill toward the Golden Gate. He motioned us to follow. Seven preceded and the rest followed. We made an odd procession, zigzagging our way between the tents, the smoke, and the noise. At first, the crowd gaped.

Some, for reasons I could not fathom, cheered, then, amazingly, put their garments in our path and strewed palm branches in our way. There were no flowers or balsam on this barren, crowded hillside to ease the stench of a thousand people, but the pilgrims had palm fronds with them for bedding and they used them to mark our passing.

Then it began. "Hosanna, hosanna in the highest. Blessed is the one who comes in the name of the Lord."

Some, from the north, from the Galilee and the area around the Decapolis, knew him, but most did not. They came for Passover from all over the empire, from Greece and Cilicia, from the area around the Gaza and southward to Egypt and the coast of Africa. A few came from as far away as Rome itself.

Passover draws curiosity seekers, pagans from around the world—the God-fearers. They stared, too. Some recognized the procession, meager as it was, as a thing they had witnessed elsewhere, part of the Osiris and Bacchus stories of their childhood. Gods made entrances. They announced themselves that way. So did conquerors, kings, and always, Romans. And now—Jesus. Many laughed. They assumed Jesus was putting on a show for them, creating a bit of theater, a comedy and making fun of the pretentious Romans. They did not often get a chance to laugh at imperial power. Others, I suspect, laughed because they saw something they thought was plainly ridiculous. A great, tall man sitting on a colt, knees tucked up and riding serenely down the hill. For them, it was a charade, a farce.

I lagged behind, embarrassed. He was making us look like fools. Someone blew a ram's horn and the onlookers laughed even harder.

"Hosanna," someone cried. "Hosanna in the highest."

My face grew as red as my hair. I lagged even more. No one could topple an empire with a dumb-show like this. He made a parody of the parade I'd witnessed just hours earlier. Jesus was no fool. If he did this thing, he did it for a reason. Did he fancy himself equal to one of the gentiles' gods? In the midst of this hilarity, I saw a significant number taking it seriously, the ones we'd seen over these last several months, the ones who cheered, and danced, and sang at the feasts on the hill, the people Jesus called "the salt of the earth." The hillside began to buzz and the cheering increased.

"Make him stop," one man pleaded. As if I could.

I knew the power of Rome first hand. They are not a light-hearted race, not when it comes to ridicule and, whether Jesus intended it or not, they would take it as such. That meant trouble.

We had never received the support of so many people before. Loud and boisterous crowds flocked to us. The day before, dozens, perhaps hundreds, stopped Jesus to say a word, or just be near him. I did not count those cheering on the hillside during his ride into the city. Where they stood and how they might respond would remain a mystery as far as I was concerned. Yet I could not shake the feeling of imminent disaster. I had the same malaise I experienced that awful day when the Greek decided to show his statue.

After the fiasco of our entry into the city, I assumed it only a matter of time before someone came to arrest us, or we would be on the run. It seemed likely the officials from the Praetorium or the palace would be looking for us. To my amazement, nothing happened. The other disciples seemed excited. Philip scolded me for being a skeptic.

"You are as cheerful as Saul at Michael's wedding," he said.

I tried to explain what I feared from our critics. I described the pomp and power of Pilate's entry and how some, maybe many, would compare the two and how they might take it to be a gesture of disrespect, a bit of Greek comedy played out in the hillside. No one listened. Was I the only one that saw these things?

"You understood about the feast, but you don't understand about prophecy—the Messiah is to come up to Jerusalem riding a white colt and entering the city from the east, through the Golden Gate. So, it wasn't as grand as we hoped. It was enough.

Many understood, even if you didn't. It's like the fish and the bread."

This from Thomas who, if I were to guess, would have ordinarily dismissed the event as comedy, something the world had in short supply as far as he was concerned.

Chapter Forty-two

The crowds streamed into the city making it nearly impossible to walk the narrow streets. We struggled through the crush to the temple's south steps, washed at the baths, pushed our way up the steps, and headed for the porches. But Jesus stopped in mid-stride, his eyes like ice. Then, he whirled and, jaws clenched, started back the way we came. We made a path through the crowds and, if I read the expression on his face correctly, headed for trouble.

"Master, what is it?" I said. His eyes flashed and my heart sank. It had begun and we were not ready.

We pushed back down the steps, provoking curses from angry pilgrims. When we reached the moneychangers, Jesus seized a length of heavy rope and without warning, lashed out at the tables, the merchants, and anyone who stood in his path. Tables crashed to the floor, coins scattered and rang across the pavement. People scrabbled around on hands and knees trying to retrieve them or steal them, depending on whether they were bystanders or traders. Doves flapped against the ceiling as their cages shattered. White feathers drifted down on us like snow. Sheep bleated, men cursed. Records of transactions, carefully inscribed on wax and clay tablets, shattered on the tiles. Papyrus fluttered in the air and landed underfoot to be crushed, smeared, and lost. Chaos. I stood in the midst of this, dumbstruck. I looked at the others, and they, mouths agape, watched as surprised as I.

"You pitiless brood of wolves. You have turned my father's house into a den of thieves. Don't you know the Law forbids charging for changing money? This is the Lord's house, not a market." He roared, he bellowed, all the while upsetting more tables and lashing out with the rope.

The merchants and their assistants recovered from their initial shock, closed ranks, and moved toward him. Passersby, drawn by the noise and, for some, the prospect of picking up a few stray coins, tumbled into the hall. They had no idea what the fuss was about, but it required only one elbow to go astray for the confusion to turn into a full-scale riot. Soon forty or more people banged away at each other, kicking, punching, and wrestling. More tables splintered on the paving. The noise was deafening. Not for the first time, I came to appreciate Peter. He may not have had the quickest mind among us, but he certainly had the biggest body, and all those years of hauling nets gave him arms like tree trunks. He tossed men around as fast and as easily as Jesus tossed tables.

Maybe the release of tensions built up over these last months caused it. Maybe I had not changed as much as I thought, but I grew excited, exhilarated even, and I threw myself into the fray. I am not big. Indeed, I am of less than average height and do not look like someone who could do much in a fracas like this one, but I learned how to handle men twice my size in my years on the streets. And so I waded into the crowd with an eagerness that surprised my fellow combatants. All of us exchanged blows with those attempting to land a fist or club on Jesus. A merchant, face red with fury, swung at Jesus but as he did so, he slipped on some coins and his feet went out from under him. He crashed to the floor as two others, also headed our way, tripped over him. I remember dropping one very large and furious Pharisee with a punch to his midsection. I cannot tell you how good that felt. Trumpets announced the arrival of temple guards, who attempted to push into the already cramped space, which by then had been reduced to a battlefield filled with broken furniture, bruised and bleeding men, and bawling animals.

"Get him out of here," John yelled. "If the guards take him, it will be over."

Peter tossed one more merchant into the pile of moaning bodies he'd built in one corner and grabbed Jesus' arm. Philip grabbed the other and somehow they managed to hustle him down the stairs and away. The rest of us scattered. By the time the guards managed to push into the melee, its chief instigator and his accomplices were gone. They were left to sort out the few left behind—mostly those who joined the fracas without really knowing why and the poor merchants who told them the real culprit decamped and they should go after him.

As I scurried through a back passage, I felt a tug at my sleeve. I jerked away thinking I had been captured, but a voice said, "Iscariot, tonight. We want to see you tonight."

I spun around to face the fat man from the street, the recipient of my letters.

"Tonight?"

"Be at the crossing of the street leading from the old wall and the one with the potter's shop, just after the guard changes," he croaked and scuttled away before I could ask him any questions.

I knew the place. It was a short distance from the house where we were to eat that night. It would be easy to slip out and meet them without being noticed.

It had come at last, and it could not have come at a better time. Finally, I could deliver to Jesus the very thing he most needed but had not been able to acquire himself—power at the center. Finally, I would succeed with these men where I had failed with Barabbas. The events I had just left behind could have easily lost us their support, but we had succeeded. And set the stage for Jesus' confirmation as Messiah.

Chapter Forty-three

We gathered in the room supplied by Mark's family. It was large enough for the thirteen of us to dine and for the women and other guests to sit on benches placed behind us when they were not serving. As usual, the table was set with shorter surfaces along the east and west walls, the longer portion along the north. Lamps were placed around the room, and their light gave it a warm, golden glow. Dishes and bowls of food, bread, and oil for dipping, lamb, and herbs, and eggs were placed on the tables. I saw the appreciative looks on the others' faces as they entered and sensed the calming effect it had on them.

As a courtesy to our Essene host, we celebrated Passover with him and his family that night. Essenes insist on using the old calendar, which necessitated a dual celebration. I had no problem with the way things were done. I had grown accustomed to this practice at Qumran. In two more days, we would celebrate Passover again with the rest of the city.

We reclined on our couches, Jesus at the left-hand table with John to his immediate right. I took the place on his left hand, and the rest assembled along the walls. Peter positioned himself opposite Jesus so he could speak without having to crane his neck. He appeared to be very sore from this morning's tussle, and there were dark bruises on both sides of his face. Andrew grinned from ear to ear when I asked about them.

"He must have turned the other cheek," he laughed.

"Teacher," I said, and dipped a piece of bread into a bowl. He put his hand on mine.

"Wait."

I breached the first rule of etiquette that governs meals. I forgot. John gave me a look. Jesus said a blessing and then took the first bite.

"Now," he said with a hint of a smile.

"I will have to leave soon. There are still a few arrangements I must make."

"Stay with us for a while. There is not much time left." He raised his voice a little so everyone could hear him.

Who has received our message? And who has seen the strong arm of the Lord? He recited Isaiah, and then with infinite patience, told out the words of suffering, of rejection, and of the death that must follow.

The Son of Man, the anointed of God, will be handed over to the Gentiles. They will humiliate him and kill him, he continued, shifting to Zechariah.

We sat in stunned silence, unsure what to say. After a pause he said, "Listen, listen carefully and remember what I am about to tell to you."

He picked up a round of bread and broke it into smaller pieces. Then, he filled a bowl with the pieces. "This is my body offered up for you," he said and held it aloft for a moment. Next he filled a bowl with wine and even though it was good wine, I had seen to that, he added a bit of water. He prayed silently and then said, "This is my blood which will be shed for you and for the many, for forgiveness."

The room became very quiet. Jesus ate a piece of the bread and passed the bowl down the table. We each took a piece and ate. Then he sipped from the chalice and passed it, too. At a gesture from him, we each drank as well. When each of us had eaten a piece of bread and drunk from the cup of wine, he said, "Remember this night. Whenever you are together and I am not there with you, relive this moment, and in so doing, I will be among you."

"When will we not be with you, Master?" Peter asked. "We will never desert you."

"Ah, Peter, my brave fisherman, you don't know what you are saying. This very night one of you will hand me over."

Everyone looked startled and confused.

"Not by me," protested Peter.

"Peter, before the rooster announces sunup, you will deny ever knowing me at least three times, and the rest of you will scatter to the winds."

The room erupted as each declared his steadfastness to Jesus, but my thoughts were elsewhere. I heard the tramp of feet in the street and that meant the guard was changing and time for me to go. I rose from my couch.

"Master—"

"I know. You must leave us now. If we are not here when you return, you will find us in Gethsemane. So, now do what you must do, Judas."

I don't think anyone noticed me leaving. Before I went, I signaled to the young boy, Mark, to take my place at Jesus' left. His face lighted up like the sun. He had done much for us, and he deserved a chance to be there. I slipped out through a side door, on my way to meet the men who could change everything.

Chapter Forty-four

I stepped into the night and paused, letting my eyes adjust to the gloom. The feeble light from a few torches spaced irregularly along the street created a forest of sharp, menacing shadows. I heard the tramp of marching feet a street or two away. It must have rained. The streets reeked of damp masonry. I waited until I could safely make my way to the intersection where I was to meet the men. I could hardly contain myself, intoxicated at the prospect.

A moment later, I found the potter's shop. I experienced a moment of panic when I realized its proximity to the high priest's house. These men knew the streets—how could they misjudge our meeting place so badly? I peered into the shadows around me but saw no one. I must have arrived early. I strained to see a movement, some sign of life, then stepped back into the shadows. The sound of marching faded away. Only the muted voices of families at mealtime along with the aroma of roasted lamb and herbs wafted out of shuttered windows and down to me. After what seemed an eternity, figures appeared at the end of the street.

"Judas Iscariot?" one said in a low voice.

Before I could answer, a voice behind me said, "He is here."

I jerked around but could not make out where the voice came from. Had someone waited for me in the darkness? When the group drew closer, a figure separated from the shadows immediately at my right.

"Follow us," one said and walked away.

I wanted to ask questions, but their backs were to me and they walked quickly. I could barely keep up with them.

To my astonishment, they wheeled through Caiaphas' gate. I was too confused to be afraid. I hesitated and, too late, turned back toward the street to run. The man behind me stood in the torch's light—a temple guard. I spun back to face the others. Three official-looking men in long robes stared at me, their faces arranged in smug triumph. More guards stepped into the light. I felt a spear point in the small of my back, urging me forward through the gates and into the flickering light that defined a courtyard. There had been no mistake.

The guard steered me across the courtyard, into the house, down some stairs, and into a large hall. A dozen or more people milled around. I could not make out who they were. Suddenly, Joseph stood by my side. "They have baited a trap for you. Say nothing," he whispered.

I turned to ask him what he meant, but he had melted into the crowd. More lights were brought. Temple officials—the room was filled with them. Joseph belonged to the Sanhedrin. What had it to do with me, and what had become of the men I was supposed to meet? I looked around frantically, trying to find a familiar face or an escape route—anything. A man pounded his staff on the floor and the men sat.

Torches set in sconces and stands guttered, filling the room with shadows, the aroma of hot pitch, and peril. Two guards pushed me into the center of the room. I studied the faces surrounding me.

Somewhere in the darkness a door creaked open. A heavy man swept into the center of the room. Not fat, not heavy that way, but big all over, larger than life, big hands, arms, even his beard.

"Stand for the high priest," someone announced out of the shadows. The high priest, Caiaphas himself, stalked into the room.

After a pause, he took a seat at the center. Then he said, not quite looking at me, "You are Judas, sometimes called Iscariot?"

I stared at the man for a moment. I wanted to know what I had gotten myself into. "I am," I said. My voice shook and my heart pounded like the drums that led the legions into the city.

"A trusted follower of Jesus, the rabbi from Nazareth?"

"Yes, I suppose so."

"The man who preaches blasphemy and sedition, wouldn't you say, Judas Iscariot?"

"No, certainly not. He preaches only the true word."

"But that is not what is reported. That is not what these men heard about your rabbi. These are men of great learning and substance. They, better than you, are qualified to make judgments, and they agree, Rabbi Jesus is a blasphemer and a troublemaker."

I decided to take Joseph's advice and say nothing. What had gone wrong? One moment I stood at the verge of making the impossible happen and the next, in the middle of some sort of hearing, heading to disaster. What had I done?

"Judas Iscariot," Caiaphas shouted. "It is in your best interest to pay close attention to what we say here. There are serious charges being made against your teacher tonight, and a few of them by you." By me? What was he talking about?

"I make no charges. I would never accuse my master of anything."

"You deny then, you believe he is the Messiah, the anointed one of God?"

"It is no crime, High Priest," Joseph interrupted, "to claim Messiahship. Many do, many have done so in the past, and many will in the future."

"Yes, yes, I know that," Caiaphas said, annoyed. "But this one also thinks he *is* the Lord. Is that not so, Iscariot?"

"He never said so." He put me in a tight spot on that point. Peter's confession, while not as stunning to me then as it had once seemed, still needed to be reckoned with. It would not do to bring it up in that assembly.

"Ah, but he did, or at least implied it. He is a lawbreaker, a defiler of the Sabbath. He puts his hands on corpses, he touches women in their impurity, even lepers, and all this is clearly against the law Father Moses gave us…and many other things as well. You agree, Judas?"

"No, certainly not."

"No? But that is exceedingly strange. I was told those were the very charges you bring against him tonight. Am I mistaken in this?"

His eyebrows shot up in mock surprise, and he looked around the room. Then his expression darkened. He held out his left hand and a packet was placed in it. Still staring at me, he opened it and withdrew some papyrus sheets. My heart stopped. My blood ran as cold as a mountain spring.

"Do you recognize these letters?"

I said nothing. What could I say?

"These things of which I speak are all documented here."

How did he get his hands on those letters? They must have captured my correspondents as well. I looked wildly around the room. Then I saw him. My fat Pharisee lurked in the corner, looking pompous and pleased.

No group of supporters ever existed. In my vanity I had been deceived and blundered into the trap Joseph said they baited for me. In my entire life, Jesus was the only person I ever knew who believed in me, who trusted me, and who loved me. But my pride betrayed him to the very people I had hoped to defeat. I closed my eyes and thought of the bees.

Chapter Forty-five

I believed myself so much cleverer than everyone—the solitary wasp. I worked the miracles with the purse. I followed Jesus' teaching without explanation. I did. I looked at the sheets of papyrus in the dim flickering light. How could I have been so stupid?

"Iscariot, I asked you a question. Do you recognize these writings?"

For a fleeting moment I thought—lie, deny the letters, claim they were forgeries—the sort of thing I might have done in the past.

"Yes, they are by my hand." The men murmured and leaned forward in their chairs.

"So we can say this is your testimony, freely given to these men?"

I said nothing. He turned to the fat man. "Did you ask this man to write you?"

"I did."

"And did he do so willingly?"

"Yes, Excellency."

"Was he paid to write any of this?"

"No, Excellency."

"Was there any attempt on your part, to have him report anything but the truth?"

"No, Excellency."

"Judas, you have heard this good man's testimony. Do you dispute any of it?"

I hung my head. "No, it is as he says."

They had used me. They'd found the weak link. If I had been one of them, I would have done the same thing. I wrote only the truth, but truth in the hands of those who believe inspires; in the hands of those who do not, destroys. My words should have brought men to Jesus. Instead they condemned him.

"Some of us have not read this man's accusations," Joseph interjected. "It is improper to discuss this as testimony or evidence until we have."

"Of course, of course, but we are not holding a trial here. We are merely gathering information against the time when such a trial might be necessary."

Caiaphas' speech was as smooth and oily as a Greek wrestler. His heart existed in the world too much and in the temple too little.

"But now we have another problem. It seems someone has let it be known to the Roman officials that the instigator of the riot in the temple this morning is this very same Jesus. Is that also the truth, Judas Iscariot?"

I said nothing. "Come, come. You were there. You had a conversation afterwards with Ehud."

He pointed to the fat man. Until that moment, I did not know his name—Ehud, the left-handed judge.

"Ehud, is this the man you spoke to this morning at the money changers' booths?"

"Yes, Excellency, it is."

"So you were there, Judas?"

"Many were there."

I studied the floor. I dared not look at Joseph. Torches guttered and flickered. The room reeked of the resinous smoke and deceit. Mine or theirs?

"Yes, as you say, many were there including your master. Listen to me, Iscariot, it is one thing to march about the countryside proclaiming one the 'Son of the living God' and quite another to start a riot during the Passover when the prefect has made it clear any disturbance would be met with swift and awful punishment. You understand we must arrest him now."

I looked at Joseph. He must warn Jesus. He would not meet my eyes.

"Now then, will you take us to him?"

"No. I have done enough already. It is not what I intended. I thought I could gain support for him by writing. I thought the truth might persuade them to join us."

The room rocked with laughter. And I played the fool.

"Yes. We know what you thought. Understand this, we chose you because we deduced you would be the easiest to snare. The others, those Galilean fishermen, have families and friends, wives and children. They are the sons of Zebedee, Alphaeus, and men of note. They have people to ask for advice. They have histories. But you—you are different. You are solitary. You have no one to go to for counsel, do you? You do not because you cannot reveal who you really are. No, you are not one of them and never will be."

In one blinding moment I realized the awful truth—no matter how close I came to Jesus, I would always be an outsider, the wasp. My friends, if I had any, were Thomas, Mary Magdalene and, perhaps, Matthew. The fishermen only tolerated me.

"And we are uncertain if you belong anywhere. We can find no trace of you, Judas, son of...who?"

"Ceamon." I said loudly, and then regretted my outburst.

"Simon...precisely. Simon who? Simon son of...who? Judas, can you enlighten us?"

I said nothing.

"You see how it is. You have no history. In this country everyone has a history. Most people think they can trace their lineage back to Abraham—some to Adam. That is silly, of course, but you, you cannot trace it anywhere. Why is that, Judas, son of Simon?"

"I am of the Diaspora. I was brought up in Corinth." At least, it was partly true. And that line worked on the priests at Masad Hasidim.

"Corinth? Not Caesarea? Are you sure? I ask only because we received some reports when we sought to uncover your history, reports of a boy and his mother living in Caesarea. You would be about that boy's age, I think. A boy of uncertain parentage, I might add."

I felt a noose tightening around my neck. Try as I might, I could not escape my past.

"There is even a question about your claim to be a Jew."

"My claim to being a Jew is as good as yours to being a high priest, Sadducee," I said.

Anger flashed in his eyes. "Ah. The Jew of the Diaspora opines about the legitimacy of the Sanhedrin. How is that possible, I wonder? Did a well-known rabbi in some great city train you, Judas? Tell us his name. We might know him."

I felt like a fish in their net about to be hauled into the boat.

"What do you want from me?"

"Ah, at last, our poor Corinthian grasps the situation. All we ask is for you to take us to your master."

"I left him at dinner not three hundred paces from here. You know where he is. Why ask this of me?"

"Well, I might say, to make it clear who gave him up. But the truth is, he is no longer there."

"I can't take you to him." I tried again to catch Joseph's eye. He could warn Jesus. I could not, but he could.

"Cannot or will not?"

I remained silent. Caiaphas combed his beard with his thick fingers and contemplated me the way a snake contemplates a mouse.

"Tomorrow men will arrive from Caesarea. They will stop here. They have been following a boy—the one I spoke to you about—and his mother for many years. They almost caught him several times, they said, but in the end, the boy, now a man, managed to slip away. They seek the murderer of an important artist and scion of an influential family. You wouldn't know about that, would you, Judas son of Simon? One might expect to find him in the company of Barabbas. Indeed, at one point they thought the bandit of the wilderness might be that boy grown up. It turned out not to be so. But who would think to look for a murderer among the shabby band following the holy man from Nazareth?

"That boy, they say, had hair much like yours. Now that is an interesting coincidence, wouldn't you say? But we do not know that boy's name. Perhaps we will be told tomorrow."

It did not matter how Leonides came to have a knife stuck in his ribs. The whore and her bastard were to pay for it. Nothing changed. My nemesis had finally caught up with me.

"Do you think I should receive the deputation? Or should I send them away because you have decided to help us?"

"I have done too much already. Do what you will with me. I will not hand Jesus over to you."

"Very brave. I admire your loyalty, however misplaced. But you see, you must." He swiveled in his chair and faced the line of men on his left.

"Joseph, tell this misguided fool that his master is better off in our hands than the Romans'. We have our rules. Jesus is entitled to representation, his own witnesses, and as long as he is in our jurisdiction, the Romans will not act. But, if they find him first...you understand"

"He is right," Joseph said quietly and looked away.

At a gesture from Ehud, guards pushed me to the front. Was there no end to this humiliation?

"Iscariot, it is required your fee be paid." Fee? I knew of no fee. At a gesture from Annas, Ehud brought me a small purse— small but heavy.

"What is this for? Am I being rewarded for betraying the man I most admired in the world? I cannot take it."

No one answered.

There it was. Like my grandfather before me, I had presumed to know the mind of God. Before the Sabbath star rose, I would likely hang from a cross and Jesus would be disgraced.

Chapter Forty-six

Guards manhandled me back to the courtyard. A wind from the north brought cold air to the city. I shivered. I am not sure whether from the chill or fear. Less than four hours remained before dawn.

"Stay here. Your life and that of your rabbi depend on your cooperation and silence."

Ehud, sounding more and more like Caiaphas, had been assigned my keeper, and we would spend the next three days in each other's company, he gloating, me alternately disconsolate and angry. What function he performed in the ranks of the Sanhedrin's bureaucracy before, I did not know, only that he had contacted me initially. One of the guards saluted him. He looked pleased with himself.

There had to be a way to escape this nightmare. I could not, I would not, lead these men to Jesus. I racked my brain. If I could slip away somehow, if I could race ahead of these men into the dark. I could run to the garden and warn him. We could leave the city under the cover of darkness. Traveling at night through the wilderness carried substantial risks, but given the alternative…

I glanced at the gate not more than ten paces away. If I dashed out into the darkness, I could lose myself in the streets. I had eluded guards and officials all over the empire, a small benefit of my upbringing. I could still do it. I began edging toward the gate, slowly, so as not to attract attention. I covered half the distance when one of my guards stepped between it and me and grasped my arm.

"He said to stay, Galilean."

"Corinthian."

A small band assembled—three or four temple guards, Ehud, one of his associates, and some others I did not recognize. They carried torches, but only two were burning. The rest, pitch still fresh, would be ignited when they took Jesus. I mulled other escapes. Once through the gate, I thought, I could push my guard off balance and bolt. Two torches would make it impossible for them to see me, or where I went. I took a few deep breaths and tightened my sandals. I would only have one chance to do it, and I must be ready when it came.

Ehud led over another guard. This one was carrying a length of rope about ten cubits in length. One end was firmly knotted around my waist, the other around his. We were tethered. Perhaps I could make a great deal of noise and warn Jesus. Before the thought fully formed in my mind, a smirking Ehud faced me.

"If we must, we will gag you, blasphemer. You will give no warning. There is a contingent of Roman legionnaires with us as escort." Ehud's smirk pushed his jowls back toward his ears making him look like an officious pig. "At a word from me, they will take your rabbi. If you value his life, you will be silent and cooperate. Do you understand?"

We left the court. Ehud, my guard, and I led the way. The rest of the black robed officials and legionnaires straggled along at the rear. The soldiers grumbled among themselves. They harbored no affection for Jews in general, the Temple Party in particular, and resented being sent on a fool's errand. We turned and descended stone steps into the valley. Somewhere down there and to the north, Jesus and the others gathered, unaware of what I had done and what would soon to be visited on them. I felt sick.

With a jerk on my rope, the guard brought me back to the moment. We started down the steps. I offered him a bribe. I had their thirty pieces of silver, I could afford one, a large one.

He might have taken it except Ehud overheard me and to save face, the guard cuffed me behind the ear.

"Think about it," I whispered.

We trudged on. I put aside any thoughts of escape and turned instead to what I might do when we got to the valley floor. I still harbored the hope Joseph had sent a warning. When we reached the valley, I aimed to take them south, away from the garden and stall until dawn. Perhaps, by then, news might reach Jesus. Then I remembered the Romans searching for Jesus. Ehud stared at me as if he were reading my mind.

"Just lead us to him," he said. "For his own good, let us find him first."

Bereft of ideas and despairing, I decided to get it over with. I took them northward toward Gethsemane.

"Please don't be there," I prayed to myself. "Please be gone."

Chapter Forty-seven

Gethsemane—the oil press—was a newly planted olive grove. Because the cuttings were still green and tender, the owner of the plot did not allow pilgrims to camp there, so it remained largely deserted. When we arrived, the moon slid behind the western hills and the torches barely lighted our way. I did not know which way to turn. Jesus and the others could be anywhere. We stumbled up the slope toward its northern edge. I almost stepped on a sleeping Simon. Someone held up a torch and I saw most of the others scattered around on the turf, also asleep. I could not be sure how many there were. I did not see Jesus.

"Is he here?" Ehud whispered.

I shook my head and we moved on. The sleepers stirred. A few woke and sat up, confused and groggy. We moved on and they were swallowed up by darkness. Farther up the path, we stumbled onto Peter, James, and John, also asleep, but still no sign of Jesus. I had the irrational hope that somehow or for some reason, Jesus had left this place and his disciples behind. Surely he could sense a threat like this. A man who could raise the dead ought to be aware of threats. I stepped around a small clump of figs and came face to face with him. He had been praying, the dirt still on his face.

"That's him?" Ehud asked.

"Yes."

Ehud signaled for the other torches to be lighted, and suddenly the garden blazed as bright as day. I heard the grunts of men waking up, followed by angry and fearful shouts. The garden degenerated into mass confusion. Ehud gave me a push. I went to Jesus. Tears burned my cheeks. My legs shook so badly I nearly collapsed. I reached for his hand to kiss it.

"Rabbi…" My throat felt like it was filled with the hot sand from Arabia.

Jesus took in the scene behind me and then, in a very tired, but, I think, relieved voice, said, "Is it with a kiss, then, that I am to be handed over?"

"Master—"

"Do what you must do."

"Seize him," Ehud said.

The others, now awake, looked on in disbelief. In the next instant the area filled with sounds of shouting and pounding feet. Disciples rushed into the well of light as the guards reached for Jesus' arms. They surged toward us but were shoved back. Fists flew. I heard the crack of a club on someone's skull. Peter swung his short sword. One of the high priest's servants yelped, and there was blood all over his tunic.

"Enough. No more of this," Jesus shouted. Everyone, even fat Ehud, froze in place. We stood in that cold olive grove absolutely still, like a field of statuary or a scene from a play stopped in midaction—men with arms raised, clubs suspended in the air, dangerously close to skulls, knees, and backs.

"It is enough," Jesus said, this time quietly, and put his hand on the wounded man. He turned to Ehud.

"Why here? Why this way? I have been teaching in the temple for days. I have been out and about in the city and in plain sight. I never tried to hide myself from you, nor have I ever evaded your questions. You corrupted my friend with your lies to bring us to this end, but you could have asked anyone where I might be found and arrested me at any time. Yet, here you are skulking about in the dark. You came for me in stealth and in the small hours of the morning because when darkness is at its deepest, that is when evil flourishes. And so the dark, not the light, is your preference, is it not?"

Ehud was momentarily flustered by this scolding but then his expression hardened. "I need no sermon from you, Rabbi. We have heard quite enough of your blasphemy."

The others, seeing no hope, no chance of rescue, drifted into the night. The guards bound Jesus, and the two of us were led away. I looked for the legionnaires, but they were nowhere in sight. Sometime during our march Ehud must have sent them away. I suppose he did not want to risk losing his prize to them, even by accident.

As we exited the grove, the rope still firmly around my waist, I sensed, rather than saw, the figure lurking near the bole of one of the larger trees. I did not need to look. I knew her as surely as if she stood in the middle of the path.

"Is it you?" the Magdalan murmured.

I wanted the earth to swallow me. I felt her eyes piercing the shadows, piercing my soul. I said nothing.

"Oh, Judas, what have you done?"

Chapter Forty-eight

Nothing stirred in the courtyard when we returned. Only five guards remained. They dragged us down several flights of stairs to a dungeon. When we reached the top of the last set of stairs, one of the guards untied Jesus and then, with no warning, gave him a shove. He tumbled down to the bottom. He managed to get his hands and arms out to break his fall. The guards laughed.

My guard said, "You next," and before I could catch his meaning, I catapulted down the steps as well. Unfortunately, he forgot the tether that still bound us together. I grabbed the length of rope, more out of an instinctive attempt to keep my balance than with any idea it could have another result. As I extended the distance between us to about a body length, he left his feet and tumbled down the steps behind me. His head hit the corner of the bottom step making a noise like a melon hitting the ground. I hurt but nothing seemed broken. I untied the tether and moved away from the prostrate guard. His friends guffawed and walked down the steps. They nudged him with their feet and poked him with the butts of their spears in an attempt to wake him, but he didn't move. Finally, they propped him up in a corner, arranged his spear in his hand, and posed him in a watchful position. Then, with more laughter, they moved away.

Jesus managed to get to his feet, but I could see he had been hurt. I started to go to him but one of the guards stopped me.

"Oh, no you don't," he said. He looked as mean and vicious as anyone I had ever seen, and that included Barabbas, who up to that point in my life, defined meanness. Not much to choose from between the two camps, I thought. They deserved each other.

He pushed me into a cubicle. A chain secured in the wall with a shackle at its end was fastened to my ankle. A stout wooden grate sealed the entry. The four guards then shoved Jesus to the end of the corridor to what I supposed would be his cell. By leaning forward and sideways, I could see most of what happened.

There is something that takes over men at the mercy of layer upon layer of superiors. In those rare instances when they find themselves in positions of power, however slight, they become monsters. They have no place to take out their rage and frustration except on the helpless and, in this case, prisoners. Those low men had Jesus, and he became the focus of all their anger and hatred. One of them struck Jesus on the shoulder while his back was turned.

"You are a prophet, so prophesy who hit you." The other three howled their approval. Jesus turned to face them.

"We heard you preach to the yokels that if someone hit them in the face they should turn the other cheek." With that he balled his fist and hit Jesus in the cheek as hard as he could. Jesus crashed against the wall and sank to his knees. In a moment, he staggered to his feet and faced them again.

"Well, here's one for the other cheek," another guard sneered, and he struck him on the other side. I yelled at them—cursed at them. One of them told me to be quiet or I would be next.

They pushed and pummeled Jesus back and forth between them the way bullies will. They spit on him, slapped him, and called him names. He never raised a hand to protect himself, never tried to strike back, as I supposed they hoped he would. It would have excused their brutality.

I glanced back at my guard. The light was too poor for me to be sure, but he seemed deathly pale and blood trickled from his ear. I called the other guards. They only glanced my way and then returned to their sport. Finally, frustrated with his lack of response, they took up the stiff laths used to flog prisoners and proceeded to beat him. Fortunately, those instruments create more noise than physical damage. After a while, their arms weary, they stopped and shoved Jesus into his cell.

"Sleep, if you can," one of them rasped. "We'll be back."

A sliver of daylight crept down the steps and into the dungeon. The cock outside in the courtyard announced a new dawn. I thought about Peter. Had he fulfilled the prediction and betrayed Jesus, too? The last I saw of any of them were shadows fleeing in the darkness. What had become of Mary? Finally, exhausted, I collapsed into a fitful sleep.

Chapter Forty-nine

Sunlight. A small beam streamed through a narrow slit window and teased my eyes. I stretched and winced. It was the first hour of the fourth day of the week, and my tormenters waited. The rooster quieted, his crowing replaced by the noisy comings and goings in the household. Cookware clattered. Voices and footsteps echoed from the several levels that made up the house. I smelled cooking. I had not eaten since early the night before.

At the top of the steps, hasps rasped and latches clanked. The guards, asleep at their posts, staggered to their feet, rubbing the sand out of their eyes—all except the one who accompanied me down the steps. He remained exactly as his companions had left him. Ehud and four men, clad in the now familiar black robes favored by lesser temple officials, descended into the chamber. They stopped and Ehud glowered at the rigid guard outside my cell.

"What is the matter with this man?" he snapped. The other guards straightened up and saluted.

"He fell," one said, and looked to his companions for support.

"I think he is hurt, Excellency," another added. The other two nodded their agreement.

"Well, get him up."

Two rushed over to wake their companion. One nudged him gently on the shoulder. He crashed to the floor, still in the sitting position. His spear clattered to one side. His shield rolled away and settled in a series of ringing loops on the paving stones. The poor man was stiff as a board. Ehud stared disgustedly at the sight of his dead guard.

"Get rid of him," he snarled.

They dragged the unfortunate guard away. His heels thumped on the steps as his two friends pulled him out of sight. Ehud pointed toward me.

"Take this man to the outer court. See that he has water to bathe in, a clean robe if you can find one, and something to eat. Do not let him out of your sight. Have him ready to travel in an hour."

My chains were removed. The guards, seeing I was now the object of some courtesy, underwent a change of attitude. They took me up the stairs to the courtyard where I washed in a basin of murky water. A guard handed me clothing, a tunic, and a cloak. They were made of coarse linen and scratched, but at least they were clean. I was grateful for that. A guard brought me a bowl of tasteless porridge. It filled and warmed me and I started to feel a little better. I chanted a verse or two from one of the few Psalms I knew by heart.

Let your love and your kindnesses come to me in the morning, for in you have I put my trust. Show me the road I must follow, I lift my soul up to you. Deliver me from my enemies, O Lord…

If I thought about it rationally, I had no real prospects, but I always began my day in hope, a habit that sustained me over the years. Even though the men from Caesarea would be arriving that afternoon to seal my fate, a new day had begun and I believed anything could happen. I had been in tighter spots than this and managed to wiggle out. I wondered what would happen to Jesus. I did not see how anything, other than his beating, was likely. Passover limited their options. And who knew… perhaps the burly Peter and the clever Simon with his Zealot friends might find a way to free him. The day had barely begun and hope, however fragile, bloomed.

Against that, dark scudding clouds defeated the sun's attempt to brighten and warm the day. Ehud reappeared and beckoned to the guards, who shoved me in his direction. I took a deep breath, assumed it might well be one of my last, and followed them through the gate and up the hill toward the city. I had no idea where we were going or why, but I savored every minute of what I believed were the last moments I had on earth.

The great hall of the Sanhedrin stood a short distance from the temple. It was not a place anyone in control of his senses would choose to visit. Trials were held there, and, even though the Sanhedrin no longer had the authority to hand down a death penalty, it remained a place ordinary men and women shunned.

The hall had a high vaulted ceiling, more Roman than Herodian, supported in part by two rows of thick stone pillars that ran the length of both sides of the room. Two high-backed chairs had been placed a pace or two from the back wall in the center facing the entryway. The wall behind them rose into the gloom of the ceiling. A round window filled with what appeared to be colored stones was set in its face. Smaller chairs were arranged along the sides and in front of the columns, a score or more on either side. Behind them, stools and benches were drawn up in no particular order. More benches and stools filled the area on either side of the massive cedar doors. The space smelled of damp and people up too early to have washed properly. Ehud's deputies led me in. The room filled as important-looking people wandered in, spoke with one another, or sat. A few stared at me. I recognized one or two from the previous night. All of them wore ceremonial robes. The High Priest had called the Sanhedrin into session.

I tried to read faces. It occurred to me that if I had any talent at divining thoughts by such study, I should exercise it now. A group stood together and passed papyrus sheets back and forth—my letters. Some turned and glared at me. Most seemed puzzled, by what, I could not tell. Either they did not see the harm in the letters, or they simply did not understand them.

I trudged to the front of the hall and was made to sit on a bench against the sidewall. The large chairs were directly in front of me facing down the hall's length. From where I sat, I could see whoever occupied them. If I leaned forward, I could see the entire row of chairs opposite, and if I leaned back, I could see along the wall as far as the stools and benches near the doors on my side of the room. Guards stood at my right and left.

I tried to recall what the law said about turning a Jew over to Gentiles. The law required the circumstances to be extreme. The thought depressed me. Murder qualifies as extreme, and they had already convicted me of that.

Chapter Fifty

The Sanhedrin and their assorted lieutenants, aides, acolytes, and attendants filled the room. The latter took positions behind in the rows of chairs and stood or sat. A clapper sounded and Caiaphas entered. His entourage processed behind him. I saw Ehud among them and another, older man, whose dress matched that of the high priest.

"Who's the old man?" I whispered to one of my guards.

"Annas," he hissed, "the high priest before Caiaphas."

If Caiaphas felt he needed to drag along his predecessor, then what would come next must be important. The clapper sounded again and everyone sat. I leaned back and discovered the area beside the doors had filled with men. They were not members, and I wondered who they were and why they were there. I leaned forward and saw the whole of the entry had filled with people.

I knew I had missed the significance of the day. They were not interested in me. Whatever Caiaphas and his party knew or thought they knew about Leonides and Caesarea, I was not on today's agenda. They had bigger fish to fry.

Caiaphas clapped his hands and the assemblage intoned their prayers. In the midst of that holy cacophony, some temple attendants entered and lighted two large braziers on either side of the main chairs. The room brightened and filled with the fragrance of incense. Caiaphas called them to order. He explained that their purpose was to hear charges brought against a particular rabbi. He did not mention Jesus by name but everyone in the room knew which rabbi he meant. He said the charges included blasphemy and sedition and required swift action on the part of the Sanhedrin. He droned on reciting bits of scripture, precedents, and bits of personal experience, which he believed relevant. When he finished, he turned to Annas and invited him to continue.

Annas, a shorter, grayer version of Caiaphas, took even more time to elaborate. If they proposed to bring about swift action, they needed to step up the cadence. I leaned back and tried to figure out why I had been dragged here—to what purpose? Joseph stood and was recognized.

"Excellencies, am I to understand you are proposing we try this man, and if so, on what charges? I read this so-called testimony, and I find no cause for action. Furthermore, we have procedures we must follow. It is not permitted to hold a trial in this manner." Nicodemas, on his left, leaned toward him, and said something. They nodded in agreement.

"Joseph of Arimathea, we are aware of your affection for Jesus of Nazareth. Indeed, there are many who share your enthusiasm, even though he attacks the very foundations of our life and, I should add, your position. But, we will not presume to have a trial. Call it an investigation, a hearing, a preliminary gathering of information that may allow us to proceed in an orderly fashion later, should one be necessary."

Joseph stood again. "But what precedents have we for such an action? I am aware of none. This whole gathering and what you propose to do is contrary to our law and custom."

"Joseph makes a valid point," Annas said, and looked at the other members seated along the rows of pillars. "We do not wish to seem out of order. But there is some urgency. And, to be sure no advantage will be taken of this rabbi or anyone else," he glanced in my direction, "we invited the people you see at the end of the hall to bear witness to our fairness and openness of purpose."

I studied the man carefully. He was up to something and it had nothing to do with fairness or openness of purpose. I shifted my gaze to Caiaphas. I could not be sure, but I believe a smirk lurked somewhere in his carefully combed beard. They played with these men. They knew what they wanted, and they would have it and make the Sanhedrin complicit in it. Except for Joseph and Nicodemas, the expressions on the faces of the men ranged from agreeable to stupefied.

Nicodemas took a turn. "Excellencies, I inspected the writings, and even if we put the worst face on them, there is nothing here remotely libelous, much less blasphemous. I pray you call off this gathering, and let us be about the business God calls us to."

"We are respectful of the thoughts expressed by our colleague, Nicodemas. You may be right in what you say. An hour or two at the most is all we require. Then, if there is nothing, as you say, we can release the prisoner—" Annas said, through drooping lids.

"—into the hands of the Romans." Caiaphas finished for him. "The riot, you recall…most unfortunate, but we have no choice in the matter."

Duplicity. If Jesus did not answer to them here, he must answer to Rome there. I looked around, craning my neck to see if anyone else caught his drift. Joseph sucked in his breath. He knew the lengths the Romans would go to make an example of those who defied them or even annoyed them, indifferent to any distinction between the two.

I leaned forward a bit more. I could see all the way into the far corner of the room where the "witnesses" were seated. One raised his head for a moment as though he had an important thought. It was John. He must have used his rabbinical connections to get in. I jerked my head back, out of his line of sight.

"Annas," Joseph said through his teeth, ignoring the niceties of address, "You are right. My apologies to you and to the High Priest. A hearing would benefit us all. I suggest further…" he said slowly, as if thinking aloud, "I suggest we reserve this day for some, as you so nicely put it, preliminary inquiries and then tomorrow, we can all study the evidence and be in a better position to make a just determination."

Joseph understood Passover would soon overtake events and after that, the Sabbath. The following day, Pilate would be on his way back to Caesarea, pilgrims would stream home, and order restored. No one would remember or care about the melee in the temple. The case against Jesus would collapse and he would be free to continue his work.

The High Priests and Joseph and Nicodemas were joined in a contest like soldiers casting stones on the pavement, playing the king's game. Only in this version, the king was Jesus. One side wanted him destroyed, the other wanted him saved. I studied Caiaphas and Annas closely, saw the looks they exchanged, and concluded Joseph and Nicodemas were no match for those two foxes. I watched as the first stones were cast.

"Well, let us see how this will unfold," said Caiaphas, his tone conciliatory, but his eyes sly.

Chapter Fifty-one

It never ceases to amaze me the lengths people will go to defame one another if they are paid enough, are ignorant enough, or angry enough. Because he held a hearing, not a trial, a distinction Caiaphas reminded us of frequently, the rules of evidence and procedure did not apply. Anyone could say anything without fearing the serious penalties that accrue if caught breaching the commandment about bearing false witness. For hours we listened to accusations from men whose contact with Jesus had been negligible or nonexistent. The high priests must have recruited them to bolster their case against Jesus. One declared he heard Jesus conversing with Satan. Joseph asked him when he overheard the conversation and the man gave a date and time when Jesus would have been one or two years old. He was dismissed. Another swore Jesus plotted with bandits to burn down the temple. But the man who brought the charge could not provide a time or date or corroborating witnesses. I heard three more variations on how Jesus threatened to destroy the temple. After a while, it became clear many were willing to tell the Sanhedrin anything it wanted to hear, but even the worst of the accusations did not warrant a trial, much less, punishment.

Caiaphas remained patient. He had time on his side, while Joseph wrestled with a dilemma. If he succeeded in having Jesus released too soon, he faced the possibility of swift and terrible Roman retribution. If he let this hearing drag on, sooner or later, someone could come forward with a story sufficiently damning to bring Jesus down.

"High priest," he said, "this is getting us nowhere. Half these stories are preposterous and the rest, inconsequential. I suggest we adjourn for the day and study what we have learned and return to this tomorrow."

Caiaphas frowned and then nodded his head. "It is the sixth hour. We will recess for an hour so that those who need to eat and those of us with other duties may see to them. When we return, we will hear from Jesus himself. Perhaps then we can consider Joseph's suggestion."

Joseph started to say something but the clapper sounded and everyone stood. Caiaphas dismissed the assembly with a wave of his hand. I stood, too, but my guards pushed me back. I stayed in that dreary, ornate room. A crust of bread, some water, and a bowl of boiled beans served as my mid-day meal. Outside, the sky hung gray and ominous over the city, which matched my mood exactly. The hope that started my day blew away with the clouds. Annas and Caiaphas moved slowly but inexorably toward a goal they shared but had not revealed. Whatever they were up to, one sure thing emerged: Jesus would not survive the inquiry and probably not the day.

The clapper's racketing woke me. I had slept very little the night before, and fatigue finally caught up with me. I slumped over on my bench, back against the cold, stone wall. Ehud, Annas, and Caiaphas had their heads together. They looked calm and in control. The hearing must be progressing to their liking. They glanced in my direction from time to time and then, a decision made, they nodded and took their seats. Everyone's eyes were on the doors, expecting Jesus to be ushered in at any moment. I leaned forward again to locate Joseph. He whispered heatedly with another member of the Sanhedrin. Nicodemas nodded his head in agreement. Joseph seemed to be lining up support. The clapper rattled a second time and everyone quieted down.

Annas stepped forward and announced, "The man, Jesus of Nazareth, will be here soon. Before we hear from him, however, we need to call another witness." He signaled my guards who pulled me out into the center of the room facing the priests.

"This is Judas, known as Iscariot. He has produced irrefutable testimony against Jesus." He waved the sheets around for all to see. Every eye in the room bore into my back. I felt the blood rush to my face.

"Judas, do you deny you are the author of these documents?"

"No."

"You affirm before this assembly that everything you have written here is the truth as the God of Abraham is your witness."

"It is not permitted to swear such an oath," I declared, with some boldness, I thought.

"Yes, yes...But you will certify that all...all you have written here is the truth, is that so?"

"Yes."

"And you gave this testimony of your own free will, there were no inducements made by anyone in this room?"

"No, but it was never intended to be testimony, I—"

"Simply answer when you are addressed. We are not interested in hearing your commentary."

"But—"

"This man," Caiaphas announced in a voice loud enough to be heard in the farthest reaches of the room, "is a close associate of Rabbi Jesus. He may be his most trusted disciple. He has been with him for many years. You can give credence to anything he says. We have his testimony and it reveals Rabbi Jesus as a blasphemer and an inciter of riots."

The crowd stirred, muttered, and shuffled their feet. They heard real evidence for the first time. My guards spun me around to face them.

"This is the man who had the courage to come forward and report these things to us so no harm can fall on the nation," he continued, ignoring my protest.

Except for the members of the Sanhedrin, and perhaps not all of them, no one had read what I had written. For all these people knew, I betrayed Jesus with accusations of such magnitude they should be overjoyed at the fortuitous capture of so dangerous a heretic.

I looked into the corner where I saw John earlier. I hoped he had not returned after the morning recess. I hoped in vain. His eyes blazed. He gave me a look of such utter contempt I flinched as if struck. Even though it made no difference—I would be dead before the Sabbath and would never be in his company again—the burden of his contempt crushed me. The others would soon hear how the deed was done and I would become the object of their enmity forever.

As I listened to Caiaphas, I swore there must be two of me in the room. The misguided and foolish spectator to the proceedings, listening and wondering how it came to be, a boy who became a man in the mean streets of the empire, the man who came to his homeland dreaming of killing oppressors, of wreaking havoc on the empire, its leaders, and bringing it crashing down. But who, instead, ended serving a man of peace. The other Judas—Caiaphas' creation—had betrayed his master. At that moment I realized that no one would ever know the former. If I were remembered at all, it would be as the traitor.

Finally, my agony ended and I returned to my bench and out of sight. I pressed back against the wall. Until that moment, I harbored thoughts, however irrational, of escape, of finding a side door or a careless guard, and somehow getting away. After being presented to the gathered masses, I prayed, instead, for a quick and merciful death.

Chapter Fifty-two

The doors swung open. Witnesses stirred and turned their heads. I leaned forward. At first I saw nothing. Then I saw him. He wore a clean tunic and a cloak of white linen. The cloak hung loosely over his shoulder, one end across his forearm. As he drew nearer, I could see bruises on both cheeks. He looked pale and gaunt. His eyes never strayed right or left. He moved slowly toward the high priests. His stature and the combination of his thin ravaged face, white garments, and onyx eyes staring straight ahead made him appear taller, more arresting, apocalyptic. He moved with such grace, he seemed to float. The hall became eerily silent, every eye on him. The only sound in the room was the soft padding of Jesus' sandals on the tiled floor. I watched his prosecutors. As Jesus advanced, they retreated deeper into their chairs.

He stopped in the center of the room. The silence lasted a moment and then a low hum, which slowly grew louder, replaced it. Annas regained his composure and raised his arm. The room quieted. He stood. His hand fiddled with a large amulet hanging from the gold chain around his neck.

"You are Jesus of Nazareth?"

"I am."

"You are accused of serious crimes and breaches of the law—accusations that might cause this assembly to bring charges against you—serious charges. Do you understand?"

Jesus said nothing.

"Have you nothing to say? Do you have any idea about the testimony they brought? They charge you with sedition. They say you threatened to destroy the temple, that you ridiculed the Sanhedrin. Your own disciple has testified…" he waved in my direction.

Still, Jesus said nothing.

"They say that by words and signs you declare yourself the Anointed One, the Messiah, and you even claim to be the son of the Blessed One." Jesus remained silent. Exasperated, face red, Annas shouted, "Well, are you? Are you? Do you make such a claim?"

"Yes. It is as you say," Jesus said.

What happened next, I will take to my grave. When Jesus said "yes," the window high on the wall behind the High Priests suddenly burst into color. What I took to be varicolored stones turned out to be chunks of Roman glass which seemed to capture the sun itself. Brilliant points of ruby, citrine, and sapphire glowed and swelled in intensity. The points merged and blended and streamed down like honey from a comb, down in a beam of pure gold. It all happened in an instant, but for me and those who witnessed it, the moment seemed elongated in time. My eyes followed the light. It pooled around Jesus and his raiment blazed, the white linen transformed into holy fire. Everyone in the room sat transfixed. Later, those not there and those who follow the cynics and skeptics would say, "Oh, well, the sun just came out from behind a cloud." But we, who witnessed it, knew better. We had seen the hand of God.

Annas sat down heavily. A low moan filled the room, the exhaling of a hundred throats. I remembered the angry man's words.

Rabbi Jesus, just who do you think you are, God?

Caiaphas broke the silence. "So you are the Messiah? You are, as you claim, the Son of God?"

"I am, and hear this: The day will come when you may see the Son of Man sitting at the right hand of the Mighty One and coming on the clouds of heaven."

No one dared speak. If any doubt still lingered in anyone's mind as to who or what Jesus claimed to be, it vanished in that moment. Many in the back of the room fled. Caiaphas grabbed the front of his robe and tore it.

"We do not need to hear anything more. Take him away."

The guards seized Jesus by the arms and trundled him out of the room. As Jesus disappeared, the light faded as well.

The spectators had served their purpose and were ordered out. The doors thumped shut behind them. Only the Sanhedrin, a few of their lackeys, and the high priests remained. Caiaphas, his expression grave and worried, walked slowly to the center of the hall. He pivoted around and then, with a sweeping look that managed to encompass everyone, began the speech everyone expected.

"You see the difficulties we have with this case. This Jesus is a charismatic leader who daily gathers followers from the countryside. Is that a bad thing? Of course not. Leaders who teach obedience to the Law, who draw people closer to the Way and the Truth, are to be commended. We have many fine rabbis who do this. But this Jesus…well, even the good Joseph of Arimathea must concede that the words we all heard and the events we witnessed here raise serious concerns for those of us entrusted with Aaron's legacy. Wouldn't you agree, Joseph?"

Joseph started to say something and then shook his head.

"Serious concerns, grave concerns, and we must deal with them. As I see it, this is our position: First, we are part of the *pax romana* whether we like it or not. No one but a fool believes we will lift that yoke anytime soon."

Caiaphas swiveled around the room, his gaze leveled at everyone. Heads nodded.

"We are given leave by our overlords to practice our faith as our fathers and their fathers have. We continue our sacrifices, our feasts, and our worship. We enforce our own laws. These conquerors from the west maintain the roads, keep the peace, and protect us. For this, they collect taxes and extract tribute.

It is not a situation we like or wish to continue. But the reality is, they are here and they will be here for a long time.

"It is wholly within their power to crush us like eggs if they wish. We have all witnessed their willingness to strike out for even the most trivial cause. Now, along comes this misguided man, besotted with Messianic zeal, who starts a riot not fifty cubits from where I stand. He threatens to bring the temple down. It says right here," he continued, waving one of my letters in the air, "right here, 'Not one stone will stand on another!' He makes a mockery of the prefect by entering the city riding on an ass with a reed for a scepter. To make matters worse, hundreds join him in this foolishness.

"How long do you suppose the Romans will put up with this? They have little patience with acts of disrespect and none with civil unrest. We all know from painful experience what Pilate is capable of. His reputation for cruelty is known throughout the empire. Even now blood stains the temple pavement, spilled by him. But as great a threat as that is, there is an even greater one we must address."

Caiaphas paused, letting his words sink in. The room hushed. I looked at a very different Caiaphas, no longer the smarmy poseur of the previous hours. He sighed, his expression deadly serious.

"There is the matter of blasphemy. Oh, I know what has been said already, 'It is not unlawful to claim to be a messiah' and you are right. In the past, many have, some do now, and, no doubt, many will in the future. But this man is no ordinary prophet claiming to speak for the Lord. No, he claims to speak *as* the Lord. When he says he is his son, he does not mean, as we do, we are all children of the Creator, he means His son—literally.

"As more and more are drawn into his web, I fear the Lord's swift retribution will become a certainty. You can appreciate, then, the grave position we are in. Our entire nation is at risk, either from the retribution of Rome or of the Lord. Either would be terrible—both will spell the end of us as a people.

"Is it not better, then, that this one man should die, than the whole nation suffer?"

As Caiaphas spoke, men leaned forward in their chairs and, one by one, nodded. Only Joseph shook his head, but with more "yes" than "no." It seemed the high priest had won the day. The room remained hushed.

One man sitting at the far end of the hall said, "But 'that this one man should die…' Even if we find him guilty of all the things he is charged with at a trial, we may not condemn him to death, high priest." Others agreed and looked worried.

"Yes, yes, I know. But you do agree, do you not, it would be appropriate, *if* we could?"

Most of them nodded. Joseph looked stricken.

"But a trial, Caiaphas. We must have a trial. We have our rules to maintain, even if, as you say, we only have them on sufferance, because the Romans let us. Still, we must keep to them."

Caiaphas only shrugged. "What must be—must be."

Within the hour, I imagined, I would be handed over to Leonides' people, and who knew what death they planned for me. I did not object to dying for betraying Jesus. That would be just, but not for the cold-blooded assassination of a foolish sculptor by a ruthless official. I bowed my head.

My guards returned and led me away, I supposed, for the long walk to the Antonia Fortress. Instead, they led me back to my cubicle in the basement of Caiaphas' house. Why? Ehud would not say. He only smiled.

"We are not yet done with you, Iscariot."

Chapter Fifty-three

As on the previous day, the sun and Ehud arrived early. He had me taken to the courtyard. I received the same tasteless paste in the same wooden bowl. I washed and tended to my needs. Then, in less than an hour, Ehud and two guards led me away. Again we climbed upward toward the temple. It was the fifth day, Passover, as reckoned by everyone but the Essenes, and only a week since I had arrived in the city. It felt like a month.

A breeze carried the scent of burning flesh. The morning's ritual sacrifices had begun. We climbed the temple Mount using the bridge at its southern end and walked northward through its vast courtyards which, even at that early hour, were filled with pilgrims. A few, heads covered with ritual shawls, foreheads studded with phylacteries, marked our passage, but most ignored us, their thoughts undoubtedly on more sublime matters than the passage of one murderer-traitor and his escort.

We passed by the porches. There could be no mistake this time. We headed straight to the Antonia Fortress. We climbed its long flight of steps. Massive cedar doors faced the floor of the mount. One had a smaller entry set in it. Ehud rapped. A moment later, a legionnaire peered out. Ehud signaled me to step in as the temple guards gave me one last shove. The legionnaire stepped out of the shadows, gave the temple guards a disdainful look, gestured for them to stand back, and slammed the door in their faces.

"Watch this man. He is a wanted criminal," Ehud said, and disappeared down a dark corridor into the depths of the building. The legionnaire escorted me to a small side room. Soldiers, crouched in the corner, cast stones and cursed the gods for their bad luck. They scarcely glanced in my direction. I counted four of them, three playing the game and an older man at a table, his armor in a disorderly pile next to him. He wore his helmet shoved back on his head. His arm moved steadily up and down as he honed his sword. The sharpening stone sang against the iron. Occasionally, he tested the edge and then rubbed some more. I waited. The thought of escape never crossed my mind.

Ehud returned with two men. I heard their voices as they approached. They spoke alternately in Greek and, I think, Latin.

"Light!" one of them barked.

The soldiers kicked their game pieces under a bench and lighted a torch. The new arrivals wore the shorter toga preferred by Roman officials. The first was blonde and stocky, the second lean and tense, his face dark, dangerous, and pockmarked. Even while standing still, hands on his hips, he looked ready to leap into action. His eyes were hazel, golden. My heart pounded and I had to strain to breathe. I knew that face. I had seen him earlier in the week, as I stood in the street, a branch of fragrant balsam in hand, watching him ride into the city. I thought then that he looked familiar. But in that room, in the flickering torchlight, twenty years slipped away. The memory had seared my mind like a slave's brand. I stared at the dark dangerous man who murdered Leonides, raped Mother, and destroyed Dinah.

He whirled around the room, spotted Ehud, and snapped, "Well. Where are they? I haven't all day to waste on your nonsensical petty disputes. Where's the idiot Caiaphas and his case?"

I thought, "Here, I'm here." But even if I wanted to, I could not make a sound. My throat clamped shut. I only managed a squeak which went unheard. Just then the large doors swung open and Caiaphas stood outside, Jesus behind him, hands tied at his waist and a rope around his neck, like a sheep being led to slaughter. A clutch of functionaries, guards, and others who had some official position or who were simply curious, bunched up behind, craning their necks.

"Here is the high priest and the man we need you to judge," Ehud said, and pointed to Jesus.

I shrank back against the wall and tried to be invisible.

"Honorable Pilate," Caiaphas began. "I bring you a matter of great concern that requires your immediate attention. This man represents a clear and present danger to the peace and order of our city."

"What has he done?" Pilate said, his foot tapping the floor.

"He threatened the temple, caused a riot, and—"

"Riot? I know of no riot. Centurion, have you heard of a riot?" Without looking at him, Pilate addressed a Roman soldier somewhere in the relative gloom behind me.

"In their temple, Prefect. Two days ago, this man started a riot in the area reserved for their moneychangers."

"Oh, that."

"Excellency, there is more—" Caiaphas began.

"Fine. As you wish," Pilate said. "Guards, nail him up. Is that all?"

"Yes, Excellency, you understand my position? I would not, except under extreme circumstances, hand this man over to you. To do so is a serious breach of our custom and some of my more militant brothers might even say—"

"I understand perfectly. Your laws foolishly allow you to betray one another to each other, but you may not turn any of your people over to me. But now you need the power only I possess, and so here you are. Never fear, high priest, no one will ever know what we do here. We will accept these are 'extreme circumstances'; or would you prefer you were never here at all? Guard, take this man out."

"A moment." The other man, Pilate's companion, spoke.

"Rufus?"

"Pilate, I beg you, stay that order for a moment, at least until we can have a word."

Pilate signaled the soldiers to wait, much to their apparent disappointment, and walked away with his colleague, away from the door, toward where I crouched in the shadows against the wall.

"Do not crucify this man," the man called Rufus murmured. "I have important information I must share with you first."

"Information? What sort of information is so critical I must delay the solution of one more pathetic little problem? This is of no consequence." Pilate had difficulty keeping his voice down.

"You would crucify this man without a hearing?"

"I do it all the time. It's not like these people are citizens or even civilized for that matter."

"As a favor to me and because of our long-standing friendship, delay this for now."

Pilate shrugged, sighed, and returned to the doorway.

"Caiaphas, what sort of man have we here? Why are you in such a hurry to see him put to death?"

"He is a Galilean who presents himself as a king, as a rival to Caesar."

Pilate burst out laughing. The soldiers joined in.

"Does he indeed? What a novelty. But, if he is a Galilean, he is not in my jurisdiction. He belongs to Antipas. Take him to your little Herod. If that nitwit can't help you, then bring him back to me."

Caiaphas started to protest, but Pilate ordered the doors closed in his face.

Chapter Fifty-four

Half light returned to the rooms as the great doors closed against the sun. Pilate passed by me and then stopped.

"Who's this?"

"An important witness. He will testify to the riot yesterday and on other matters," Ehud said.

"Very well. You…" The old soldier leapt to his feet.

"Prefect?"

"Watch this man. If he gets away, you, and not the Galilean king, will die." And with the words trailing over his shoulders, he strode away, his colleague close on his heels. I was dumbfounded. What else could possibly happen? The old man was staring at me.

"You all right?" he asked.

"Is there a privy I can use?" I had an urgent need of one.

"*Latrina*? Go through that portal and down the steps. You can only get in and out through that door, son. Don't be long," he laughed.

The privy was a marvel. A long trough ran the length of the room. At one end, perhaps half of the full length, marble slabs had been laid over the trough to make a box-like enclosure. Slots were cut through the vertical face that joined those on the horizontal, which then opened into smooth holes that enabled one to sit. Water ran through the trough cleaning it constantly—a practical benefit of Pilate's aqueduct.

I inspected the room carefully. Narrow horizontal windows pierced the walls where they met the ceiling. I stood on the lip of the trough and could just make out the walls of a building opposite and hear the noise from the street below. I could not squeeze through them if I wanted to. Smaller openings pierced the inner walls as well. They must have been designed to aid in circulating air. I walked the length of the room, inspecting the writing scratched on the wall. I could not decipher the Latin, but most of the Greek was readable—soldier's humor—and crude drawings of men and women with impossible anatomies. At the far end, I heard voices. I moved closer to the source. Pilate and the other man, Rufus, must have been in a room just above me.

"These are all of the dispatches you have for me?" Pilate said.

"Yes, that's all."

"Not much here. They usually send me a camel's load of these things. Nothing from the emperor for me?"

"No, nothing. He—"

"Very well, I certainly can live without more orders from your crowd, no offense, Rufus. Now, what of this other matter? What is so urgent I had to spoil my legionnaires' fun?"

"Pilate, we have known each other for a long time."

"Yes, a very long time…get on with it. It can't be as bad as all that."

"No, well, not bad, a warning only. There is talk in the senate, in the emperor's councils…well, there is talk."

"Talk? There is always talk. You people have nothing better to do than talk. You and your friends in the capitol should come out to places like this and try to hold the empire together for a change instead of nattering about estates, the price of wine, and whether that demented boy Caligula will succeed Tiberius. Come out here and try to rule for a month or so in my place. I should like very much to stand in the forum in a long toga and talk about the state of the nation."

"Well, you may get your chance."

"Meaning what?"

"You have developed a reputation. You are said to be needlessly harsh in your treatment of the people you rule. There is talk of recall."

"Harsh? Do those soft, self-righteous ninnies have any idea what it takes to keep order in a place like this? Oh, they're happy when we crush a rebellion threatening their borders or making sailing the Great Sea risky. 'Thank you, Pontius Pilate, for ridding the seas of the pirates…Thank you for keeping the barbarians from our estates…Oh, but now, don't upset us by being harsh with the Jews.'"

"You know I have served the empire as you. I know it is not always easy. But that doesn't change what they are saying."

"Yes, you know. But I tell you this, in all my postings, I have never run into a people like these Jews and their infernal god. Rebellion is everywhere. I think these people are born with it. They absolutely refuse to be civilized. You remember Sepphoris? We crushed that uprising by nailing up every male we could find and sold off the rest into slavery. There has been no trouble there since."

"Yes, I know. It had to be done that way then, but now —"

"Do you know who was in charge of that rebellion? An old man. Not a general with a trained army—not a Jewish legion—just an old man. There could not have been more than a hundred men. They took on two of our hundreds and held out for three days. Three days! They are born to it, I tell you. The only way to keep order here is crush it as hard as you can, as often as you can.

"You saw that king person? He started a fracas in the temple. Do I care? Of course not, but do you know what? If I don't make an example of him today, who knows how many more old men, presumptive kings, or their friends will think they can raid another armory tomorrow. By Jupiter, I keep order here. I do so by being harsh and by keeping these people divided. You saw the high priest, Caiaphas? There are those who wish him deposed. There are those who believe he is right for the times. There are parties of every stripe and color here. By keeping them at each other's throats, they haven't time to come at ours. So, I will do this Caiaphas a favor, and the other parties will know I did. It will make them hate him more. Division, Rufus, we rule the world because we have mastered the art of division."

"My friend, I can only tell you what I hear. Recall is the word they use. If you do not want to be called back to Rome and put out to pasture in some out-of-the-way corner of the empire, you will find a way to keep order without the appearance of cruelty. That's all I have to say."

They moved away and I did not hear the rest. I went back to my guard. He sat at a low table eating his midday meal. He offered me a crust of bread, a piece of salt fish, and some wine. The wine, the cheap sort sold in the streets, had already turned. I added a generous splash of water to it and we ate. After a while he said, "You're not one of them, are you?"

"No, I am not." I guessed it must be true now. I was not anything anymore. "Why do you ask?"

"You aren't wearing one of them boxy things on your head, now, are you? So why did the fat man bring you in?"

"They think I killed a man."

"Did you?"

"No."

"Doesn't matter. If they have a witness who'll say you did, the Butcher—that's what they call Pilate—will nail you up, anyway. Too bad the fat man wouldn't take a bribe, huh? Peculiar people, these Jews—but the women…" He grinned and his eyes flickered with old memories.

"The women?" I asked. I do not know why, a simple grunt of assent would have taken the conversation elsewhere.

"Juicy," he said. I did not want to know what "juicy" meant in soldier talk. I could guess.

"You're not from around here, are you?" he said.

"No, I come from Corinth."

"Never been there. Hear the women there are juicy, too."

We were on a single track and I could not think how to get off, but I tried.

"How long have you been in this country?"

"Oh, twenty years, can't always remember. I came out when Augustus was still Caesar. There was a lot of rebellion then. I was here no more than a week and off we went to Sepphoris. Big to-do up there—some old fool raided the armory or something. We went and sorted them all out. What a show. Must have nailed up seventy of those crazy people that night, took their women in turn, and then hauled off the young ones. I had one of them for a while. Kept her for about a year. Then we were called up north and that was that. Had a little bastard, we did. First of many little red-haired bastards I've seeded this land with."

He slapped the table and cackled, his mouth open wide. Crumbs tumbled out onto his chin and onto the table. He took off his helmet to wipe his brow. I saw patches of red streaked in matted gray hair. I tried to collect my wits. My heart raced. I did not want to follow where my thoughts tried to take me.

"Are there many of you, of us," I pointed to my hair, "in the service of Rome?"

"Us? Oh, I see. Ha. Us. That's a good one. No, hardly any. We'd rather fight against Rome than fight for her."

"Then, why—?"

"Well, you and me have something in common now, don't we?"

My heart skipped another beat. "Do we?"

"Let's just say there's a dead man back where I come from and I can't go back. So I take my chances with Rome."

Something in common? If he only knew. I stared at his battered but familiar face and thought I would like to kill him.

Those thoughts were knocked aside by pounding on the great doors and the clatter of armor, footsteps, soldiers, and officials.

Caiaphas had returned from Herod's palace.

Chapter Fifty-five

Heavy bolts were thrown back and the doors opened. Late afternoon sun streamed into the fortress, lighting its dim interior. I ducked back into the safety of the shadows. Caiaphas and his entourage stood at the entrance. He looked hot and tired and, judging from his sour expression, exasperated. Jesus stood in the center of a group of men, his hands still bound together, face battered, eyes defiant. Pilate inspected the group, paced up and down, and stopped in front of the high priest.

"The noble tetrarch not in sympathy with your needs, Caiaphas? No luck in the palace of the brave Antipas?"

"The tetrarch says he has scruples."

"Ah. Well, of course, he does. He is no fool. Did you take him for a fool, high priest?"

"No, I did not. I did your bidding, and now I am back with the same request I brought to you this morning."

"And what was that? My memory is not what it used to be."

Caiaphas gritted his teeth. His face turned a brighter shade of red. The soldiers behind me snickered. High priest of the temple of the god of the Jews or not, those men were not about to show him even a small measure of respect. Caiaphas shot them a dark look, and they turned away, still grinning.

"This man mocked the great Caesar, threatened the temple, caused a public disturbance, and instigated a riot. He deliberately disobeyed the prefect's stated demand that no disturbances should mark the Passover. He is a threat to the peace, a known heretic, and notorious blasphemer. He must die that others will not be tempted to do the same."

"You wish me to kill this man? Is that the essence of the thing?"

"As you say."

"Send him in here. I wish to examine this dangerous person myself."

Jesus was pushed forward and made to stand before Pilate.

"They say you are the King of the Jews—*Iesus Nazarenus, Rex Iudaeorum.* Do you know what it means, King? In the civilized tongue of the empire, it means 'Jesus of Nazareth, King of the Jews.' That's what you say you are, am I right?" He pivoted around on his heel and faced the assembled Roman contingent.

"He says he is a king. Bring him a robe and a crown." The soldiers grinned and disappeared into the room where I spent the afternoon. They returned with a dirty purple robe and a crown fashioned from tree branches. Some of the branches had long, sharp, protruding thorns. It seemed they had played this king game before. The robe was draped over Jesus' shoulders and the crown pressed down on his head. Some of the sharp branches pierced the skin of his forehead, causing it to bleed. They laughed.

"There. Now, that's much better. Now you look like a king. You are a king, then?" Pilate circled Jesus, pulling at the wrinkles on the purple robe and giving the crown an extra downward push.

Jesus looked at Pilate with black fathomless eyes and responded, "Is this nonsense your idea or are you repeating someone else's?"

Pilate flinched, taken aback by Jesus' sharp tone. His eyes flashed with anger and then amusement.

"The king is defiant. So you are a king. Tell me, king, where is your throne? Where are your armies? Where is your palace?"

"My kingdom is not of this world. If it were, we would not be having this conversation. My subjects would have risen up by now and delivered me from these corrupt temple dogs… and from you."

"But they didn't, did they? So your kingdom is where—in the sky, perhaps? Then, why are you causing these good people so much trouble? I really need to know that. You understand, these men here want me to kill you?"

"I came to testify to the truth."

"Oh. It's the truth you bring us. Tell me, king, what is truth? We'd all like to know the answer to that. Yes?"

Pilate turned away and went back to Caiaphas.

"High priest, I can find no crime here, nor does your Antipas. I cannot crucify someone just because you think he might get you in trouble with that ridiculous god of yours. No, I won't do it."

"Prefect, he must die," Caiaphas said softly.

"Must? You say must? You are mistaken. That would be too harsh. Don't you agree, Rufus? We are not harsh people. Rome is famous for its sense of justice."

"He mocks the Caesar. He threatens."

"Well, yes, there is that to consider. I tell you what I will do… for the acts of disrespect and the riot—of course, mustn't forget that—a good flogging is in order. That should do it. Guard, bring the scourge."

Again the guard ran out and returned with a whip. I'd heard of Roman scourging but I had never seen it. The whip, or scourge, had a short wooden handle, no longer than a man's forearm. Attached to the end were about a dozen thin leather straps and fastened to the ends of the straps and along their length were small, sharp stones. The guard twirled it around his head and it sounded like he had released a bevy of angry wasps.

"I want everyone here to note that Pilate is merciful. Let it never be said he treats his people in a harsh manner. Proceed."

Jesus was stripped of his purple cloak, his robe, and tunic. His hands, still bound, were fastened around a pillar.

"How many, sir?" the man with the whip asked.

"How many? Three, I think. Three should do it."

Three lashes. It would hurt but three could not be too bad. Ehud, who is standing next to me, sucked in his breath. "It will kill him for certain," he said.

"Kill him? Three lashes? I don't see how."

"Not three lashes—three sets. Three sets of thirteen. It will flay the skin off his back. If he is lucky, the pain will be so bad, he will pass out after the first half dozen."

"Why do you care? Isn't this what you wanted?"

The man wielded the whip with great expertise. He flicked his wrist at precisely the right moment. Instead of simply laying down a set of stripes, the stones raked across the flesh and tore at it. Six lashes and Jesus' back was torn and bleeding. After a dozen, it was laid bare. Jesus never flinched or cried out. Anyone else would have been screaming for mercy. At the twentieth stroke, he slumped against his ropes, unconscious. The soldier continued the beating. Blood splattered everywhere. At the thirty-ninth stroke, the beating finally ended. The scourge dripped with blood, its wielder with sweat. A guard cut Jesus' bonds and he fell on his face.

"Get him up," Pilate snapped. "Get the king on his feet and get him out of here."

A legionnaire brought a bucket of water and poured it over him. Two others grabbed him by the arms and hauled him to his feet. The dirty purple robe was thrown over him. I saw it darken with blood from his wounds.

"There. We all feel better now, king," Pilate said.

As the soldiers steered Jesus toward the steps leading from the fortress, Caiaphas raised his hand.

"Stop. Prefect, this will not do. This man must be put to death."

"What is it with you people? Thirty-nine lashes aren't enough?"

Caiaphas drew in a breath. He looked very old at that moment, old and tired. Then, with all the dignity he could muster, he faced Pilate.

"You have your duty, prefect, I have mine. This man threatens the whole of our nation. I am fully aware you think our worship and practices are ridiculous and even primitive. But I tell you this, we have been faithful to the Lord since the beginning of memory. We worshipped him in the high places when your ancestors were still turning over rocks looking for food. Whatever you may think of us, we are not a bloodthirsty people. The Covenant calls us to obedience, and we know if we stray from it, the Lord will punish us. I do not relish this moment, Prefect, but this man, who believes *he* is the Lord, has drawn many to him. Soon, I fear, our Lord will respond."

Caiaphas sagged. His headpiece sat crookedly on his head. He had laid out his case to the prefect. He believed he was right. If I were anyone else and hearing this for the first time, I might have agreed with him.

"So he thinks he's a god. Tell me, high priest, what king doesn't? Very well, I will crucify this dangerous man for you."

Rufus cleared his throat. Pilate glanced his way and smiled. "It will be fine, you will see." Then returning to the high priest, he added, "Let us understand each other. If I do this thing for you, you will be in my debt."

"Yes, prefect."

"Deeply in my debt. I can expect you to guarantee the parties who now wrestle with one another for position and power will continue in that exercise in futility, with your help, of course?"

Caiaphas swallowed hard and said, almost in a whisper, "Yes, as you say."

Chapter Fifty-six

Rufus stepped forward, took Pilate by the arm, and walked him to the back of the room where I stood.

"This will get back to Rome. A crucifixion on one of the people's holiest days—you can't."

"You worry too much. I am not going to pass judgment on this man—they are. Trust me. I am the new Pilate, 'Pilate the Merciful.' You will see." He spun on his heel and strode back toward the doors.

"Guards, bring up the other prisoner we took last week, the bandit and assassin."

"Barabbas?"

"That's the one. Bring him up here. Oh, and fix him up with a king's robe, too. Caiaphas…?"

"Prefect?"

"Get all those people in the court over here so they can hear what I have to say."

Caiaphas spoke to his guards' captain who, in turn, sent his men into the courtyard. Soon the people massed at the foot of the steps. A commotion broke out behind me. Two guards shoved Barabbas, kicking and cursing, into the room. He started to strike out at the guards but was knocked to his knees. The soldiers hauled him to his feet and told him to be still or die. Another filthy purple robe was produced and thrown over his shoulders. He glanced in my direction. There was a brief flicker of recognition in his eyes.

"Bring them out here. Put one on my right and one on my left."

Jesus and Barabbas were led out on the platform in front of the doors. Each had a soldier at his side. The old soldier, my putative father, stood next to Jesus and the wielder of the whip stood next to Barabbas. A moment frozen in time followed as I took in that scene. The setting sun glowed golden and silhouetted the four men who defined my life—Pilate, Barabbas, my father, and Jesus. One way or another, I was related to each of them through blood. I would gladly kill three with my bare hands if I could, but I would be responsible only for the death of the fourth.

Pilate called for a bowl of water and a towel.

"Caiaphas," he said, "I am about to relieve you of any possible repercussions coming to you for what you have done to your countryman." Then, out of the side of his mouth, he muttered, "Watch and learn, Rufus."

Turning to the crowd, he raised his hands for silence. At the urging of the temple guards, the crowd quieted.

"People of Jerusalem, both of these men have been found guilty of crimes so serious, they require the death penalty." He paused for effect. "But it is your Passover Feast and Rome would show mercy. We have a tradition, do we not, on such important days, that one prisoner shall be set free?"

The crowd stirred. Caiaphas and the temple officials frowned. What tradition? No one had ever heard of such a tradition.

"Yes. And we will honor tradition today. However, it is difficult to choose, so I give the choice to you. Which of these two would you have me free?"

He pointed to Barabbas. "Shall it be Jesus Barabbas?" He slurred the 'bar' but said Jesus very loudly and clearly, Jesus bar Abbas. It came out sounding like Jesus, son of the Father.

"Or shall it be this man, *Iesus Nazarenus, Rex Iudaeorum?*"

The new, merciful Pilate now played the cruelest joke of his bloody career. No one in the crowd spoke Latin and he knew it. All they heard was something akin to "Jesus, son of the Father" and then a name that made no sense. The two men above them on the platform were both bowed and beaten. If anything, Barabbas looked better. After a brief pause the followers of Barabbas, seeing their chance, shouted, "Jesus Barabbas." Others, followers of Jesus—my Jesus—thinking they could rescue him, took up the chant and shouted with them, "Jesus."

Pilate waited, his snakelike face wreathed in smiles.

"You have chosen this man, Barabbas. So be it. Let him go."

Barabbas, stunned by the turn of events, watched in amazement, as his hands were untied and his dirty royal robe was stripped from him. Fearing a possible change of heart, he raced down the steps into the arms of his supporters.

"What shall I do to the other?" Pilate looked at the High Priest and surreptitiously signaled to him with his fingers.

Again he waited. Then Caiaphas, finally catching his drift, shouted, "Crucify him." His people repeated it and soon the crowd joined in, "Crucify him."

Pilate looked for a long moment at the crowd in mock amazement and announced, "It is your decision then, not mine. My hands are clean in this."

He dipped his hands in the bowl of water and dried them with the towel.

"We are finished here," he said to Caiaphas. "Go away."

"The crucifixion?"

"Tomorrow."

"But I thought—"

"It is your feast day, high priest. Go and celebrate your deliverance out of the hands of the enemies of your god. Go."

He gestured for the great doors to be closed.

"Lock up the king. Give him water but no food. Tomorrow, be prepared to take him and the other two out and crucify the lot of them."

He started to leave the room. Ehud, who had lingered, stopped him.

"Prefect, there is one last thing."

"There is more? You people amaze me."

Ehud pushed me forward. "This man needs to be dealt with, too."

"The witness? Why, what has he done?"

"There was a murder in Caesarea some years back—a famous carver in stone. You are no doubt familiar with the case?"

Pilate's eyes narrowed dangerously. Ehud sailed on, oblivious to the change.

"This man is party to that crime."

Pilate gazed at me with the snake-like eyes I remembered so well. "You know something about it?" he said. There was no doubting the threat in his voice and the danger in those golden eyes.

"I know nothing of it." We stared at each other for a long time. Then, he nodded and turned back to Ehud.

"Get out of here. I have no interest in old crimes involving silly Greek sculptors. Get out."

Ehud's jaw dropped. He hesitated for a moment and then scuttled out the small door and disappeared.

Pilate looked at me for a long moment. "You were very wise just now. Guard, this man has earned a reward."

"I ask for nothing."

"Nevertheless, you shall have something. Where are the things we took from Barabbas?"

The guard placed a bundle on the table next to the wall.

"There will be something suitable here. Ah, just the thing!"

He handed me a heavy purse and a knife. Not just any knife—my knife—the one I took from the dark desert man, the one Barabbas took from me. I loosened it from its sheath and tested the edge. Barabbas had honed it to a sharpness it never had when I carried it. I could have drawn it and with one slash, avenged Jesus, my friends, my mother, my sister, and the hundreds, the thousands of men, women, and children this butcher destroyed. One lightning stroke and I would have been free. Before I could act on those thoughts, Pilate wheeled around and headed into the depths of the fortress.

"Leave now before I change my mind," he said over his shoulder.

I stepped out of the fortress and on the street, free. I could not believe it. I had money, a lot of money, and my knife. I shook my head in disbelief. I stood there in the exact state I arrived in when I came to this peculiar country. Except for the ache in my heart, the previous six and a half years might never have happened.

Chapter Fifty-seven

Freedom. For the first time in two days I could move about as I pleased. I stretched my arms out and spun on my heel. I looked right and left. I did not want to meet any of the disciples closest to Jesus, or any of our supporters, in fact. I did not know what they knew about my role in Jesus' arrest and impending crucifixion, but I knew if he had not already done so, John would tell them, and no amount of explaining on my part could ever reconcile us. I wanted to flee, to go as far as I could, as fast as I could, anywhere. But instead, I wandered aimlessly around the city, my mind numb, and my spirit broken.

As darkness fell, I found myself wandering the hills north of the city, a short distance from the Fish Gate. Travelers covered the area with their tents. I settled near a family from Thrace. Their horsehide tent with its streamers and gaily-colored poles spread over a substantial piece of ground. I counted nearly a dozen people coming and going through its bright red flaps. I caught the aroma of cooking, some sort of meat.

The head of the household motioned for me to join them for Passover. His wife looked dubious, but when I offered a few coins, she beamed and waved me in. They had never heard of Jesus, were only dimly aware of the commotion at the temple, and eager to eat and sing and celebrate. I was not very good company, I fear. Afterward, I spent the night in the rocky hills not far from their tent. Sleep, the great healer, avoided my earnest pleas, so I watched as the stars made their circuits in the heavens and finally gave way to the sun.

Before I left, I traded a few more coins and my cloak for one of theirs and a head covering. The cloak, like their tent, was made from finely tanned horsehide and decorated with loops and swirls along its edge. Anyone seeking me would not be looking for a man from Thrace. I wished my host a safe trip and set out, intending to go away from the city. Instead, my steps turned toward it as if a great force willed me back, back to the temple, back to the fortress, back to my shame. I wondered if I had finally gone mad.

I entered the city and made my way to the north side of the Antonia Fortress. A large crowd had gathered at the stout door that fronted onto the street. They pushed and shoved and a few minor fights broke out. Soldiers moved into the mass of people to quell them. Even though the crowd vastly outnumbered the guards, no one dared attack them. The sun cleared the eastern walls—the second hour of the sixth day. With an eye trained to spot them, I noted the cutpurses were out in force.

A soldier on the wall above shouted an order to those below. They moved to the door, pointed their spears at the mob, and drove them back. When they had cleared a space, one of them banged his fist on the door and it swung open. More soldiers led out three men. The crowd began to curse and throw rotten fruit. Neither pilgrims nor worshippers, this mob came from the threadbare hem of society that delights in public hangings and crucifixions. They would jeer and harass the prisoners all the way through the city. Whatever the other two had done or not done held no interest for me. My eyes were only on the third man, Jesus.

He wore the same dirty purple robe, but now it was stained dark brown. The dried blood from his wounds glued the cloth to his torn back. There were dark circles under his eyes. A piece of pomegranate glanced off his forehead. Only when an errant apple struck a soldier's helmet and its recipient whirled, sword in hand, did the pelting stop. People laughed.

The soldier nearest Jesus grabbed the purple robe and, with a jerk, tore it away. I swear I could smell blood. Jesus cried out. Everyone could see the horror the scourge had made of his back. Even those slow-witted street denizens were subdued at the sight. His old linen robe replaced the purple one across his shoulders and, eyes wet, I watched as new red stains spread across it.

The soldiers then dragged three heavy wooden beams from the fortress, each half again as long as the men were tall. They banged and bumped across the rough cobbles. From the new bark on them I guessed they had been cut from green wood and would be very heavy. Next, the soldiers hoisted them up onto the shoulders of Jesus' companions. The two trudged away, bearing their crosses, but Jesus remained. Most of the oafs and their baskets of fruit followed the first two. Only a smaller, quieter crowd remained. It looked like the soldiers wanted the other two prisoners away before they started down the street with Jesus. I thought I saw Joseph nearby. Perhaps he had arranged it. Perhaps he, like me, felt deep shame for our lack of courage.

The soldiers placed the crossbeam on Jesus' back. He collapsed under its weight. He was jerked back to his feet and given a drink and the beam lifted on his back again. This time he managed to stagger down the street, one painful step at a time. I stayed at the back of the onlookers, moving slowly with them. The street twisted down into the Tyropoeon Valley, the valley of the cheese mongers, which divides the city. Just as he reached the bottom of the street where it veered to the left, he fell. The crossbeam bounced off his torn back and clattered several paces away. He lay motionless in the street. A soldier kicked him and he stirred. He struggled back to his feet but as soon as the beam was replaced on his back, he collapsed again.

One of the soldiers, the one in charge, it seemed, shook his head, frustration creased his face, and looked around for help. Apparently they had orders to deliver Jesus for execution and they were determined to do it. They would not allow him to die beforehand. The soldier walked into the crowd and grabbed a man. By his dress and demeanor, I guessed he came from Africa, perhaps Cyrenaica or Tripolitania. The soldier told him in broken Greek to pick up the beam.

Whether the African understood what the soldier was saying or not, he knew better than to argue. He picked up one end of the beam Jesus carried on his back. They trudged along single file, sharing its weight, for a short distance, before Jesus fell again. The crossbeam tumbled away. The soldier hit the man with his scourge, not hard, but enough to draw a cry of pain.

"If this happens again, man," the soldier shouted, "it will be very often you will feel these lashes."

While this exchange took place, a woman knelt at Jesus' side and wiped his face. Another gave him a wet cloth to suck on. Another soldier cursed at the women and shoved them away. I saw tears in their eyes. For the first time, I noticed the people around me. I recognized many of the faces from the last three years—honest Galilean faces. Men, women, and children stood silent and weeping as Jesus reeled past them with his cross, as though he carried their burdens, their pain, on his back as well. A few mocked him, but others stared them into silence. One small group of men started to sing softly. Others joined them.

The man required to carry the cross positioned himself immediately behind Jesus and took nearly all the crossbeam's weight onto his own shoulders. If Jesus should fall again, the beam would not. They continued slowly and deliberately through the valley, climbed the steep slope past Herod's palace, through the Gannath Gate, and out to the hill the local people call by its Aramaic name, Golgotha—Skull Hill.

Chapter Fifty-eight

Golgotha is a low hill just outside the walls and at the east end of an abandoned quarry. Its stone contained too many fractures and, therefore, was deemed unfit for cutting, so the masons left it, a small rise at the end of an otherwise flat valley, now turned into a rough garden. At the far end, where the quarry face remained, tombs had been cut into the stone for wealthy families.

We arrived about the fourth hour. Jesus and his helper staggered, lockstep, up the hill. The other two men—thieves, I was told by one of the regulars to these occasions—had already been raised up. Their cries rent the morning air.

I have witnessed crucifixion many times—who hasn't? You cannot live in the Roman Empire for very long and not see that peculiar Roman institution. But no matter how many times you see it, nothing prepares you for the horror. There are a variety of ways to nail someone to a cross—all of them terrible. Some are more appalling than others. A few soldiers relish the moment, inventing new ways to inflict pain when they draw the assignment. Most, however, get down to business and do the task as quickly as they can. I never saw a woman on a cross. Romans have more humiliating ways to punish them.

To survive, the victim must pull with his arms and push with his legs against the pain of the nails. In time, he weakens. Then, strength drained and no longer able to withstand the pull his tired body makes, his knees bend, his arms dislocate from the shoulders, he sinks, and suffocates. The whole process may take hours or days. It is an awful way to die.

I watched as soldiers stripped Jesus of his clothes and lashed his crossbeam in place in a notch prepared for it on a long vertical. With a quick blow to the back of his knees, they dropped him in place, stretched him out on the assembled cross and extended his arms to their limit on the horizontal. He looked almost relieved to lie down. He was whiter than the linen cloth they had taken from him. His back, now rubbed by the rough wood of the cross, began to bleed again, adding new stains to the already bloody crossbeam.

Usually nails are driven through the wrists, less often through the tough sinews of the palm. Driven through the wrist, there is no chance the nails will tear out and have to be replaced. But, if the intention is to create the greatest distress, they are driven through the palms of the hand. To stay alive, the victim must make a fist and grasp the very nails that send searing pain up his arms and into his shoulders. They nailed Jesus through his palms.

The soldier raised his maul high over his head. There was a collective intake of breath. The hammer swung down and rang against the spike. We all exhaled. Each stroke of the hammer sent a shock through my body as if I, not Jesus, had received it. I covered my ears, but it did not stop the sound. I think God wanted me to hear every ringing blow.

Next, Jesus' knees were bent to the right and spikes were driven through his heels. The men stood back and inspected their work. At the signal from one of them, the cross was raised up and dropped into its hole. The vertical hit the bottom of the hole with a loud thunk and Jesus' body jerked violently downward. Whether he groaned or not, I could not tell, as the onlookers, those who came to mourn and those who came to jeer, moaned in unison for him.

The hecklers turned their attention from the thieves and had their time with Jesus. I could only hear a few words. Jesus managed to hold himself erect.

"He is praying," a woman near me said.

"It is one of David's Psalms," another corrected her.

My God, my God, why have you forsaken me? Why are you so far from my cry and my distress?

I looked around for the other disciples. Mary, his mother, stood off to one side. John and the Magdalan and some of the other women hovered nearby. I saw no sign of Peter or James or anyone else. One of the thieves wailed at Jesus, "If you are the Messiah, deliver yourself and us, too."

But the other thief rebuked him, and turning his head, said something about being remembered in his Kingdom. Jesus paused in the midst of his chanting and said, "Today you will be with me in Paradise." It sounded like paradise, although I could not be sure. It was not an expression I had ever heard him use.

The sun neared its zenith, the heat bordered on the unbearable. A dry southerly wind gusted through the crowd but it brought no relief. The air felt like the blast from a furnace. People nearby laughed and threw the last of their fruit. Jesus continued to recite the Psalm.

All who see me laugh at me with scorn, they sneer and shake their heads and they say—

"He trusted in the Lord—let's see the Lord deliver him. Let's see the Lord rescue him," one of the temple officials shouted, as if on cue.

People laughed but Jesus remained upright on his cross. I could only imagine what that must have cost him in his weakened state. After a while, the crowd tired of their sport and began to drift away. A few stayed bearing silent witness.

Be not far from me, for trouble is near, and there is no one to help. Praise the Lord, you that stand in awe of him, offspring of Israel, you of Jacob's line...

At the sixth hour, the sun disappeared and it turned dark as night. The wind shifted and blew from the north, a cold, biting wind that made people clutch their cloaks close about them. I saw worried and fearful expressions on the faces of the spectators. Even those sanguine Roman soldiers, for all their ferocity, were nonplussed at the temporary disappearance of the sun.

When it finally returned, many had scurried back to their lairs like wolves at the sight of a lion. Only the few loyal to Jesus remained. I looked up at the cross again, silhouetted against a copper sky. Jesus struggled to hold himself erect.

At the tenth hour I heard a faint rumble, and then I felt it under my feet. For what seemed a long time the ground rolled and trembled. Women screamed and the soldiers, who had managed the darkness with relative aplomb, leapt to their feet and looked around frantically. Red smoke rose on the skyline in the direction of the temple.

The Sabbath would begin soon. The priests assigned to oversee the executions approached the centurion in charge and asked him to break the legs of the three men so they might die quickly and be buried before sundown. It would not do to have them hang there on the Sabbath. Much to the disappointment of the soldiers, who had bet on the order of death, the centurion agreed. One soldier prodded each man with a spear. The two thieves jerked as its sharp point pierced their flesh. A second soldier then crushed their legs with a heavy club. They screamed and crumpled. In a moment, they were still. Jesus did not respond to the spear. The soldier then stabbed harder. Finally, he pressed the spear into his ribs. Only a little blood and a clear fluid poured from his side.

"This one's dead already," the soldier reported. A collective groan rose from the few people left on the hillside. Jesus' mother fainted. The Magdalan knelt down next to her, buried her face, and sobbed. John stood near them, his shoulders slumped in defeat, and then looking up, shook his fist at the sky. Nearly everyone wept, except the soldiers who noisily divided the prisoners' belongings. The centurion muttered something to his aide who looked startled and then nodded.

I turned to leave. I had no idea what to do next. I no longer had a purpose for my life. My friend, perhaps the only real friend I ever had, lay dead as the spikes were removed from his broken body. In despair, I turned and headed back to the hillside.

Chapter Fifty-nine

I resisted the temptation to return to our rooms and find out what the others knew. I reckoned the last person they wanted to see, now or ever, would be Judas, the thief, the traitor. But I lingered nearby out of sight. Shortly after sunup, I saw Mary rush into the rooms. Moments later, those few who had not fled the city poured out and raced in the direction of Golgotha. When I saw Mary reappear, I signaled to her. She looked my way, hesitated, and then came to me.

"Judas," she said. She had the same expression on her face my mother had the day we parted. "What you have done…you cannot stay here." Again, a memory that refused to fade.

We cannot stay here.

She added, "You must go."

I retrieved my few belongings and slung them in a bundle over my shoulder.

"There is one last thing I must tell you," she said as I turned to leave. "He is risen." She saw the blank look on my face. "Jesus was not in the tomb." She stopped and looked at me, her eyes pleading.

"Are you sure?" I thought of Thomas, and his resemblance to Jesus, *Didymus.* I wondered if she had mistaken the one for the other.

"I spoke to him. He…What are we to do?"

I tried to return the silver but the high priest refused to see me. He sent a clerk who would only speak to me through a bronze grating set in the door.

"That is blood money," the clerk said. "We cannot accept it."

"But it is the money you gave to me less than two days ago. If it is blood money now, it was blood money then. I do not want it. It is like fire in my hand." I shouted at him and threw it through the grate.

"Very well," the smug clerk said, "we will use it to buy a burial field near the rubbish pile, and we will buy it in your name."

◇◇◇

At the seventh hour, I found myself outside the city walls with no place to go, no one to speak to, and no future. I had finally become the murderer the empire wanted me to be. I did not kill Leonides, I did not push that boy over the sea wall in Cenchrea, and I did not kill the Roman soldier, but I had murdered Jesus as surely as if I stabbed him in the heart.

As I walked away from the city, an assortment of petty merchants and artisans caught my eye. They were haggling with one another over the price of this or that. I paused to listen; I'm not sure why. I let my eyes wander over this gaggle of honking geese, wondering about each in turn. Did the one with the red nose drink too much wine? Did the sylph-like servant attending a fat wife also serve her master in another way? My eyes fell on a woman, the wife of a leather merchant who, to his credit, seemed calm and deliberate. Her back was to me. She had her hands full with a fussing child. Something about her seemed familiar—the curve of her neck, the arch of her back—something. A plump Israelite matron absorbed in her child, her mind miles away from the men's haranguing. She turned and faced me. I don't know why, but I caught her eye first. Our gazes locked like tiles in one of Zakis' mosaics, unmoving, unmovable.

My mother stared at me across thirty cubits of open space and a lost decade. I stood motionless, unable to breathe. I spent years searching for her in all the wrong places. I thought to find her in the brothels or under the shadowy arches of the city, the places where men seek a quick release for their lust. I sought her in the eyes of every woman who came to us from her broken profession. But she had escaped that. Somehow she had reinvented herself. Unencumbered by children and Darcas, she left the streets and found respectability. All those wonderful fantasies spun for me so long ago in Caesarea; she'd made one of them come true and found someone to believe her. Did this leather merchant think she came from the priestly class, that she was a widow of means? I don't know. It didn't matter. She was free.

I started toward her but drew up short when I saw the look of panic on her face, the quick jerk of her head. Her eyes slid first to the boy, then to the man, her husband. Then I understood. "You are dead to me," she once said. And so I must remain. How would she explain a grown son to her husband? She had found her way home without me.

Our eyes embraced one last time. Disengaging was more painful than the beating I had taken at the hands of Barabbas and his men. I wanted to tell her about Dinah, I wanted to tell her how much I missed her, about the years I looked for her. But all I could do was smile and lift my fingers to my lips. She glanced uneasily at her husband and her son and, seeing them both momentarily distracted, smiled back. I walked away and Jesus' voice whispered in my ear.

Have you found your treasure yet?

The morning's early chill gave way to scorching heat. Although spring, it felt like summer in the valley of the Salt Sea. Lost in my thoughts and feeling sorry for myself, I did not notice where my footsteps had taken me. Only when I stumbled did I realize I had wandered to the rubbish heap outside the city walls. All the city's trash, garbage, and offal was deposited there along with animal carcasses, the contents of thousands of chamber pots, mixed in with shattered dreams, lost lives, and broken promises. Fires smoldered here and there. Gehenna they called it, the Hinnom Valley—Hell. Sensible people avoided this place. The only signs of life were dogs—the pariahs—digging through the rubbish, snapping at rats bold enough to challenge them, and rooting for something to eat. Occasionally a fight broke out over a bone or a scrap. Then, teeth bared, they tore into each other with desperation known only to the starving. I knew that feeling, had even fought like that—pariah dogs and Judas, cousins.

I noticed other pariahs as well, human refuse from the city—abandoned children, the infirm, lunatics, all of the city's unwanted human surplus. They, like the dogs, scavenged through rubbish. Each carried a club or stout stick used to poke in the piles of trash or to protect themselves from the dogs and each other.

I made a wide circuit around the stinking pile and plodded onward, up and away from the city. It occurred to me I ought to be near the field purchased in my name by the clerk and his masters. I may even be standing on my own land. That was something I had never been before. Imagine—Judas the Red, landowner.

As I neared the crest of the hill, I saw a small boy sitting by the side of the path—one of the denizens of Gehenna. As I drew near, he leapt to his feet. He may have been asleep, startled by my approach, or just frightened. I raised my right hand, palm out, to show him I meant him no harm. His face was so incredibly dirty, when he looked up at me his eyes glowed like twin moons in the night sky.

"I wouldn't go up there, sir."

I took in the sores and the bruises on his body and I saw in him all the children I had known in my past. I thought of Gaius and his pack of urchins working the streets of Cenchrea—all of them dead before they were twelve.

"Why should I not go up there, boy?"

"There's a dead man up there, sir."

"A dead man? What sort of dead man?"

"Soldiers come up here last night, and when Barak thought they were sleeping, he tried to steal their things. They woke up and caught him. Now he's dead."

"That was very foolish of Barak. Was he a friend of yours?"

"No sir, he's just one of us what lives up here. Sometimes he was nice to me. When he found some food, he would sometimes give me some, that's all."

The boy was dressed in rags so filthy it was nearly impossible to tell what color they were. His sandals were an adult's and his cloak dragged on the ground. I reached in my purse and gave him a few coins. His mooneyes waxed at the sight. It will hold him a week or two, I thought, if someone does not steal them from him in the meantime. Unfortunately, the sores on his legs were already festering and I did not hold out much hope for him. I wondered…what would Jesus have done? Probably healed him and told me to get him clothes and food. Then he would have sent him to Bethany to the women. But we could not do that anymore. Whatever power I had to heal had surely been taken from me.

"Run along boy. Get away from this place. Go to the Jericho Road. Do you know where it is? Yes? When you get there, go down to Qumran, Masad Hasidim. They will help you. Do you hear me? Masad Hasidim. Go."

He dashed off and, I hoped, away. It is never easy to leave the familiar, even when you know it will eventually kill you.

What would Jesus have done?…What had he done? I stopped in my tracks…dumbstruck.

He knew!

He knew what the consequences of my foolish pursuit of Ehud and his cronies must surely be. He knew, and yet…he sent me on my way. At the meal in the upper room, a simple word from him and I would have stayed. Yet, he sent me out. He *wanted* to set in motion the events that led to the cross. He'd chosen me to be the instrument of his destruction. Did he think I shared that knowledge?

Did I?

How could I have missed it?

I don't know how long I stood there—heartbeat, an hour? I will never know.

He knew!

Epilogue

Barak swung slowly in the slight breeze, suspended by the cord I guessed once served as his cincture. A large boulder was positioned a short distance behind him. The soldiers must have stood him on it, drawn the noose tight, pushed him off, and watched as he swung back and forth, desperately trying to get his feet, his toes, back on the stone. He probably struggled like that for a long time. I could almost hear the soldiers' laughter and see the terror in Barak's eyes.

Carrion crows, their beaks red with his blood, flapped, croaked, and scattered when I drew near. He hung there naked. Barak had been the object of other scavengers as well, it seemed. I recognized the source of the boy's over-large sandals and cloak. Barak's face had turned a hideous shade of purple. The heat of the day caused his body to bloat. He looked as if he might burst at any moment. His own mother would not recognize this Barak.

It should be me...

Barak must have been about my size and age. In his condition who could tell? I moved around to get upwind and away from the odor of corruption. As I did so, something—perhaps the wind—caused him to swing around and I saw again what was left of his face. In addition to the ravages made by the crows, I could see he had been beaten badly. The hanging may have come as a relief. Blood caked on his scalp and in his hair. I missed the hair at first because of the blood. But as he swung on his noose, the late afternoon sun glinted off the same awful red hair as mine.

Could this be one of my father's "red-haired bastards" he had seeded this land with? This Barak could be my brother. Where else were the bastards of these Roman brutes to go but to the streets, the rubbish piles, and the gallows?

It could be me…

It seemed indecent to leave him this way—my newfound brother. I stood on the rock and cut him down. I expected a thump or a crunch when he landed, but what I heard sounded more like a large, half-filled wineskin hitting the ground.

The sun hovered just over the western horizon, and I still sat *shiva* with poor Barak. The air cooled and, in the half-light, he looked almost peaceful. Some might say he went to a better place, better than when he rooted in the garbage like a pig.

I heard a footstep and the crunch of pebbles. I do not know why, but I felt Him, felt his presence, and I knew. Another footstep and his shadow captured the sun at my back.

"Lord? Is it you?"

"See for yourself."

"I cannot. I cannot face you."

"Do you think your denial worse than Peter's?"

"They will say so."

"But what will I say?"

"That you willed me to this place."

"I sought the cross so all might live, do you see?"

"All, Lord? Surely not all; how can I live?"

"Do you believe that I am here with you now and I live?"

"Yes."

"Then you must live, too. You did not walk all those miles, did not proclaim the Kingdom, and did not see the wonder of God's mercy, to die alone on this hill. What did I tell you that morning?"

*You of all who come to me will be asked to sacrifice the most and
receive the least. It is why you were chosen, because you understand
these things.*

He was gone.

◇◇◇

I sat on the boulder a little distance from poor Barak and contemplated the turn of fate that brought the two of us together.
What if we had met earlier?

I untied my bundle. I put my old sandals on Barak and
covered him with a tunic.

*If you have two tunics and your brother has none, give him one
of yours…*

I put the few remaining shekels into my old purse and placed
it beside Barak's body. It was probably the most money he ever
possessed. The other coinage I put in the now empty purse the
temple money came in. I dropped my wax tablet, the one on which
I did my accounts, by his hand. I would not need it anymore.

I left my brother, Barak, in my stead. It was time to leave,
time to be about the business given to me. My mother found her
way home and so would I. I had my treasure. Now, I needed to
spend it.

I would go west, across the Great Sea and the land beyond. I
would take from my father the one thing he could not give me at
birth, the only thing he had of value, the thing that could have
set me on a different path…I would take his name. I would be
Ceamon, Ceamon the Red. I would travel first to the temple of
Aphrodite in Corinth and then to the land across the seas where
even the mighty Roman Legions dared not go. I would go where
all the men have red hair and paint their bodies blue and I would
tell this story. And someday, when it has been told enough times to
enough people, the Romans and those like them—the oppressors
of the world—might yield to it. Then his Kingdom will come.

In the distance I heard the grunts of camels assembled in
a caravan on the Joppa road, then *"Sah, Sah, Sah,"* from the
caravan master. If I hurried, I could catch them.

Notes

The Antonia Fortress

The Antonia Fortress was a large building that formed at least one half of the north wall of the Temple Mount. It was built by Herod the Great and named in honor of Marc Antony. It served as a garrison for the Roman troops and occasionally, during high holy days, the residence for the prefect when he was in Jerusalem. The fortress would serve as the *praetorium* (barracks) for the Roman legionnaires stationed in the city. It is in this building that Pilate would determine the fate of Jesus and any other non-citizen prisoners under his jurisdiction. The *Ecce Homo* arch in modern Jerusalem marks the site of the fortress and the place where Pilate is said to have announced, "Behold, the Man."

Some contest the fort as the site of Jesus' trial, insisting that he would have been taken to the palace instead. They further assert that the trial must have been held in public with the rules of evidence found in the Roman codes of justice. That this was not done is evidenced by the description of the events in the gospels. Furthermore, Roman law was not codified until well after the first century and applied only to Roman citizens. Other races and nationalities received only that portion allowed them by the emperor and interpreted by the local governor or legate.

Barabbas

One of the more ironic coincidences in the Gospel narrative involves the person of Barabbas, the bandit, robber, and possibly one of the forerunners of the *Siccori* or assassins. The gospel tells us his full name was Yeshua Barabbas, that is, Jesus Barabbas. In Hebrew the word *bar* means son of, and *abba* means father. Therefore, Yeshua Barabbas could easily be translated, or heard as, Jesus, son of (the) Father, particularly if enunciated by a non-Hebrew speaker.

Caesarea Maritima

Caesarea Maritima served as the seat of the occupying Roman government and later as the capitol for Agrippa. It is one of Herod the Great's most ambitious and successful building projects. Desiring to rival Alexandria, he built a magnificent port on the site of Strato's Tower. The harbor was formed by huge jetties which extended out into the Mediterranean. It is thought to be one of the earliest examples of the use of poured concrete on any grand scale.

Chronology

Most scholars date Jesus' birth prior to the first day of the first millennium. Therefore, the use of the older B.C. and A.D. to designate years becomes problematical. Obviously, Jesus could not have been born four years "before Christ." Thus, the usage of the newer and probably more informative B.C.E.—before (the) Common Era and C.E.—Common Era.

The chronology used follows the now generally accepted idea that Jesus was born between 5 and 3 B.C.E. Using that as a starting point, it is then possible to date the events of the crucifixion at 30 C.E. The remaining dates then follow logically from that.

The Jesus Years

5 B. C. E.	Jesus is born in Bethlehem.
4 B. C. E.	Herod the Great dies. His sons are named his successors as tetrarchs.
6 C. E.	Judas of the Galilee raises a revolt and storms the armory in Sepphoris. Prefects (procurators) replace client kings.
7 C. E.	Judas (Iscariot) is born somewhere on the Via Maris.
14 C. E.	Tiberius becomes emperor.
26 C. E.	Pontius Pilate appointed prefect of the Judea.
27 C. E.	John baptizes Jesus at the Jordan River.
30 C. E.	Jesus is crucified in Jerusalem. His resurrection is widely reported.

Passover Week	
The First Day	Jesus enters the city riding an ass to the cheers of the people.
The Second Day	Jesus teaches in the temple.
The Third Day	Jesus cleanses the temple and celebrates the Essene Passover.
The Fourth Day	Jesus is brought before the Sanhedrin.
The Fifth Day	Jesus is brought to Pilate and Antipas. Orthodox Passover.
The Sixth Day	Jesus is crucified.
The Seventh Day	The Sabbath.
The First Day	The Resurrection.

Corinth

Corinth was the capital of the Roman province of Achaea. Located on an isthmus that separated mainland Greece to form the Pelopennisos Peninsula, it was a major shipping hub and transfer point for ships and their cargo. Attempts at digging a canal fell short and were replaced by the construction of the Diolkos, a paved tramway that led from Cenchrea on the southeast to Corinth and then on to Lechaeum on the northwest. At one time Corinth was considered so corrupt that the verb (in Greek) *to corinthianize* meant to indulge in sexual immorality. It was destroyed by the Roman Republic in 143 B.C.E. and rebuilt by Julius Caesar a hundred years later.

Crucifixion

Crucifixion was a punishment peculiar to Rome and it was only applied to noncitizens. The several variations described in the text are authentic. Some authors doubt the placement of the nails in the palms of the hand. There is a very tough membrane in the palm, the *palmar fascia* that is quite capable of supporting the weight of a man for some time.

It is unlikely that Roman guards would be involved, as some suggest, in a conspiracy to spare Jesus' life or allow his body to be stolen. The Gospel of Matthew (27:62 ff) says that Pilate, at the suggestion of the temple party, placed a guard on the tomb soon after the second day. In the following chapter, we are told the guards went to the high priest to report the body missing and Caiaphas, after bribing the guards, invented the story of the body being stolen. He promised to "keep them out of trouble" if they did so.

It is highly unlikely that any Roman soldier would report to the high priest under any circumstance and even less likely that the latter could in any way affect the punishment they might receive for their dereliction of duty. If we accept Matthew 28:12 ff., then 27:64 may not be true. The guards would have to be from the temple. Similarly, if we accept the former, then we must ignore the latter. In either case, anyone familiar with the circumstances would assume that the guards would "hot-foot" it out of town when confronted with an empty tomb.

Feeding the Multitude

There are several versions of this miracle in the New Testament, including a repetition for different audiences. The numbers of people in attendance and how often the event occurred is secondary to the message implicit in the act. The Messianic expectations held by the Israelites in the first century varied widely but, common to them all was an expectation of a Messianic feast. This would signal the declaration by the principal of his claim as Messiah. For some this was the replication or an anamnesis of Moses calling down the manna from heaven. For others it represented leadership that could figuratively provide sustenance for the nation.

Infancy Gospel

There are many stories relating to Jesus' childhood. Only the brief mention of his lingering in the temple to speak to the learned rabbis and his parents' subsequent frantic search for him is in the canon. The story of the clay birds related in this narrative is the most often repeated, in noncanonical gospels and elsewhere. Because it is so widespread, both in "gospels" and in some traditions, it is tempting to believe it to be true.

Judas Iscariot

Judas, like Jesus (Yeshua) was a common name in the first century Israel/Judea. One tradition holds that the Apostle Thomas' full name was Judas Thomas Didymus, which would mean the two had at least that in common. Iscariot, on the other hand, has been variously translated. The traditional treatment assumed Judas was from a village named Kerioth, presumed to be in the southern part of Judea. No satisfactory location for the town has ever been established, however. An alternative translation for *kerioth* is "neighborhood" intimating that Judas was from the suburbs (of Jerusalem, presumably). Other scholars assume Iscariot is an adulteration of *siccori*—the assassins. In John 6:71 Judas is clearly designated as son of Simon Iscariot, which could make Iscariot a patronymic.

This book's interpretation assumes Iscariot is a variant on the Aramaic word *skyr*, which is roughly translated as red or ruddy. Thus, the plausible notion the reference is to the color of Judas' hair—Judas the Red, as in Erik the Red and so on. Or as John writes, Judas son of Simon the Red.

A mixture of the Aramaic and a Greek suffix –ote (like, -ish) would yield: η σκιριοτε and pronounced as eh-skiri-ote, Iscariot, Judas the Red [ish]. Early Byzantine icons commonly depict Judas with red hair.

Judas of the Galilee

Little is known about Judas of the Galilee except he is mentioned in Josephus with regard to the raid on the armory in Sepphoris. This insurrection resulted in the crucifixion of many men and the town itself being razed. There is an additional reference in the New Testament (Acts 5:36 ff.), which reports Gamaliel, the teacher of Saul, later to be Paul, and a great rabbinic figure of the day, describes Judas of the Galilee as a false Messiah.

His uprising in 6 C.E. is thought by some scholars to be the opening battle of what would culminate in the Jewish Wars in 66-67 C.E. and finally the destruction of the temple and the leveling of Jerusalem in 70 C.E.

Judas' Death

Judas is reported to have died in one of three ways. Two are found in the Gospels: He committed suicide by hanging (Matt. 27:5) or he swelled up and burst (Acts 1:18). The Apostles all assumed he was dead, and in order for the number of Apostles to remain at twelve, Mathias was chosen by lot to replace him. Peter spoke of Judas in far less damning terms than the other evangelists, in particular, John, who seemed to hate him. Peter says:

> *…Judas who served as a guide for them that arrested Jesus, he was one of our number, and had his place in this ministry…*

Of course, Peter's own betrayal of Jesus by denying him three times may have something to do with his more generous assessment of Judas.

The third is recorded in a fragment of Papias (an early church father) identified as III, and reads as follows:

Judas walked about in this world a sad example of impiety; for his body having swollen to such an extent that he could not pass where a chariot could pass easily, he was crushed by the chariot, so that his bowels gushed out.

An unlovely image but deemed an appropriate one, apparently, by those who remained with Jesus and needed to assure their listeners of the dire consequences attendant on anyone who would betray God's anointed.

The Kingdom of God

In the first century, the phrase, "The Kingdom of God" meant different things to different people. For the contemporaries of Jesus, a Messiah, the anointed one, was a growing expectation. But the nature of the Messiah was hotly disputed. One group looked for a prophet to announce it, a second Elijah. Others looked for someone who would lead them to it, a second Moses, and still others expected someone who would rule it, a second David. It is fair to say that few were looking for the kingdom Jesus proposed, a kingdom God would create by changing the hearts and minds of his creation.

Little People

One of the most persistent legends of Northern Europe and of the British Isles, in particular, concerns the Little People—gnomes, dwarfs, elves, fairies, and leprechauns. For many, the Little People were believed to be the imaginings of a superstitious era fed by the occasional appearance of genetic midgets, pygmies, and dwarfs. But their stories persist even today. The recent finding in Indonesia of a race of little people suggests the possibility that similar beings might have existed in the environs of Europe and offer some substance to the myths.

Mary Magdalene

Next to Judas, Mary Magdalene is one of the more intriguing characters in the Gospel stories. She was the first to see Jesus after his resurrection. She stood with Mary the Mother of Jesus at the foot of the cross as Jesus' life ebbed away. Contemporary thought assigns her the role of a "fallen" woman, perhaps confusing her with the prostitute who poured oil on Jesus' feet at the home of Simon the Pharisee. It has become a popular pastime to speculate on the possibility she was married to, or bore children by, Jesus. There is no credible evidence or tradition to support this view. Matthew simply describes her as a woman from whom seven spirits were exorcised.

Masad Hasidim—Qumran

Masad Hasidim, or the community at Qumran, that of the Dead Sea Scrolls, was a group of dissident Jews—a denomination not unlike the Pharisees. Commonly identified as the Essenes, their theology seemed to incorporate some Zoroastrian characteristics, an influence acquired, no doubt, during the Exile. They were as fiercely nationalistic as the Zealots and looked for the coming of the Messiah at the end times when the forces of darkness and light would clash. They viewed themselves as an elite group, the remnant of God's covenanted people. They were known to use an older calendar to calculate Holy Days and Feasts. Thus, they would have celebrated Passover on Tuesday rather than Thursday of the week now referred to as Holy Week or Passover. That would explain the textual differences between John's Gospel and the Synoptics. It also allows ample time for the events described in the Passion Narratives to take place. One major criticism of those narratives hinges on the time and the process guaranteed Jews accused of serious crimes, as Jesus was. It is highly unlikely that his "trial" and condemnation could have happened in one twenty-four hour period.

The Naming of God

Jews of this era would not have used the term God, or in Hebrew, Yahweh, in referring to the Creator. The word was too holy for human utterance. Instead, they would have used *Adonai*, in English, Lord. In the book, I used Lord up until the time when Jesus asserts his filial relationship to God. From that point forward, with a new relationship in the making, his disciples are released from the proscription on the name.

Picts

"Blue men" is a reference to the ancient Picts who occupied the area now thought of as the highlands of Scotland. They were fierce fighters and were such a thorn in the side of imperial Rome that the emperor Hadrian finally built a wall across parts of Scotland to keep them out. Tradition holds they dyed their skin blue and were predominantly a race of red-haired people.

The Twelve

Jesus gathered around himself a substantial group of disciples. Some stayed with him throughout his ministry while others drifted in and out. At some point he identified twelve as his core group, who were subsequently denoted as the Apostles. Who they were is a matter of some small confusion.

Part of this confusion derives from the lapse in time between the events narrated in the Gospels and the events themselves. And, secondarily, further confusion comes from the translation of the narrative from Hebrew, Aramaic, or both into their final form in Greek.

The four gospels identify the Twelve by name, but there are some minor discrepancies in the listings. Luke's is as follows: Simon (Peter), Andrew (his brother), James and John (sons of Zebedee), Philip, Bartholomew, Matthew (Levi), Thomas, James (son of Alphaeus), Jude (son of James), Simon (the Zealot), and lastly, Judas Iscariot.

Matthew and Mark list Thaddeus instead of Judas, son of James. John, while not listing the Apostles in any particular order or place, adds Nathaniel. Most scholars also assume the men were known in different congregations and churches by variants on their names. Thus Bartholomew was thought to be Nathaniel's patronymic, Nathaniel son of (bar) Tolomai, etc.

The important concept to keep in mind is there were *at least* twelve central players in the story and several (we don't know how many) others as well, so that Mathias (who replaced Judas), and Joseph called Barabbas, who was surnamed Justus, are described as "having been with us from the beginning."

Discussion Guide

Frederick Ramsay, Ph.D. and Connie Collins

To get the most from this rich spiritual *midrash*, it is suggested that the book be read completely, then reread section by section, answering the questions as you go. A few chapters have no assigned discussion questions, but they are important to read because they carry the story forward.

The discussion guide is divided into seven sessions. If your group desires more in-depth sharing, consider dividing each session into two.

Session I
Background to the story

This first session should be devoted to a general discussion of the times and place in which the New Testament unfolds. There is a dissonance between what many people perceive the Roman Empire to have been, and what it really was. We have been raised on a diet of Shakespeare and Hollywood clichés representing the times and personalities, of Richard Burton and Charlton Heston, and we forget that the twentieth century's greatest admirer and imitator of the empire was Nazi Germany. The times were oppressive for any who were not citizens. Rome was a class-driven society and rank, as they say, had its privileges.

1. Judas would have been the lowest of the low at the outset of this story. How would that jibe with your understanding of Jesus' mission?

2. The disciples moved around a great deal in the course of their work. What about this is related to the nature of the Roman Empire?

3. Is this important later on, when Paul begins his journeys?

4. Crucifixion is a peculiarly Roman custom. What do you know about its application?

5. To whom?

6. Were women crucified?

7. Rome kept its peace, the *pax romana,* by the application of force through its legions. How were they assembled?

8. Was there a hierarchy among them as well?

9. Can you name the Caesars who ruled in the era just before, during, and just after Jesus' mission?

10. Who was Caligula, and what relationship did he have with Pilate? With Caiaphas? Other thoughts about Palestine, Israel, Judea?

11. What were the differences?

12. Who ruled?

13. What is a client king?

Session II
Caesarea and Corinth, Chapters 1–12

Define *midrash*.

Chapter 1

1. The book is written in the first person. Who is the narrator?

2. Why did the writer establish Judas' family history immediately (second paragraph)?

3. *"There are risks attached to presuming to know the mind of God."* Explain what this statement means in this context. Does it presage the action to follow?

4. What is meant by the following statement? *Many swore silently that some day, somehow, they would avenge this indecency. God would raise up a Messiah, a new David, who would lead an army against the blasphemy from across the sea and cast it out forever.*

   Describe the Messiah the Israelites were expecting God to send. Whom did He send? Were there others who made that claim?

5. At the end of the chapter, Judas says, *"This chaos was my birthright."* What kind of man grows out of a childhood of such chaos? Does he have choices?

Chapter 2

1. What do you think the narrator meant when he said, *"It was to be expected, this betrayal of the betrayer."*

2. What is your understanding of the value of human life at this point in history? Is it different now?

3. What thirty pieces of silver was the storyteller referring to?

4. What approximate value, in today's reckoning, does this sum represent?

Chapter 3

1. Discuss Judas' relationship with his mother. How is your experience different?

2. What is Judas' surname and what does it mean? (Check the notes in the back of the book.)

3. Does the translation of *skyr* sound reasonable?

4. If you have a chance, look at the evolution of Judas as represented in art through the ages. What is the predominant color artists use for his hair?

Chapter 5

1. Leonides: who was he in history? What is the symbolism in this chapter?

2. People of that era frequently named their sons after heroes and great figures in history. Can you think of others?

3. What is Jesus' name in Hebrew?

4. How do you think the religion of Judas' mother differed from that of the pagans in Caesarea?

Chapter 7

1. *"Shadowy figures rose up near us, then drifted away. We wanted to run, but which way—and where?"*

   Put this statement in the context of the story. Have you ever felt this way? What did you do?

Chapters 8–12

1. Summarize the story thus far.

2. We spoke of the culture of the times in session I. What have you learned about the culture since?

3. What new insights do you have regarding what Judas may have been like?

4. If you were reading this for the first time, what direction would you predict the story would take?"

Session III
Essenes and John the Baptist, Chapters 13–24

Chapter 13

Briefly describe the class system and Judas' place in it.

Chapter 14 and 15

1. Judas' statement to Nahum: *"I am the grandson of Judas of the Galilee. I intend to pick up where he left off."*

   Who was Judas of the Galilee? (Acts 5:37) What did he mean? Speculate on how this may have affected the end of the story.

2. Read the last two paragraphs of the chapter.

   What do you think Judas was really yearning for? Have you ever experienced such a yearning? What do you think is meant by the expression, "a hole in the soul?" How can it be filled?

3. What were the Israelites' expectations of a Messiah?

Chapter 16

1. What seems to be Judas' mission?

2. He says, *"But the stars were set in their courses, and so was I."* What does this say about Judas' mindset? Is this a Christian or a Pagan concept? How does modern thought resonate with this idea of fate?

Chapter 18

1. From this chapter, *"And yet, I lived—why? I really needed to know the answer to that question."*

   What is your insight into Judas' question? Have you ever asked yourself the same question? Explain.

2. Read Luke 10:25–37. Compare it to Judas' experience in this chapter. Comment on the author's intention.

Chapter 19

Read the second-to-last paragraph in this chapter. Discuss your understanding of the meaning of the phrase, *"some divine current…"*

Chapter 21

1. *"…but it was through Reuel I found God."* What does that statement mean to you? Relate this to the second question in Chapter 14.

2. Discuss the last paragraph in this chapter in light of John 14:6.

Chapter 22

1. Read the first section of this chapter. What is meant by the "forerunner?"

2. What do you think the "new mission" is? Describe the Essenes' intensity.

3. For future reference, note John, son of Zebedee's, opinion of Judas.

4. In the second section of this chapter, Judas states, *"I had changed."* What indication did he have of change? What changed him?

Chapter 23

1. Why was John the Baptist quoting Isaiah 43:19 (third paragraph)?

2. What was the purpose of John's baptism?

3. What did Jesus have to say about it to John?

One of the most powerful spiritual principles in the book is in this chapter. It is John's admonition to *"...inspect the things in your heart that do not please God."*

What was in Judas' heart that needed to be purged?

4. What is the purging process for hatred?

5. Discuss all that goes into forgiveness. Consider Matthew 6:9–15.

6. What is in your heart that needs to be purged through forgiveness?

7. What did John the Baptist mean in this chapter when he said, *"It is not Rome who destroys us. We destroy ourselves."*?

Chapter 24

1. In whose company was Judas at this time?

2. Read Luke 3:13–17 and compare it to the author's narrative. How do you think Judas felt as he observed all this?

3. Why did Jesus want to be baptized?

Session IV
Jesus in Galilee, Chapters 25–34

Chapter 25 and 26

1. Why did Judas follow Jesus? Who went with him?

2. Why was Judas confused about the Messiah and what to expect...David, Elijah, Moses?

3. Read Jesus' words in Luke 4:18–19. Find them in this chapter. Read Isaiah 61:1–2.

Why are the words in Luke and Isaiah the same?

4. Read Luke 4:20–21. Who did Jesus claim to be?

5. What was the response of the listeners?

6. What is meant by a *minyan?*

7. Simon (Peter) and John both called Judas a thief. How did their opinion of him differ?

Chapter 27 & 28

1. The man hearing Jesus preach calls out, *"Who do you think you are, God?"* What did he mean? What was Jesus doing in that sermon?

2. What is the Torah?

3. For Jews, the Law is the way, the truth, and the life. What does Jesus have to say about himself in that regard? (John 14:6) (ref. to Ch. 36.)

4. Review Jesus' conversation with Judas. How were Jesus and Judas alike? How were they different?

5. What did Jesus say was their deepest yearning? How did He say it would be fulfilled?

6. What did Jesus mean by *"Our futures are woven on the Father's loom and into the fabric of our lives."*?

   Compare this to the statement discussed earlier in chapter 16, question 2.

Chapter 29

1. Read Luke 7:40–43 and find the story in this chapter. Discuss the hierarchy of sin and God's forgiveness.

Chapter 30

1. What is Sukkoth?

2. How did the Baptizer die? See Luke 9:9.

   What effect did that have on Jesus' followers? On his enemies?

3. Read Luke 4:1–13 and compare it with Jesus' conversation with Judas. What do you think of the way the well known Temptation account was used in this context?

4. Do we sometimes have this kind of conversation with God ourselves?

5. The story of Gideon that Jesus and Judas discussed is in Judges 6:11–16. Read it and discuss the question, *"Why, if God stood with him, do people suffer?"* What was Jesus' response?

6. Jesus told Judas, *"The Kingdom of God will come when the hearts of men are changed."*

   What did He mean? Discuss the radical surgery in Ezekiel 36:26–27.

Chapter 31

1. Jesus uses Judas' experience on the road to Jericho (Chapter 18) and the story of the woman about to be stoned for adultery as teaching tools. What two lessons can be gleaned on living a life pleasing to God?

2. What is in it for us in living a life that pleases Him?

Chapter 33

1. Read Luke 8:22–25 in relationship to the story in this chapter. Answer the two questions in verse 25 (Where is your faith? And who is this?).

   Who is seated in the back of your boat?

2. The story of the man with many demons is in Mark 5:1–13. Read it and discuss it as it is told in this chapter. What effect did this experience have on Judas? (See last paragraph of this chapter.)

3. Demons can be both real and metaphorical. Discuss.

Chapter 34

1. In the first section of this chapter Jesus says, *"What is important is the circumcision of the spirit."* What did He mean?

   How would this be received by the Jewish community? By the Pharisees?

2. Can you identify the source of this quotation the author attributes to Jesus?

   What can you say about its authenticity?

3. Jesus asked Peter, "Who do you say that I am?" What was Peter's answer?

   Why did this drop them to their knees (Luke 9:18-20)?

   If asked that question today, how would you answer?

4. In the fourth section of this chapter, Jesus introduces a new idea on living a life pleasing to God. What is it (Luke 10:1)?

Session V
Beginning of the End – Chapters 35–45

Chapter 35

1. A quote from Mary Magdalene: *"Women are far less trusting than men in matters of the world. In matters of faith, the reverse is true. Women are naturally spiritual and men must be drubbed into faith."*

   Do you agree or disagree? Why?

2. In Islam, men must pray five times a day to Allah, facing Mecca. Women are exempt. It is assumed they do not need to as they are naturally spiritual. Is there a lesson for us here?

3. The miracle of Jesus feeding the five thousand with two fish and five loaves of bread is found in this chapter (Luke 9:12–17). Why is this story included in this book? In scripture?

Chapter 36

1. Why did Jesus say to Peter, *"Get behind me?"*

2. What did Jesus mean when he said, *"My kingdom is not of this world?"* Why did Judas struggle with that truth? Do you?

3. As presented in this chapter, what are Jesus' views about women? Do you think the author fairly represents the scripture in this?

4. Discuss the Law, as explicated by Jesus in this chapter.

   How does this take on the law differ from what you were taught? Is there room for debate with various faiths, given this interpretation? Is it more inclusive than you want? Discuss.

Chapter 37

1. What is "the Passover" that Jesus, Judas and the other followers were celebrating? Refer to Exodus 12:1–13.

   How is this relevant to the Christian faith?

2. What is the significance of having Jesus celebrate the Essene Passover on what would be our Tuesday?

3. What does John say about the time of Jesus' arrest and trial? Is it the same as the reported in the Synoptic gospels?

Chapter 38

1. What two authorities are working at odds with Jesus at this point in the narrative?

2. Is this within the will of God—or against it?

3. Consider again the statement in chapter 27, *"Our futures are woven on the Father's loom and into the fabric of our lives."* How does it relate to the above question?

Chapter 39–40

1. Compare Pilate's entry into Jerusalem with that of Jesus and share your insights.

2. Read Matthew 21:1–5 and Zechariah 9:9. Is fulfillment of prophecy important?

Chapter 41

1. What prompted Jesus' anger when he lashed out at the moneychangers in the temple? (Luke 19:45–46)

2. When was Judas' last act as a moneychanger? Imagine how he must have felt. Discuss.

Chapter 42

1. Relate Luke 21:14–20 and I Corinthians 11:23–29 to the story of the Last Supper as told in this chapter.

2. Explain your understanding of the Eucharist, also known as Holy Communion. How does it affect your relationship with Jesus?

3. What is transubstantiation? Consubstantiation? The doctrine of the Real Presence?

Chapter 43

1. Agree or disagree: The author portrays Judas' betrayal of Jesus as innocent and well-intentioned. Recall Judas' self-appointed purpose, which was introduced in the beginning of the book. Discuss this statement from Chapter 1: *"There are risks involved in presuming to know the mind of God."*

   What are the implications of this statement in the context of Judas' part in the crucifixion narrative? How did pride figure into this incident?

2. Has your own pride ever gotten you in trouble? Explain.

3. What was happening in Judas' heart as he remembered the bees (refer back to Chapter 36)?

Chapter 45

1. Consider Caiaphas' interrogation of Judas. How important was it for a Jew to know his lineage?

2. What did Judas mean when he answered, *"I am of the Diaspora"*?

3. Why would Jesus be better off in the custody of the Sanhedrin than the Romans?

4. How was Judas like his grandfather?

Session VI
The Trial, Chapters 46–51

Chapter 47

1. Describe the scene when Jesus said, *"Is it with a kiss, then, that I am to be handed over?"*

2. Consider and discuss the emotions of Judas, Jesus, the Disciples, and Ehud.

3. For what was Jesus being handed over?

4. Consider again how this statement of Jesus' relates: *"Our futures are woven on the Father's loom and into the fabric of our lives."*

5. Explain what Jesus said about darkness. Discuss Luke 11:33–36.

Chapter 48

1. Read Psalm 143:8. It is the scripture that Judas chanted. Following this in the narrative he said, *"...but I always began my day in hope, a habit that sustained me over the years."* How did the verse from Psalms help Judas?

2. Have you experienced the strength and hope that comes from knowing scripture?

3. What scripture verse do you use to bring strength in a time of crisis or need?

Chapter 49 and 50

1. Describe the "legal proceedings."

2. What was Judas' purpose in following Jesus all that time?

3. Is it "fair" that Judas be remembered as a traitor?

4. What did Judas pray for at the end of Chapter 50? Why?

Chapter 51

1. What were the charges against Jesus?

2. Who did Jesus claim to be?

3. Read Caiaphas' speech. What did he mean by *"Way and Truth"*? Relate that to what Jesus said about himself in John 14:6. What do you suppose was the reaction of the Jewish leaders to Jesus' claim?

8

4. What is *Pax Romana?* What did it do for Jewish culture? Were the Jews happy with it?

Session VII
The Crucifixion, Chapters 52–58

Chapter 52

1. What reason did Caiaphas give for taking Jesus to Pilate?

2. Describe Pilate's demeanor.

3. How did Pilate refer to Herod? Why did he assign the Galilean to Herod?

Chapter 53

1. Who was Rufus and what was his plea to Pilate?

2. What role did Pilate previously play in the history that so deeply marked Judas?

3. Who was the old soldier, now Judas' guard?

4. Describe how Judas must have felt upon making this discovery. Put yourself into the story. What would you do? Does forgiveness come into play here?

Chapter 54

1. Why would the eyes of Jesus—the Son of the God of Love and Forgiveness—be defiant?

2. What did Jesus mean when he said, *"My kingdom is not of this world"*?

   Are you a part of His kingdom? Why or why not?

3. Why was Jesus tortured and crucified after Pilate said, *"I can find no crime here?"*

4. Think about Caiaphas' statement, *"You have your duty, Prefect, I have mine. This man threatens the whole of our nation."* Discuss it in light of the context of the entire paragraph.

5. What is the real purpose of the brutal crucifixion? What does it mean to you?

Chapter 55–56

1. Did you realize the brutality of the crucifixion?

2. Do you think the author's depiction is accurate?

3. Why did Jesus say to the thief on the cross next to him, *"Today you will be with me in Paradise?"*

4. Examine your feelings after reading these two chapters and share them with the group.

Chapter 57

1. Jesus quoted Psalm 22 from the Cross? Why? Is it prophetic?

2. Do you think quoting the psalm helped Jesus? Why?

Session VIII
The End and the Beginning: Summing up

Chapter 58 through Epilogue

1. What did Jesus mean when he said, *"I sought the cross that all might live…"* and *"Then you must live, too"*? Is this part of the story possible?

2. Explain your understanding of the Resurrection. What does it mean to you?

3. Was Judas the betrayer or was he the betrayed? Discuss.

4. Judas is the disciple we love to hate. How do you feel about him after reading the book?

5. Did Judas find his treasure?

6. Does the author draw an accurate picture of Jesus, as you've come to know Him?

7. Jesus seemed to be able to read the disciples' thoughts. Is that consistent with Scripture? Can He read yours?

8. Spend some time thinking about what thoughts can be hidden from God and discuss them with the group.

9. What have you learned from reading *Judas, The Gospel of Betrayal*? How will it change your life?

10. After reading this fictional gospel, has it changed the way you think about the authentic one? If so, in what way?

11. In the end, do we need Judas in the gospel story at all? Why? Why not? If we don't need him, why is he there?

Tell us what you think about
Judas, The Gospel of Betrayal.

- Would you recommend it to a friend?
- Do you think it is an appropriate book to introduce a skeptic, nonbeliever, or hesitant Christian to the Gospel?
- Are there other topics or personalities you would like to see depicted this way? For example, could you see St. Paul in a novel of this sort? Peter?
- How does this book compare to other Biblical fiction you may have read?

Contact us at ramsaybooks@cox.net or write to us at:
16027 W. Sandia Park Dr.
Surprise, AZ 85374
www.frederickramsay.com

To receive a free catalog of Poisoned Pen Press titles, please contact us in one of the following ways:

Phone: 1-800-421-3976
Facsimile: 1-480-949-1707
Email: info@poisonedpenpress.com
Website: www.poisonedpenpress.com

Poisoned Pen Press
6962 E. First Ave. Ste. 103
Scottsdale, AZ 85251